Night of the witches

"Tell me"—she paused, looking at his name tag—"Spider. Very goth, by the way, Spider." She tried very hard not to snicker. "Is Mr. Bright in this evening?"

"Should be." Spider tried to look tough, but she could use him to pick spinach from her teeth with one hand so the effect was lost on her.

She nodded, taking her tag and sauntering past the line and through the doors. The bouncer took one look, a smile settled over his features and he stepped back, letting her pass.

Once inside, the scent caught her attention. Mmmm. *Humanity.* Sex, lust, greed, anger. *Beautiful.* The hard-edged beat vibrated off her skin as she prowled through the crowd. In every flash, flash, flash of the strobe lights bodies moved, arms up in the air.

Magick drifted through the large room, catching her attention, drawing her to its source. It wasn't hard to find the go-between, the place normals wouldn't see but others would be drawn to, and through, into their own private club.

Heart of Darkness—not a bad name for a club, really. One of her favorite books too. Too bad Gage wasn't here. The women would have been falling over themselves to get to him. Her [...] ard Meriel had [...] corted, but for g[...] k to a thief in pu[...] een a long time [...] any taking care [...] her mother havi[...]

continued . . .

Heart of Darkness

LAUREN DANE

BERKLEY SENSATION, NEW YORK

THE BERKLEY PUBLISHING GROUP
Published by the Penguin Group
Penguin Group (USA) Inc.
375 Hudson Street, New York, New York 10014, USA

Penguin Group (Canada), 90 Eglinton Avenue East, Suite 700, Toronto, Ontario M4P 2Y3, Canada
(a division of Pearson Penguin Canada Inc.)
Penguin Books Ltd., 80 Strand, London WC2R 0RL, England
Penguin Group Ireland, 25 St. Stephen's Green, Dublin 2, Ireland (a division of Penguin Books Ltd.)
Penguin Group (Australia), 250 Camberwell Road, Camberwell, Victoria 3124, Australia
(a division of Pearson Australia Group Pty. Ltd.)
Penguin Books India Pvt. Ltd., 11 Community Centre, Panchsheel Park, New Delhi—110 017, India
Penguin Group (NZ), 67 Apollo Drive, Rosedale, Auckland 0632, New Zealand
(a division of Pearson New Zealand Ltd.)
Penguin Books (South Africa) (Pty.) Ltd., 24 Sturdee Avenue, Rosebank, Johannesburg 2196,
South Africa

Penguin Books Ltd., Registered Offices: 80 Strand, London WC2R 0RL, England

HEART OF DARKNESS

A Berkley Sensation Book / published by arrangement with the author

PRINTING HISTORY
Berkley Sensation mass-market edition / November 2011

ISBN: 978-0-425-24451-7

BERKLEY SENSATION®
Berkley Sensation Books are published by The Berkley Publishing Group,
a division of Penguin Group (USA) Inc.,
375 Hudson Street, New York, New York 10014.
BERKLEY SENSATION® is a registered trademark of Penguin Group (USA) Inc.
The "B" design is a trademark of Penguin Group (USA) Inc.

PRINTED IN THE UNITED STATES OF AMERICA

10 9 8 7 6 5 4 3 2 1

This one is for Linda Sue
who always puts her family before herself.
Love you, Momma.

Acknowledgments

I want to thank Laura Bradford for knowing how much I wanted this and going way above and beyond to help make it into a reality.

Thanks also goes to Leis Pederson, whose edits always make me a better writer.

To my husband, who makes my heart beat faster and brings me home Thai food just because—I love you!

And to all the people who have supported me with so many kindnesses—thank you. Thank you for buying my books, for talking about them, for the notes you send and for coming to see me at events. It means so very much!

And for a moment it seemed to me as if I also were buried in a vast grave full of unspeakable secrets. I felt an intolerable weight oppressing my breast, the smell of the damp earth, the unseen presence of victorious corruption, the darkness of an impenetrable night.

—JOSEPH CONRAD, *HEART OF DARKNESS*

Chapter 1

MERIEL sat, taking notes as her mother spoke from the head of the table. The pale, late autumn light spilled through the windows of the seemingly normal conference room, casting shadows on the far wall. The tastefully expensive clock and nondescript black-and-white framed photos made the space look like a law firm instead of the headquarters of a witches' clan. A boring, non-offensive space that seemed to lack any point of view at all. This was most likely a deliberate choice, but Meriel thought pretending not to have a POV when you were someone as opinionated as Edwina Owen was absurd. But it wasn't her place to make decorating choices. Not yet anyway.

So she sat in a moderately comfortable chair around an intentionally imposing table with the same fifteen people she'd spent her days with for as long as she could remember. How sucky was it that it was days like this that made her wish for law school again? What sort of whackadoo actually *missed* law school? But in law school when she excelled, it was without the context she carried in her life here. The next in line. The princess. Magickal royalty. Blah. There, she'd just been another overachiever struggling with the realities of being in a room full of people just as smart, and in many cases, smarter, than she was. That sort of bumpy ride had been a novelty.

But this was her future and she took it seriously even if she had a stack of other things to do at the moment. Meriel really didn't have the time for this assignment, but Clan Owen's investigator, who also happened to be Meriel's best friend, Nell, was still out on her honeymoon and wouldn't be back for another few days.

Really, Gage, who was Nell's second-in-command, would be a fine substitute. But as far as Edwina Owen was concerned, as the next in line to run Clan Owen, Meriel was expected to pick up the slack when necessary. Rather like working in the mail room or running the copiers, it trained in the overall running of the clan.

Whatever, at least she'd get out of her house for the evening instead of sitting around reading legal briefs or ordering a movie on demand and eating too many spring rolls. *Mmmm, spring rolls . . .*

The lull in sound meant her mother probably expected an answer and it was time to pay attention instead of thinking about fried carby goodness.

She sat, back straight, and met her mother's eyes. "I have the file. Nell briefed me before she left. I'll head to the club tonight to see for myself what's going on." She continued to hold her mother's gaze. It wouldn't do to show Edwina Owen, the leader of Clan Owen, any weakness. Some predators ate their babies, Meriel knew. She'd actually said that to her mother once. Her mother had replied, "Then you should never give me a reason to do that." Not really warm and fuzzy, Meriel's mother.

"Take Gage with you." It wasn't a request. Very little of what Edwina said ever was. In this case, as was most often the fact, she was right. It wasn't like Meriel was unused to having guards with her. She wasn't helpless, but she had no problem having an expert on the job with her.

"I'll be picking Meriel up this evening at ten," Gage spoke from his place near the door.

Edwina looked very pleased the whole world was following her command and Meriel fought the smile edging the corners of her mouth.

"Excellent. Brief me in the morning then." Edwina dismissed her with the flick of her fingers. Meriel gladly took her up on it and got out of the room as quickly as possible.

"She scares me," Gage said as she passed him in the hall on her way to her office. She totally did not look at his butt or the way the denim was faded in all the right places. That would be wrong. Heh.

Meriel, who was *not* having nasty fantasies about a coworker, tried to emanate total professionalism for about five seconds before she simply rolled her eyes. "Whatever. She wants you to be scared, she likes it. Gets off on it even. Some men like that. My dad for instance and I don't know why I brought that up because, um, *ew.*" She shook her head to dislodge that thought. Oh yeah, Gage's ass. She smiled at that much more appetizing mental image. "I'll see you tonight then? So you can protect my honor and stuff?"

He grinned. "Your stuff is awesome and I'm sure you can protect it yourself. But yes, I'll be there with bells on. Or not with bells, that would be noisy and annoying, but I'll be there." He sauntered off and she snuck one last peek at his ass. She wasn't a saint after all. It was a spectacular ass and, like any great work of art, should be admired. It was her sacred duty as an American. And stuff.

EFFICIENTLY, she made her way through the office to her side of the building. Clan Owen's headquarters took up the entire thirtieth floor of a high-rise in downtown Seattle. They were much like any other business, with a secretarial pool, legal department, accountants, sales reps even. Only their employees were all witches.

Twelve generations of Owen women had run the clan. The first Owen witches came to California in 1847. They'd come a long way from the dry-goods stores and illegal booze operations that had given them their first financial roots in the region. Now, the clan was a multimillion-dollar business and an unquestioned powerhouse in the world of witches.

Like every firstborn daughter of the leader of Clan Owen, from birth, Meriel had been shaped to lead. Taught, formed, molded into the kind of witch, the kind of woman who could hold the clan together and keep it prosperous and powerful for the next generations.

Edwina had not been the kind of mother to kiss boo-boos and bake cookies. She'd raised Meriel to be hard and canny. Meriel liked to believe she got the canny part without the hard.

And one day she'd kiss boo-boos and bake cookies and still manage to run the clan just fine.

She stopped by her assistant's desk, picked up mail and messages and closed her door, and the rest of the office out.

The day was nice enough and she let it pull her attention from work for a moment to take in the beauty of the water glittering in the sun, of the ferries dotting the Sound.

With a happy sigh, she kicked off her shoes and opened the file folder on her desk—the dossier on the man she'd be speaking to that evening.

This man had just appeared in Seattle and had set up a nightclub in the middle of Owen territory. For months it appeared he only ran the club for humans, which is why they didn't notice him at first.

She didn't know exactly when he'd opened up the part of the club for others, but he'd been using magick from Clan Owen's font to power some wards for a few months and it had *just* been noticed two weeks before.

One, it agitated her that it took so long to be discovered.

Two, despite her annoyance, she was impressed.

Whoever he was, Meriel understood that it wouldn't do to underestimate him. She hadn't achieved bonded full-council status yet, but she wasn't stupid.

She *was* curious though.

A knock sounded on her door and before she could speak, her mother came in. Not breezed in, not strolled or barged or anything of the sort. No, Edwina came in and occupied nearly all the oxygen in the room.

"I've just received an interesting phone call."

Meriel didn't bother to ask her mother to sit. Edwina would do what she wanted to do. She pulled out a notepad and a pen and looked up, ready to take notes.

"There've been some developments in New Mexico. Three witches are missing from a local coven just outside Albuquerque."

She'd been an attorney long enough to know silence got you more information than a lot of leading questions when you were interviewing someone. So she simply waited for her mother to give her all the details.

"One of the women has been missing for eight months. They believe she is dead. Another male gone for six months and this last one went missing two weekends ago."

"Were they all active within the coven? Or loners? Drugs? Trouble at home or work?"

Her mother nodded her head once, as if reassuring herself Meriel was indeed not a total idiot.

"None of the three is very active. They don't have a font, but the parents of one of the women are leadership. Which is why it got to me at all I expect." The unspoken was that no one would have cared about the other two because no one was watching out for them.

The very idea of it burned in Meriel's belly. The very fact that her mother wasn't similarly offended also burned. This could be a totally nothing issue, or a big problem. Simply refusing to examine it very closely wasn't, to Meriel's mind, a very effective way to run things.

"Why these people? Is it connected to some of the similar stories we've heard lately?"

Her mother simply went forward as if these questions meant nothing. "I know you like open communication with other witches, even those who are clanless. I'm going to have you be the point person on this for the clan. Until Nell returns on Monday, work with Gage." She stood and then handed a file folder to Meriel. "That contains all the details." Again she paused, taking a breath. "I'm not convinced this is a problem. People disappear, Meriel. We don't know enough about any of them to get worked up."

It must have been a herculean effort to not show the sneer in her voice on her features. Meriel bit her tongue and reminded herself she'd run the show differently when her time came.

She took the file, looking over her mother's beautiful and very precise handwriting. Edwina may have thought the call was crap, but she took good notes. Meriel would head over to talk to Gage about it to get his opinion once her mother had gone.

"If they were in a clan, they'd have taken better care of their people. This may not have happened. People do themselves all sorts of damage. You know this as well as I do."

If she spoke, she'd say something bitter and she didn't want to. Didn't want to spend any more negativity on the day. Or on her mother.

One brow rose in challenge. "Go on. Say it. If you're going to take over for me, you need a spine."

It was difficult, but not impossible to rein her magick's response to her mother's taunt. There was no winning by Edwina's rules. So she refused to play by them. "I'm not playing this game with you. Also, there's no *if* and you and I both know it. Thank you for this information. I'll handle it from now on." And she was sure the witches in New Mexico would appreciate not being made to feel as if it were their own fault for getting kidnapped or killed or whatever may have happened down there.

Edwina narrowed her gaze and Meriel gave her blank face right back. She'd groomed her blank face over many, many years. Considered it perfect. It was the only way to win with her mother, who pushed to get a response. One of these days though, oh, Meriel would give it to her, all right.

"Thank you." Meriel said it again, holding her mother's gaze.

Edwina sighed and moved to the door. "Keep me apprised." And left.

Meriel read through her notes and headed to Gage.

Chapter 2

GAGE looked up as she tapped on his door. Meriel liked this part of the office. Back in a far, infrequently used corridor, Nell ran the investigative and law and order arm of the clan. They had a pinball machine. Hello.

Gage sat, boots up on his desk, a phone to his ear as he looked over whatever he had in his hands. She waved when he looked up and made to leave, but he waved her in to sit and wait.

"I have to go. *No.* Nell, if I so much as get a whiff you're back in town before Sunday, I will kick your ass. And I'll tell Meriel." He grinned up at her as he paused, clearly getting an earful. "Bye." He hung up, laughing.

"She can't possibly be coming back early. William has to be more attractive than anything she could find here. William in swim trunks. Yum!"

He rolled his eyes. "I had to call her about this New Mexico stuff. I take it your mother spoke with you?"

"Yes, that's why I'm here. It could have waited until Monday, you know. Nell's only going to obsess about it now."

"I know. But she made me promise to call if anything

unusual came up. I found a way around it for the investigation at this club. That's not new." He shrugged and Meriel
laughed, delighted.

"I love the way you two are together. You keep her in
line."

"William told me marrying Nell was like getting me too.
But then he confessed that he was glad because it would
take more than one person to keep her in line. He said as
long as I had no designs on the parts he liked to keep in line
we were good."

Meriel always had wondered why Gage and Nell hadn't
hooked up. But she imagined it was one of those great, totally
non-romantic partnerships. They teased, but there wasn't
an ounce of sexual tension between them.

"He's a smart man." She held up the file. "So what do
you know about New Mexico?"

"I spoke with the person who called your mother. They
don't have a clan organization so no law enforcement to
speak of. No investigative team. They're not going to bring
in anyone else. I did offer," he added at her questioning look
before continuing. "Missing witches. No real connection
they know of. But there's too much they don't know for me
to be really comfortable with the situation."

"We need to be sure we're keeping a good eye on everyone. Even the outclan." This would make her mother insanely
angry, but just because those witches didn't want to join the
clan didn't mean the clan should simply leave them without
any protection. They used the font. They obeyed the clan
rules. They deserved some benefit.

"I agree. We have something in place, as you know. But
I think it can be stepped up. I'm going to work with section
five to see if we can't monitor through the font. You know,
see who is taking and filling. Look for gaps."

The font was the collective energy bank for the clan. All
witches within it were keyed in so that their magickal energy
should be part of it, if not every day, at least several times
a week. An absence could be detected; she just didn't know
how hard it would be to do it.

"Good. That's a good idea. They'll tell you if it can be done or not. Keep me apprised. I've been named the point person on this."

Gage's brows went up a bit.

"I know, I'm surprised too." She couldn't very well say she was shocked her mother had let go of the power. Her mother had a way of hearing lots of things. Most likely, her mother thought this was all bullshit so it was fine to give it to Meriel, who'd also end up with a reality check that would smack the notion of working with other witches and protecting against external threats by banding together right out of her head.

Ha. Edwina had no idea. None. Which bugged Meriel. For heaven's sake, she was Edwina's child—canny and strong willed, just like her mother. The future didn't involve this continued self-segregation and her mother could pretend Meriel didn't know any better or that she was naïve, but they both knew that wasn't true.

"Totally hypothetical question here. Do you think this might be connected to the situation in Minnesota? With the mages?"

A witch had been found nearly dead and had recounted a horrifying tale of being kidnapped by a group of mages who'd spent days siphoning her power. She had only been able to escape when she'd managed to grab back enough of her magickal power to siphon the air from the room and the mages had passed out. She'd crawled nearly a mile before someone found her and took her to the hospital. By the time the police had arrived at the house, everyone had gone.

The human authorities were looking for human monsters. Human monsters could be taken down. But mages were not human, and they had no code of ethics like witches. No, they stole power and magick to twist it and use it like a drug.

And what if they'd decided to hunt witches for that drug?

BY the time she'd made ready to leave for the day, the sun was down. She'd had plans to duck out early but of course

that hadn't worked out. As it was, she still had the opportunity to stop at the little boutique just down the street from
her apartment building. She wanted something new for that
night. Wanted to find an outfit suitable for club wear.

Her phone was ringing when she came out from her bathroom and she ran to grab it. It had been Gage's mother,
Shelley, calling from his house where he was currently suffering the throes of food poisoning. She'd assured Meriel
that Gage would be fine by morning, but there was no way
he'd be accompanying her that evening.

Meriel had almost felt sorry for him as he'd attempted to
order her to wait until the following night and she'd refused,
promising to be safe and check in the following day before
telling him to get well and hanging up.

She'd made the choice to go and, she thought as she put
in her earrings, that was that. It hadn't simply been a matter
of their font being stolen from. It had been bigger.

No spiky-heeled sandals that night. She needed to be able
to move easily and quickly. So she opted for her cowboy
boots. Thankfully they went well with the outfit she'd
picked up.

The skirt was a little shorter than she usually went for,
but it wasn't so short she'd be in danger of showing any of
her bits. And the shirt was snug and a little stretchy; the
sequins accenting it here and there would catch the light.
Feminine. Sexy. And it all emphasized her best parts and
hid her worst.

In the garage she looked at what she'd picked up two days
before. Nell's car. Nell's beautiful, cherry-red classic 1967
Camaro. All shiny and powerful.

Her own car was nice enough and all, but this, well, this
was part of the whole night. Unexpected like the short skirt
and this mission she went on. Silly, but it was thrilling all
the same.

She traveled across the lake toward Seattle, feeling as if
there was a reason she felt nearly driven to do it. Though
Meriel was as rational and logical as they came, she still

believed in following her gut. Her gut was where her magick lived and it wanted her at that club tonight.

There were no reasons to expect a violent response from Bright. He'd been peaceable since he'd arrived in Owen territory, though still a thief. He had to quit that, of course. And the opportunity to do something so unexpected—to act on behalf of her clan with this witch to make him stop— well, that excited her.

It could wait, of course, for the next night, or the next week for that matter. Restlessness had settled into her bones over the last year. Before that she'd been pretty much single-minded with her studies and her job.

Ambition came to her naturally. Her foremothers had created Clan Owen from nothing and built it into one of the most powerful organizations in the world. Meriel accepted that the blood of these women ran in her veins for a reason and that she was supposed to use every gift she'd been given to protect and serve her people.

From infancy there had been one path and she greeted that with joy and a sense of duty. But things were changing. The older and more experienced she got, the more the witches in Clan Owen expected her to lead and many had begun to look to her first, before Edwina, and that had created a rift. Most though weren't sure she could be as brutal and ruthless as Edwina. So she'd have to show them. But in her own way.

For the first time in her life it was hard to wait for what was next. She wanted to go out and greet it. Wanted to make things happen. Wanted to see what this heady sense of expectancy was all about.

She supposed at this point in a full-council witch's life, it was about finding her bond-mate to finally ascend to her full power. She was in limbo until that happened. Until a full-council witch performed the ascension spell with her bond-mate, she wouldn't achieve her full power and take her seat on the ruling council of the clan.

It wasn't so much that Meriel was aching to find her

bond-mate. It was more than the magickal ascension, though
she did want that very much, it was a lack of soul-connection.
It had only gotten worse once she'd seen Nell with her new
husband, had seen love in her best friend's eyes.

Things were about to change. She could feel it.

DOMINIC tucked his shirt into his jeans and gave himself
one last look in the mirror on the back of his office door. He
had a to-do list as long as his arm and the sense of impend-
ing *something* lay heavily in his gut.

He hated that. He didn't want this special-sense thing.
He liked his gifts well enough, but it was just fine with him
to be an ordinary guy with a little bit of magick. He didn't
want foresight. Tom, the closest thing Dominic had to a
father and the man who deserved the credit as one, got on
his case for being a slacker and not living up to his full
potential. That's what fathers did, Dominic knew. But he
had a successful bar, didn't he? Was he not giving a place
to go to both others and humans alike? It wasn't like he was
still living on the edge the way he had those years before.
No probation officer. He was a businessman now. No more
running from bill collectors. Hell, he even had employees.
As far as Dominic was concerned, he was a useful member
of society and Tom should be satisfied with that.

It wasn't so much that he never used his magick. Just that
he used it the way he wanted to. This whole clan business,
having to be a member and obey rules, none of that was his
scene. He didn't need to be told what to do. Not by anyone.

After finally growing tired of the violence and
hand-to-mouth nature of the lifestyle he'd lived for the early
part of his twenties, he'd landed in New York City where
he'd learned how to run a business. When he'd saved for a
few years, he'd come back home to the Northwest.

He'd made something of all that energy and ambition.
He took an empty space and with some magick, okay some
borrowed energy too, had created Heart of Darkness. At
first glance it was an industrial nightclub but through an

arch, hidden to non-magickal eyes, was *the* spot for Others in Seattle. Part café, part bar.

The place was packed every night and as Simon pointed out just that day over lunch, they were bound to get a visit from some clan witches very soon. There was no way word of the place hadn't reached them and there'd be a bill come due from using their precious font. Even an outclan witch like him knew he was breaking their laws by using their magick without being keyed in. Until then though, he'd continue to do so because he needed to and they couldn't possibly have a use for all that spare power.

And because he still liked to play on the edge.

Chapter 3

MERIEL stretched her legs out the open car door, unfolding her body to stand beside the shiny curves of steel. Part of the reason people stared was the car, and she totally got that. Normally, Meriel drove an Audi. Low slung, sporty and temperamental. Sort of like she was on a good day. Heh.

Still, maybe a little bit of Nell's sexy-momma mojo would rub off on her.

The valet tried to look sullen and bored as he approached with an outstretched hand. A *valet* at an industrial nightclub? What was the world coming to?

Sullen and on the verge of tears seemed to be similar looks for this boy. No way was he more than a hair this side of nineteen. His skinny jeans only emphasized just how thin his legs were. It must have been a serious workout for him to move in those big boots he had on. Couldn't have been more than a hundred pounds soaking wet. Probably why his guyliner was running. Or maybe that was on purpose. Whatever, she didn't really care. Emo boys were not her cup of tea anyway. As long as he didn't scratch the car, he was free to weep and write bad poetry all day long.

She dropped her keys into his palm and raised one eyebrow. Might as well put on a show all the way and throw a little Edwina in there. "Do be careful, won't you?" She added a touch of magick to be sure he was.

He nodded, Adam's apple sliding up and down as her magick tickled his skin and permeated his brain. She briefly toyed with also telling him to eat a sandwich, but let that go.

"Tell me"—she paused, looking at his name tag—"Spider. Very goth, by the way, Spider." She tried very hard not to snicker. "Is Mr. Bright in this evening?"

"Should be." Spider tried to look tough, but she could use him to pick spinach from her teeth with one hand so the effect was lost on her.

She nodded, taking her tag and sauntering past the line and through the doors. The bouncer took one look, a smile settled over his features and he stepped back, letting her pass.

Once inside, the scent caught her attention. Mmmm. *Humanity.* Sex, lust, greed, anger. *Beautiful.* The hard-edged beat vibrated off her skin as she prowled through the crowd. In every flash, flash, flash of the strobe lights bodies moved, arms up in the air.

Magick drifted through the large room, drawing her to its source. It wasn't hard to find the go-between, the place normals wouldn't see but Others would be drawn to, and through, into their own private club.

Heart of Darkness—not a bad name for a club, really. One of her favorite books too. Too bad Gage wasn't here. The women would have been falling over themselves to get to him. Her mother would also have a cow when she heard Meriel had disobeyed her orders and had come out unescorted, but for goodness' sake, it wasn't that dangerous to talk to a thief in public. And hello, she wasn't fifteen. It had been a long time since Meriel had looked to a mother to do any taking care of her. And last, it amused her to visualize her mother having a cow.

Despite her amusement and admittedly, no small amount of admiration for how much talent it took to set this place up, Heart of Darkness had the potential to be dangerous for them all. Dominic Bright took risks he had no right to. Not on Owen ground and certainly not with Owen font magick.

Though the Weres had been out for a decade and the vampires discussed it endlessly, witches were far less enamored of the idea.

They'd been there and done that and many of them hadn't survived. In fact every time humans focused on them it involved hanging or drowning or being burned alive so they were obsessive about keeping what they did quiet. Pagans and Wiccans already got enough hatred; if humans knew there were witches like Meriel, well, she didn't like thinking about it overlong.

This place was a risk of exposure on top of the fact that one simply didn't just steal from Clan Owen and not face consequences. Clan witches *loved* rules. Rule breaking was frowned upon because risks were dangerous.

Mr. Bright needed to be taught that it was the height of offense to a clan to come in this way. Some of them would have sent enforcers in and he'd never have been heard from again. Lucky for him, Meriel thought that a big show of aggression would be an overreaction. At least until she learned more.

And then, if he needed to be disappeared, Nell would make it happen. The weak got preyed upon and Clan Owen wasn't weak.

Already she knew he had some sense. The closer she got to the go-between door, the more the repulsion spell increased in intensity. The entrance looked like a back door and the presence of two large bouncers looking like bartenders would stop interlopers.

The nature of the club would tend to have their kind blend in, although she didn't know a single vampire who actually looked like the ones she saw in movies. Still, she'd have to talk to Bright about it.

Ignoring the stares and touches from men and women alike as she passed through the crowd, she moved with single-minded purpose toward the warded entrance.

The bouncers didn't bother removing their sunglasses. They wouldn't need to. Even with shades on, they'd see the magick crackle over her skin with their othersight. With the patented bodyguard nod, they stepped aside and let her pass.

The sound dampened and the energy changed as magick of all sorts sparked against hers. The wards recognized her and she passed through the human part of the club and into the domain where her people walked. She recognized the flavor of the magick as Owen font magick. This was *their* power being used to hide that doorway. *Oh, that naughty man.* Against her better judgment and a lifetime of training, instead of apprehension, a glimmer of excitement slid through her. A challenge.

BY contrast to the press of humans out front, this part of Heart of Darkness wasn't such a crush. The pulsing lights and dark ambiance outside had been abandoned. Within this world created just for them, it was more like a restaurant/ pub than a dance club, though there was a dance floor too. She imagined later tonight and on the weekends it would probably be busier and noisier. Magick of all sorts danced through the air. Were, vampire, witch—even a bit of Fae. Bright might be breaking the law by stealing magick, but she couldn't deny the place had appeal.

Moving through the crowd, Meriel realized the dark interior and the light effects would hamper her ability to sight Dominic Bright easily. Still, the club was filled with pretty, shiny men and women from all sorts of backgrounds so a bit of people watching would add to the fun. This was far more interesting than take-out and a movie.

She may as well head to the bar and grab a drink as she looked around. Meriel didn't need a picture to know who Dominic Bright was. She'd recognize his magickal signature if he was there. She just needed to be patient and look around.

"Hello there, witch."

Meriel looked up into the face of a very handsome Were. His looks matched the low bass of the voice, masculine, hard. Not a run-of-the-mill shifter, this one smelled of Lycia. Royalty even. Lycian pack royalty on this side of the Veil was an unusual sight. They liked to keep to their own realm instead of having to deal with humanity and all her complications.

"Hello there, Lycian."

He laughed, showing straight, white teeth, as he leaned against the bar behind him and held out a hand. She reined in the urge to goggle at how big the aforementioned hand was. "Simon Leviathan. Can I buy you a drink?"

Oh sure, she knew she was there to find Dominic Bright, but no one said she couldn't enjoy the attentions of a very handsome Were while she looked.

The warmth of his power rolled through her as she took his outstretched hand. He held on just a bit longer than simple courtesy dictated, letting the warmth of his energy roll over her playfully. The possibilities with this man could bear some thinking on. She let him have the smile she'd been holding back. "Pleasure to meet you, Simon Leviathan. I'd love a drink, thank you. I'm Meriel Owen."

Meriel leaned around him and told the bartender she wanted a Jack and Coke. When she straightened, Simon's hand found its way to her waist. Lycians were very to the point.

Recognition lit his eyes. "Ah, an Owen. What brings you here this evening, Meriel?"

His scent, rich and spicy, tickled her senses and tightened things low in her belly. Alpha males were a double-edged option. Who didn't like a man who was self-assured? But she didn't think she had the time to manage one.

"Just looking around." Tool came on and she let the sound roll over her as she opened her magick, letting it float up and out over the crowd, seeking. Dominic Bright would be a very powerful witch to work those spells on the door. Merely the stolen energy from the font wouldn't be enough. The magick that had to be melded together and woven into that sort of protection and deception was complicated. Only a very talented and powerful witch could manage it. It wasn't just the amount used or borrowed, it was the ability to *use* it and build it into other things. In any case, the odds of that meant there would be very few with that kind of power in the room. Namely Meriel and Dominic.

"Holy shit, what is that?" He leaned in, taking a deep breath. "I like your magick, witch." Simon leaned down to murmur in her ear. "Then again, you're not any old witch are you, Red?"

"I'm not *any old anything* at all, Simon. Just like you're not any old werewolf. You're Lycian and your daddy is alpha of a pack back home. You're marked."

She paid attention to all that supercharged alpha male energy while keeping her seeking spell anchored. It wasn't hard when she was surrounded by so much raw energy. All that sex in the air, all the Others in the room and the magick they bled off as they went about their evening fed her way more than enough. So much she was a bit giddy with it.

"Don't run into too many people who'd know that."

"I like to know things. I'm a curious woman." Another thing she thought Owen should be doing better was reaching out to all groups of Others. Those Others who originated from the other side of the Veil—the Fae and Lycians—were far more powerful than those paranormals from Earth. They could move back and forth into other dimensions and their magick was unique.

Just how much Meriel didn't know because they were just as secretive as witches and there wasn't a lot of information sharing. She wanted that to change and if it came all wrapped up in this attractive a package, well, that was icing.

"I like a curious woman. Now, other than a drink, I think there might be a few other things I'd be happy to give you." The smile he gave her promised all sorts of tingly things.

Before Meriel could respond, there was a definite tug at the end of her spell. She turned and saw the smudge in the energy of the magick. It'd snagged over at a booth on the far side of the room. *There he was.*

Sadly, she turned back to face Simon. "I'm sorry to have to do this, but the person I've been looking for is here, just when I'd begun to hope he wasn't. I need to go deal with a problem."

His face changed a bit as he looked in the direction her attention had been. "I'm sorry to hear that. I'll be here for another hour or so if you wrap up your problem. I come most nights. Or, I'm at the W if you find yourself in need of some company."

She smiled, taking a long look from the top of his dark-hued hair to the tips of his expensive boots. Long and lean, broad in the right places. He sure was pretty to look at.

"Thanks for the drink. Maybe I'll be seeing you around." She touched a fingertip to her lips and took one last look.

He pushed a hand through his hair. Such a bad boy there. She winked and turned, swaying toward the tug on her spell.

The crowd moved aside as she walked, her magick brushing against them, tendrils of their energy drawing back into her, strengthening her as she took a taste of all that paranormal strength in the room. Heady stuff.

Chapter 4

SHE wasn't surprised that he knew she was there. His awareness of that fact was quite clear as she approached. The energy of his focus on her pricked at her skin. Not painful, but clearly could be if necessary. Still, nothing could have prepared her for the sight that greeted her. She knew his eyes were pale green even though the room was dim—eyes locked on her like a predator.

Dominic Bright in the flesh was a punch to the gut. A sensory wallop of total and unbelievable hotness.

Sprawled in a booth in a roped-off VIP section, his physical presence was nearly as large as his magickal one. The dark T-shirt he wore stretched over tight muscles and broad shoulders. Black boots peeked from the bottom of his jeans. Long legs stretched out before him.

Masculine. The man was breathtakingly masculine. Sharp features marked him, heavy-lidded, sexy eyes, a goatee; his shoulder length hair was thick and she wondered what it would feel like between her fingers. His lips promised such carnal delights she had to take a deep breath to steady herself.

His energy was immense. He had reserves she'd lay odds he had no idea how to use. She wondered if he even knew he was a council witch. So much raw power emanated from him she wanted to lean in and take a long sniff.

Since that would undermine her own position and power, and since most people didn't smell each other in public, she refrained from the aforementioned sniffing and found her own center.

His gaze caressed up her body and settled upon her face. "Welcome to the Heart of Darkness, pretty witch."

His voice was deep and scratchy. He didn't yell over the music and yet she heard him perfectly.

She continued her approach, steadying legs that may have buckled had she been a lesser woman, stopping finally when her thighs touched the table. The scent of his magick hung about him like a heavy cloak. And fed her like she'd been starving.

"Mr. Bright, you've been a very naughty boy."

"So I've been told a time or two. I take it you're Clan Owen here to spank me."

"I bet you have." But she wasn't there about *that*. Not until she finished this other business at the very least. She modulated her voice, not yelling, but whispering on the wind. "You tapped into Owen property without asking."

His eyelids slid down just a little and she nearly moaned when he licked his lips. "Very nice. All that sex and magick . . . potent."

One of her brows rose as she favored him with a smile. This one was a charmer.

"But you're not a hunter."

He knew enough to understand at least something of the structure of a clan. Ignorance wouldn't be his excuse for theft then. "If I was, we wouldn't be talking. We don't want to kill you. We're not like that. Most of the time. We just want you to ask nicely when you take our property."

"Would you like to sit?" Goddess, his mouth was an ode to the creator. The way it quirked up just a bit when he finished a sentence was a sight burned into her retinas.

Her gaze flicked over the women splayed on either side of him before moving back to his face. She wouldn't spill Owen business in public. Nor did she want to share his attention with anyone else. "I'd prefer to speak with you in private."

He stood, stepping over the women carefully, and Meriel tried not to gulp like a sixteen-year-old girl. He moved the few feet to her, his energy barely leashed. It was a good thing she stood nearly six feet tall because Dominic easily topped six and change.

"Shall we go to my office?" He motioned with his hand and she allowed him to steer her, his hand at the small of her back. That touch nearly undid her.

Dominic had felt the Owen witch the minute she walked through the doors out front. Her power rolled through the building, slid through him, velvet and warm. Her presence coursed through his veins. She'd sent out her spell as he watched her drink with Simon at the bar.

He liked the way she tasted on the air. Bright and spicy. Dusky and earthy too. Her spell was clever and apparently effortless. Something like that might take him a few hours to create. He admired it, even as he kept out of range.

Unreasonable anger sparked when Simon did what Simon did best. Dominic had stewed as the Were put his hand on her waist and she responded, standing close and flirting. The closer she moved to Simon the more agitated Dominic had become until finally grabbing her spell and tugging hard to snag her attention. When she'd turned and he saw her face, really saw her face, he'd hesitated a moment, fascinated. Beauty and power, a very potent combination in any woman.

Watching her approach had been worth giving her his location earlier than he'd planned. She moved like sex, rhythmic, smooth like honey. Generous curves filled out the snug shirt and he liked the look of her legs with the short skirt and mid-calf Frye boots she wore.

Shit kickers, those boots. They sealed the deal as far as he was concerned. Another woman would be teetering in sky-high stilettos, but this one looked just as hot and she'd have been able to run his ass down if he gave her trouble.

He didn't know a whole lot about the universe of clan witches, but he'd done some digging on Owen when he'd decided to use the back rooms there as a club for Others. This one was the daughter of the leader Edwina Owen. Next in line.

In a world of beautiful women, this one lodged herself in his attentions. He wanted more of her, which was interesting in and of itself. Powerful, so powerful he fought the urge to drag his tongue up her throat to get a taste. She held it to herself, snug. Tightly controlled just like the rest of her. He wanted to muss her up. Repeatedly.

Unbelievably, after less than ten minutes of seeing her, he had a mighty big want on for the delicious Ms. Owen.

He usually avoided sexual interludes with other witches. He was outclan and his unaffiliated status tended to make clan witches territorial. Before he'd been with them a few months they started talking about clan affiliation.

And he wasn't a joiner.

But he couldn't shake the image of her spread beneath him, naked, writhing, her body offered up to his hands and mouth like the feast she so clearly was. Without a doubt, he knew he needed to sink balls-deep into this woman's body, and as soon as possible.

The hallway from the club back to his office was far quieter than in the club itself. He caught the sound of her breath, the hiss of fabric as they walked. Her scent wisped in her wake, seducing, teasing, but not giving him enough to satisfy.

He found himself wanting to slow down. Wanting to stretch out all the time he had with her. He must have done it because she reached his office and turned back to him, waiting.

He approached, not hiding the way he ate her up with his gaze. But when he reached around her body to use the small spell to unlock his door, their magick mingled for long moments. Tugging low in his belly, mimicking sexual attraction.

Interesting.

"Please, have a seat," he said as they entered and he closed his door.

"I'm Dominic Bright, I didn't properly introduce myself out there." He bowed slightly, remembering he had some manners.

She waved a casual hand. "I know who you are. I'm Meriel Owen. We both know who the other is. Now, care to explain why you're drawing from our font without permission?"

Up-front, this witch. He should just get it over with. He knew it. He needed to pay his dues or whatever. But the flavor of her magick all around him made him crave more. He wanted to spar, to whet his appetite for her.

"The wards here are for the good of all. I can't see why you'd begrudge me that tiny bit of power." He shrugged, spreading his hands out to appear reasonable.

She exhaled, clearly annoyed. It only spurred him on.

"Begrudging." She rolled her eyes. "Really, Mr. Bright. If we begrudged you, we'd be teenage girls." She shrugged. "Certainly we wouldn't be powerful enough for you to be concerned when you shoplift from our font." When she cocked her head, her hair slid forward, red, burgundy, threads of gold glinting in the light. He wondered what it would feel like. Before he reached to find out, he busied his hands with a pen.

"You're using our magick and you haven't asked. Clearly the nature of this place mandates strong wards to prevent exposure. And you know our position on exposure. So while Clan Owen is certainly sympathetic to your problem, the bigger issue remains."

Yes, he knew the prevention of exposure was paramount to their people. And yes, he tended to agree that keeping what they were on the down low was a very good thing.

"Lastly, you're a businessman, Mr. Bright. If I had a drink here, I'd have to ask for it and offer some sort of payment for it."

"Or be so fucking sexy a Lycian prince buys you one."

She smiled and he felt a corresponding tug in his groin.

She shrugged and went on, "We all have our little bonuses in life. But in any case, you get my point. The font exists to be used by all witches *within* this clan. We don't quibble with another witch using it. But there are rules and even an outclan witch knows to ask."

He didn't like asking any more than he liked rules. Damned witches and their rule obsession. Plus, he knew he'd have to give them information about himself, an in to his own magickal signature. He didn't like anyone having knowledge about him that they could use.

Perceptive brown eyes looked into his. Reading him. Knowing. Saw through the outer façade, right into his soul. He didn't like that she got him so well, much less the fact that he'd known her all of twenty minutes.

Just for the briefest of moments, she caught her bottom lip between her teeth. But that brief moment was enough to send shards of desire splintering through his system. Her presence affected him so much he'd have suspected magicks, but there were none. He had excellent personal shields; he'd have known if she had attempted to ensorcell him. Just being near, the taste of her magick on his skin, had rendered him slightly punch-drunk.

He didn't trust it. Didn't trust anything that fast and intense.

She finally spoke, breaking the silence and saving him from the urge to blurt out that he wanted to take her back to his place and strip her naked. He wanted to see what sunrise looked like on her neck, what shadows it would create in the hollow of her throat, the dip of her belly button.

"I can close my eyes when you share magick with me, if that helps. That's it, right?"

He paused, the words stuck in his throat. Perceptive. So much so he found himself ruffled by it. He cleared his throat. "I don't share magick very often," he said, his annoyance clear in his voice. Enough that her eyebrows rose in response.

She sat forward, choosing her words carefully. "Look, I get that you're probably unaffiliated for a reason and we respect that. We're a clan, not a cult. We're all members by choice. Others make different choices and that's fine too. *I* respect your choice. But the font is powered by *every* witch in the clan and they all agree to let others use it as long as everyone shares. That's how it works. We all pay in. We all can use it. If we let you shoplift, others will too. And then what's the point? You don't want to be in a clan, that's your choice. But it's *not* your choice to steal from us. We won't allow it."

She paused, letting what she'd said sink in. He'd never mistake her for a pushover, pretty face or not. She was a smart, savage woman who'd kick his ass from Seattle to Toronto if she had to. Which only made him want more.

Her voice softened, "No one can get into your head. No one can steal your magick."

"But that's how the font works. You take power from witches in the clan."

She made a face, first annoyed, then confused. Strangely, he wanted to laugh.

"No, that's not how the font works." She twisted the bracelet on her left wrist and he saw her clan mark. A pretty, stylized *O* for Owen. "Has no one ever explained it to you?"

He shook his head. He didn't need her pity. "I've been told enough to get by. I wasn't raised in a clan. My foster father was my teacher but he's unaffiliated."

She nodded, tucking her hair behind her ear. "Fair enough. I'm not insulting your intelligence or what you were taught, but you don't understand how it works. When you expend magick—if you're keyed into the font—the magick once performed will absorb back. It's a collector of sorts."

She must have seen his confusion.

"Okay, so you know energy never dies, it simply turns into something else. That's physics. It's not like I made it up. Anyway, the font doesn't *steal* your magick. It collects whatever the magick dissipates into once the function is served. Like a cistern collects rainwater, for example. Only the dissipated energy once collected, will mature into magickal energy over time and be there should anyone need it.

"Essentially, if you were a registered user of the font, each time someone walked through those wards, a glimmer of energy would travel back to the font. But it can't because you're not keyed in. It's either wasted or it amps up the witches here in the club. I don't own a nightclub but I know enough to think that's a dumb idea. Alcohol, pheromones and added magickal power is an unstable combination."

She sat back, crossing her legs, flashing a slice of pale inner thigh. Good goddess, any minute he was going to drool or something. Even so, he wasn't so far gone that he failed to notice the intelligence she possessed, the calm confidence with which she carried herself.

"We're not like some of the other clans. I'm not here to hurt you, although I'd like to bite you, right there on your biceps. Just because it looks tasty." She blushed a little bit, like she was surprised by her own words. He understood the feeling, being off balance at the moment as well.

"You should feel welcome to bite any part of me you like. Within reason."

"I'll keep that in mind." Then her flirty nature disappeared as she clearly got back to business. "You have to key in or we'll cut you off. We don't negotiate on this. If you try to get into the font again, I won't be back but our hunters will and they're not nearly as nice as I am." She shrugged after relaying the threat.

"You say no one has to be clan but clearly they do."

She made a face, disappointed in that response. "You're too pretty to be a whiner. Look, you're powerful, I can see that, but you don't have enough skill to ward this place on your own. You can key in with me, which I hasten to add will not automatically make you a member of Clan Owen. You'd have access to the font and, let's be honest, shall we, some goodwill that might allow this place to stay open in our territory. Or you can try it on your own, without our font. You and I both know how that will end."

"And then you'd be really hard to convince to go out with me."

She paused and blushed, just a little. The openness of the moment slowed that time in between them for long moments.

She'd spent every day of her entire life around witches. There was always something comfortable about that. Sometimes it was also exciting or even arousing depending on the other witch. But this connection they had, the way she couldn't stop thinking about touching him, the way the stamp of his magick caught her breath, that was something different. Deeper. A little scary and a lot exhilarating.

As it happened, she liked this man a lot and it pleased her to know he felt the same. He flirted really well too.

"Yes, very likely I'd be quite annoyed if you made me come all the way down here and refused to key in and then called me to ask me on a date. Say to *Turandot*, which is in town and something I quite love." Her lips twitched into a breath of a smile before she resumed her best attempt at a calm expression.

"And, if you like, I can give you a bit of a primer on other things you may not know or understand about us."

"I could key in with you?"

"Of course." She waited for him to think over his answer. She wasn't going to push him to rush his choice. He was a businessman, he'd know he had to do it to keep that doorway hidden. But he'd have to find a way to accept it because she had plenty of power to cut him off right then and there. One brief spell and she'd unravel all those ties to the font and his spellwork would slowly die off without all the energy he'd been thieving.

"And other things? I could do other things with you?"

She couldn't deny it. When they did end up in bed, there'd be teeth marks and no few scratches. There was so much something between them. Energy? Yes, but that wasn't quite it. Chemistry, yes. Attraction, sure. *Potential*. Yes, that's what it felt like.

"Let's start with keying in and we can discuss your definition of *other things*." Her insides jittered, thrilled at the idea of working magick with him. Her power flowed, building within, filling, filling as she drew her shields away. Never had it been like this with anyone before.

Normally her magick would rise as she let her shields down, but this was a rush of energy. Surging in reaction to his. She knew she teased him now with hers. Knew tendrils of it slid over his, seducing. It brought her to her metaphorical knees.

The building could fall down around them and it wouldn't matter. There was nothing else she wanted to do in the world but share magick with Dominic Bright.

"Do I have your permission to ward this room and set a circle?"

He'd been caught by the looks of her. Fascinated and ensnared by all the parts of her. Been impressed by her demeanor and intelligence. But the surge of her energies had washed over and through him with such force it was physical. His own shields had slid aside and his magick rose in response. The pleasure of it shocked straight to his toes. And another place or two.

Clearly working magick with a council witch was a far more intense thing than with a commonwealth witch. Whatever it was, it felt awesome and he wanted a lot more.

Admittedly, her explanation of how the font worked had made him feel better. Not that he really had that much of a choice. She'd been absolutely right when she'd said he didn't have the skill to keep the wards and other spells working on his own. And he didn't want any part in exposing his own people by being a selfish sloppy asshole.

"Yes. My permission is freely given."

Chapter 5

SHE nodded and took a deep breath and her energy actually moved, like the tide, around him. Wow.

"Freely taken." Efficiently, she took her boots off and padded over to the door, drawing sigils in the air as she spoke under her breath. He only had the barest knowledge of the sort of magick she made as he watched her work. So much skill. She worked the spell, weaving it all together, fitting it perfectly together until it caught hold and came into being.

What he'd tasted of her just moments before had been a whisper of what it was like now. It was as if what he'd experienced had been through a filter, and he supposed that was true; shields were created to keep a witch's power under control.

He'd never had a taste of another witch so powerful. His skin itched as he watched her set the circle. His body ached for her, drawn to her. His power pressed against his skin.

"I invite you into the circle." Her eyes lit with the power she'd unleashed, her creamy-pale skin took on a pearlescent glow. Taking in that beauty for long moments, he snapped out of it and stepped in with her, clasping her hands. And for a second everything in him and all around him settled and was totally silent, as if holding a breath.

"I'm just going to key you in. It shouldn't take very long. Let my power recognize yours and get your signature. Open yourself and let me in." She paused when he didn't comply right away. He wasn't sure what to do. It wasn't like he ever let anyone in like she was asking. And that tautened sense of something about to happen rode his senses so hard it made him suspicious of it.

She pressed a hand at his sternum. "Your magick lives here. And our shields are a sort of cork, right?"

He nodded, following the logic.

"So it's useful to have a visual for some witches. Me, for instance. Even when you remove your shields, your tendency will be to hold it back. Those control lessons are the first most of us learn. I sometimes think of a handful of sand. Just unclench and the magick will spill. I'll catch it."

Looking deep into her eyes, he knew he could trust her. Not the whys just yet, but he rarely ignored his gut. So he took her advice and threw the locks on his power. It opened up and she flowed in. Like, literally. He felt her energy float into his and suddenly, the circle expanded, tightening to the point of near bursting as magickal feedback screamed. He held on, not knowing what would happen if he let go. So he kept feeding her power to try to even things out.

Her eyes, which had been blurred as she worked, snapped into focus and she looked at him, surprise ghosting over her features before she tipped her head back and laughed. The sound of it filled the circle, stroked his skin, tingling. Their magick suddenly eased and mingled in a way so intimate it felt as if it whispered sweet nothings in his ear.

He'd never felt so exposed in his life. Laid bare and undone and yet it felt so good that it was her who'd drawn away all his defenses and left him this way.

"It's the energy of all the witches who give to the font. The flavor of Clan Owen." Her murmured words reassured and soothed him past that panicked spot as he let himself truly examine this new connection he had to this font of theirs.

MERIEL looked at him again as he keyed into the font and all that magick and community settled into his system. The wonder and confusion on his face told her that he had no idea it would feel so lovely to be connected to a font. And most likely that he had no idea why their individual magicks had interacted that way.

But she'd grown up around witches and in a clan. She knew what it felt like to share magick, both sexually and metaphysically. Nothing she'd done could compare to what she'd just shared with Dominic.

Not only had every last bit of her magick sprung to her intent nearly instantly, but her ability to work the spells had sharpened. She saw the spell glimmering around them. Vibrant, with all the threads she'd used humming with real-ized magick.

All in reaction to and in conjunction with his power. It was the combination of their magicks that had ripened into something far more powerful and intense. Dominic Bright was her bond-mate. He clearly had *no* idea, but it made her happy nonetheless. Simply being with him in a circle made her nearly drunk with the way their power intermingled and caressed.

"This feels amazing," Dominic murmured. "Does it always feel this way when you work magick with a full-council witch?"

She shook her head. "Working magick with another witch usually feels good, yes. But . . . Have you never done that before? Felt this level of interconnectedness and power lev-els with another witch?"

He took a deep breath, leaning in closer and she had to lock her knees to keep from swooning.

"Yes, yes, of course, I've worked magick with other witches. My foster father taught me growing up. I've learned from teachers. Other witches I met here and there. Though

I've not let anyone in as far as you. It never felt this good in the past. Christ, Meriel, when it feels like this I can sort of understand why witches get stuck."

Stuck was slang for a witch who'd become addicted to magic. *Magick* came to a witch naturally. Each is born with a set of gifts. Some have very little power. A very small group had a great deal of power. Most had aptitude for certain kinds of magick and excelled on some level but overall were just everyday witches with moderate power levels.

Some people got off on that rush of pleasure when magick rushes through your body. And she got that; it felt good after all. But some witches couldn't get enough and started stealing energy through rites and spells. This unnatural and stolen energy was magic, like what a magician uses. Less powerful and didn't replenish. Most involved theft of energy from other beings. Most involved pain or blood. Sometimes worse. The more they resorted to magic over their own inherent magickal gifts, the quicker it stripped a witch of their power because it attacked their connection to the earth all around them. Without that connection, the natural connection between witch and ground is broken.

What she had with Dominic wasn't anything at all like being stuck. Though he had no idea what it was he was feeling, it galled her nonetheless that he seemed unaware that it was special. Which was unfair because he'd clearly felt something major happen and she was all over the map with her emotions.

She mentally slapped herself. "Stealing magick and destroying everything we stand for wouldn't feel like this. This is something specific and right." She hesitated for a moment, wondering how exactly to tell him just exactly why.

"There's something you aren't saying. Tell me."

So much for that. Best to be blunt and hope he knew what she was talking about. "We're bond-mates, Dominic. *That's* why it feels this way. Our magick was made to work together. Meant to, as it happens."

He stood up straighter. "*Bond-mates?* Sorry, but from

what I understand that's only for council witches. I'm not full-council, Meriel."

Of course it wasn't going to be easy. She'd just coached Nell through a mating with a man who despite wanting it couldn't admit it for some time. "Yes, you are. Or you certainly wouldn't be my bond-mate. Or anyone else's. Someone in your line was full-council at some point."

She touched his temple, the warmth of his skin against her fingertips. A lock of his hair brushed against the back of her hand. She only barely resisted her urge to laugh at the look on his face. Confusion, wonder, anger, denial. He was such an open book. As a full-council witch, she'd grown up knowing at some point she'd ascend to her true power level once she united her magick with her bond-mate. Part of her had figured her bond-mate probably wouldn't even be a romantic or sexual mating, but one of power only, like the one her mother had.

But the man just a foot away was *far* more than just a compatriot in magick. This man was meant to be hers in a way she could see on his face he did not begin to understand. Hell, she'd grown up expecting this and she wasn't sure she completely understood it all.

Nor did it look like he wanted to deal with it just yet. He leaned into her touch nonetheless, feeling the same irresistible lure she did. It would always be that way between them. Now that she'd tasted his magick, she'd crave more.

And to be honest with herself, she was sure that regardless of the bond, she'd be drawn to the man she stood so deliciously close to.

The storm of *what ifs* and *when will it bes* that had been laying waste to her thoughts, churning in her gut, had all quieted. Gone. It wouldn't be easy with this man. She knew it like she knew her name. He had trouble written all over him.

But there was something else too. Something beyond the beauty of the skin stretched taut over muscles. A body she wanted to caress and lick from head to toe. Beyond the cant of the smile that promised very bad and enjoyable things. He was so incredibly beautiful, cocky, self-sufficient. And yet there was a vulnerability there she'd just seen glimpses of. There was something in his eyes that gave her an absolute surety that he'd be worth the struggle.

She expected scientific proof of many things. But sometimes fate was just fate. And he was hers.

Sliding her fingertips down his temple, she found the warmth of his jaw, the softness just beneath, the fragility of him just there. His pulse thundered against her touch as a sound broke from his lips—a ragged moan that tore at her self-control. Opening her hand, she luxuriated in the feel of him against her palm when she slid it around his neck, the hardness of him sending need through her, flooding, intoxicating.

The warmth of his body brought his essence, man and magick, rising to her nose and she shivered at how delicious he was. Her mouth watered as she wanted. Wanted to taste, to lick and kiss and to be licked and kissed.

His eyes, half-mast and burning with some inner light, locked onto hers and nearly sent her to her knees. She paused, not a bad idea really. She wanted to devour him. It hit her with so much force her hands began to tremble.

And then she closed her eyes. Just for a moment.

A vision of him above her, of sliding against him, sweat-slicked skin. Of him inside her hit her and rebounded back to him. With a gasp she opened her eyes, needing to see him, needing to know if she was alone or if he had, indeed felt what she had.

The pale green gaze she found locked on her face told her she wasn't alone, which sent heat through her anew. His eyes darkened. The flutter of his pulse at the base of his throat caught her eye and she licked her lips.

With a soft intake of breath, he banded her waist with his arm and hauled her against his body. His mouth covered hers and the sweetness of his desire bled through her, saturating every single cell. Need ravaged through her as he drove out all the emptiness in a way she was certain only he was capable of.

She swallowed his ragged moan and dug her nails into his biceps. She'd never wanted anyone before with such raw power, such craven greed. Her skin itched with it, her insides melted as the flames of his energy licked through her.

He tore his mouth away, chest heaving as he strained to breathe. His cock burned into her lower belly where it was quite clear he felt the same way she did.

"I can't be your bond-mate." The statement was laced with desperation, but he knew it wasn't true.

She laughed. "You are and you know it. But it's sudden. I get that. I can wait until you're ready." He would be. It'd just take time. He'd need to get to know her before he could commit. In the meantime, there was no reason at all why they shouldn't be together, get to know each other. And, um, have sex and stuff. A lot of it.

But not right away. Sex would only make the need grow, only strengthen the connection they had. And there was no way she wanted him to ever wonder if he rushed into things or if he'd been swayed by the scorching-hot sex. And she knew without any doubt at all it would be just that.

She cleared her throat after her mouth had gone dry at the very idea of what they'd be like in bed. "I need to break the circle, all right?"

He nodded, his arm still banded around her waist, making it absolutely clear he had no plans to let go. *Yum.* Gooseflesh worked over her. She loved an in-charge male and this one spilled magick and testosterone until she drowned in it.

Even when she broke the circle, the intensity of their attraction still made it hard to think straight.

"Just so you know this, whatever else is happening between us, I need you." He pressed his mouth to the place where her neck met her shoulder and took a long, deep breath.

Swoon.

"I plan to need you more than once."

His voice made her nipples harden to the point of pain. Yep, not just a bonding of like powers. This was a deep, DNA tingling, supercharged fuckfest of a bonding. Two lives united to heighten power was a given of the magick bond. But Dominic Bright was her heart's mate as well as her magick's mate, even if he wasn't ready to know or accept that part yet.

But she was certain. If he was simply a magickal mate, their connection wouldn't have been sensual or sexual at all. But it sure as heck was sexual. All her parts paid attention in an oh-let's-make-babies sort of way when their energies mixed.

That knowing appealed to the organizer, the control freak within, satisfied her in a way she'd been totally surprised by.

She shivered when his lips brushed over the outer shell of her ear as he whispered, "Six blocks. I live six blocks from here. I'd take you right here if I didn't know the door would be pounded on sixteen times in the next hour. I'm in no mood to be interrupted."

"I'm across the lake in Bellevue." She tried to move back but he held her in place. "We need to take this slowly. We can talk at your place. Unless it's all stunk up with other women."

He laughed, taking two handfuls of her ass and snugging her against him even tighter. "I don't play with women at my apartment. But I'm going to play with you there."

"Play?" She swallowed. What had she gotten herself into and could she get there faster? No! No, she needed to keep her mind above her waistline and be smart, damn it.

He let go, only stepping a few feet away to pick up the phone, giving directions as his gaze greedily roved over her body like a roughened caress. "I can get us a taxi or we can walk. It's up to you. Tell me and I'll make it happen."

Goddess, she wanted him to kiss her again.

She cleared her throat, lecturing herself to hold it together. She was a powerful witch, a smart woman and if she rushed into this without thinking, she might miss something good. This man was the rest of her life; it would be a crime to not pay attention.

Yes, what they had together was intoxicating, but there were real-life considerations to be made. He didn't trust or apparently understand much about clans and it would be a wedge between them if they didn't address it.

Clans were everything Meriel was. She was proud of what her foremothers had done before her to protect their people. As next in line, she'd run Owen one day. If he accepted her, he'd have to accept that too.

But none of that was necessary right at that moment. Just then she wanted to be alone with him, to touch and be touched. She needed him all to herself.

She smirked up at him. "My car is in valet. Some sad little wannabe named Spider, who'd piss his pants if a real vampire ever showed him fang, parked it. Better not have scratched it either. Really, Dominic, *Spider*?"

His lips quivered as he tried not to smile. "I don't name them. They come with names you know. I walked so I'll let you drive, although I sense that may be a mistake. Give me the tag, I'll have it brought around."

She handed it to him, both of them shivering a bit as their fingertips brushed, and he called quickly. A tap on the door sounded. Meriel opened the wards and Simon walked in. He took in the sight of her and cut his gaze to Dominic, looking mighty annoyed.

"Damn it, Dom. You're poaching." He looked very hand-some and territorial standing there. Until his nostrils flared and his spine lost its rigidity. "She's got your damned scent all over her. Outclan witches like you have mates? You're like one of those full-council guys and you didn't tell me?"

Dominic snorted. "I didn't tell you because I didn't know and I'm still not convinced." Meriel locked her jaw, holding her words back. Instead she rolled her eyes.

Which Dominic didn't notice as there was some sort of dick-measuring moment taking place between the two men. She sighed loudly and grabbed her bag. This startled them both and Dominic put his hand on her elbow.

"Simon, you've met Meriel. I hope you enjoyed touching her because that was the last time it'll ever happen. We're going now. I'll see you tomorrow. Keep an eye on the vampires near the back bar."

Dominic put his body between them, his arm tight around her and walked her out the back door where her car waited. Interesting. She'd never experienced that level of possessiveness before and goddess help her, she liked it.

He stared at the powerful Camaro rumbling there. Waiting. "You said car. This isn't a car. This is a dream. I'm impressed." He moved the valet out of the way to hold her door open himself.

She walked around and got in. "It's not mine. It's my best friend Nell's. She's on her honeymoon so I'm driving it in her absence."

He slid inside, his large form looking hot, even as he also appeared completely capable of violence if necessary.

"Oh, I'm so going to fuck you in this car, maybe on it as we're both tall. I'm at 2nd and Broad. The garage entrance is on Broad."

She didn't tell him Nell would kill her for having sex in or on this car. It sounded really hot anyway. She followed his directions and they arrived in under two minutes. Neither spoke in that short time but for a few directional words from Dominic. The tension felt unbearably good.

The building had good security but she still worked a protection spell around the car. Nell would also kill her if that car got scratched. They'd been friends since both could walk so it would be bad to kill each other over a car scratch.

Meriel wished she could call Nell right then, to ask for some advice about this whole situation. Meriel could probably track her friend down. Nell would take the call and not ever complain. She was sure no one would give her better advice, but Meriel wanted her friend to have a honeymoon free from work or drama. She'd tell Nell about it when she returned. It was just a few days. Until then she was on her own. She handled lawyers and psychos all day long; it wasn't like she was ill equipped to deal with this guy.

He held a hand out.

She took it, swallowing back a gasp as their contact reawakened the spark between them and their power surged again.

Chapter 6

IT wasn't until she stood in his living room that she made a decision and one she knew was right, even as she hated to say it out loud. "We can't have sex tonight."

He froze, blinking at her, disbelief on his features.

"What? Why? Did you hit your head on the way up from the garage?"

She allowed herself a long look at him. Holy crap was she in over her head here. He was so freaking hot. Long and tall, stylish. All the expensive clothes in the world couldn't hide the very real fact that he was a predator though. He'd look delicious in a tux, but the brawler within would always be there, hinting at the edges.

So much more than he appeared on the surface. Which made her hungrier for him. She wanted to know his story. That longing to know was as powerful as her desire to be naked and sweaty with him.

That visual was *so* not helpful in her resolve. She twisted her fingers and ordered her hormones to knock it off. For all the good that did. They were doing a conga line and had two kegs tapped.

"I don't know if I can explain this right."

"Give it a try. Because I know you want me. I can feel it. I can taste your desire in the air." He waved around agitatedly.

"Once we give in and have sex, this need between us will only get stronger."

He interrupted with a sharp movement of his hand. "And this is bad why?"

It helped that he was being a cock. "Interrupt much? Seriously, do boys just say anything they have to to have sex? It's like you're all frozen at age fifteen." She began to pace and he tossed himself on a nearby couch, arms crossed, glowering in her direction like she'd told him he couldn't have a cookie until after dinner.

He made a sort of snorting sound that still managed to be smooth. "Please do enlighten me on why it's bad to want each other more. And I'm *going* to have sex with you so I don't need to say things designed to compel you."

Smug bastard. He couldn't know it, but she found boys to be utterly charming. Not because they tried to be. But because they were just totally from another universe. All that focus on sex, when they weren't dickheaded manwhores like some men could be, was cute. She wisely withheld that commentary though. *Stern.* Yes, she needed to be stern.

"It's become quite clear to me that you don't know much about my world. You may or may not believe the whole bondmate thing. I want you to want me for me. I want you to want what's between us tomorrow and the day after. I don't want to go forward and have sex and then next month or next year have you wonder, even just in the back of your mind if you would have made a different choice had we not rushed into sex."

"Meriel, come here." He held a hand out and she looked at him carefully. He was the human equivalent of sour cream and onion Pringles *and* egg rolls. So very good, but man, oh, man, could she be in trouble if she allowed herself to gorge on him.

Dominic started to laugh at how she looked at him. A few memories of what it was like to be a fifteen-year-old boy came back. "I promise we won't do anything you don't want to. I'll stop when you say to."

She snorted a laugh and moved to him, keeping some distance. "Next you'll tell me you'll only put the tip in. I'm onto you."

Not liking the space between them, he grabbed her, pulling her boots off and freezing at the sight of her socks.

"You're all business and then you reveal some small thing, like these socks." He looked back to the Hello Kitty socks. He'd noted that she had socks on back at the club, but he was too busy looking at the legs and being bowled over by her presence to see the detail. The cat had on a ninja outfit and was wielding a sword looking silly and fierce. Just like she was.

"I like socks." She blinked at him, he could tell, not sure whether to take him seriously or not. And he couldn't really blame her. He wasn't used to this whatever it was between them. He wasn't an overly serious man any more than he was a silly one. He'd dated and he'd fucked a lot of women. He had women friends. But this was different and totally new territory for him. She made him feel things, want things he'd never imagined before.

"I like socks when they're on you." He slid his hand higher, over the curve of her calf, up her thigh, all while she watched him, clearly torn between interest and suspicion. "You're taking me right back to high school, Meriel. What's your middle name?"

Her brows knitted as she tried to figure out his game. She was out of her league, he was a con man, a master player and she didn't have a chance against him.

Thank the heavens for it.

"Patrice. Why does this take you back to high school? Did you trick girls into sitting next to you and while complimenting their socks all innocent-like, you slid your hand up their thigh until your fingertips were just a whisper away from their panties? We're all trained to foil your gender's tricks, you know. I was a whiz at deflecting wandering hands."

He sent her what was supposed to be a reassuring smile but she snorted so he knew she was on to him.

"I'm sure I said something like, *I know you're nervous, but I promise you'll like it*. Let me make you feel good,

Meriel. I'm not teasing you now. I want that. How can it be wrong for me to want to give you pleasure?"

Her breath hitched when he pressed ever so lightly, the heat and wet of her a siren song. The simplicity of that moment felt so very right. Goddess he wanted her, wanted to possess her in every way imaginable.

Just a bit more and the heated crotch of her panties rested against his outstretched fingertips. Her lips parted on a soft sound of pleasure, a murmur, a groan, a wordless gust of expression that needed no interpretation.

Keeping his eyes on hers, he slowly pulled the silky material back until she was bared to his touch. He had to swallow and count to ten and then twenty-five when all that glorious sweet slickness met his fingers. *He'd* made her that way.

Her eyes found focus again and she started to speak.

"Ssshhh. Let me. I want to give this to you. We can talk more about your no-sex thing when I've made you come." To underline his point, he stroked from side to side until her gaze went glossy again and she relaxed.

"This is a very bad idea. With your hands on me, it's hard to think. All I want is more."

"Then let me give it to you," he nearly purred it as he touched her. Covetous. She brought out an intense greed in him. It filled him from head to toe.

"Are you listening to me? Sex is a deeply intimate act. Once we bare ourselves to each other like that it's going to bind us on a basic level. Once it happens, our connection will only get stronger."

He backed off slightly, not removing his hand entirely, but ceasing to stroke her.

"This is big. I know it and you feel it, but you don't know enough about it to truly accept it. The way we feel together is intoxicating. Truly. Our chemicals and our magicks are meant to mix and work best as a unit. You don't have to believe me, but I need to tell you." She moved his hand back, out of her panties and he acquiesced, but stayed close.

"In a very real way, we're drunk on each other. I'm certain about this bonding between you and me. I was raised in a world surrounded by people with bond-mates. I know it exists because I see it every day.

"But you didn't grow up in a clan and you don't seem to know a lot about us. So while *I'm* sure of the bond, I want you to be too. If we do this tonight, you'll wonder one day and that would break my heart."

At those last words her bottom lip trembled just a bit and he ached to make it better.

That and he had to admit he understood her point.

"You're going to kill me." He moved her so that she fit against his side, not willing to not be touching her. "It's going to be midnight shortly. Does that count as not rushing?"

She frowned at him, but then shook her head with a slow smile. "You're going to be trouble."

He laughed, surprised by her.

"I want to fuck you." He sighed and then that intensity of his focus was back and she shivered. "And just so we're clear, I *will* fuck you. But I understand your perspective and it can wait. Not a long time or I'll explode."

She snickered and he didn't resist the urge to play his fingers through her hair. He liked being around her. She was the kind of woman who had her shit together. The calm and hyperefficient type he rarely ended up with and now he wondered why. He dug the self-sufficiency and the desire to ruffle her feathers and see just how wild she could be once he got down a few layers was nearly overwhelming.

"Why don't you tell me about the bonding?"

"All right, I will." She sniffed, slightly snotty and he dug it. "I'm going to give you the basics. You may know some of this so cut me some slack."

He didn't know much, he admitted inwardly.

"In every clan you've got two types of witches. Commonwealth witches, essentially ninety percent of the clan. And council witches."

"Why the disparity? Why so many of them and so few of you?"

"*Us.* We're freaks of nature."

He narrowed his gaze. "What?"

"Most science points to a genetic anomaly. And a percent-age of that percentage is compatible with each other. And when they connect their magick with the ascension—a spell that'll unite our magick—they rise to an even greater level of power by several orders of magnitude. It's our function, and our honor to use that extra power to run and protect the clan for the benefit of its members."

He tended to see that point and yet it bugged him that the few ran the clan for the many. And he said so.

"The wards at Heart of Darkness? I've seen only a hand-ful of witches who can work spells like that. You're already powerful and unique. Now, me? I could have done it and not tapped into the font. Because I've been trained. If you choose to ascend, you'd be able to do it ten times over without much of an effort. So it's not much of a surprise is it? That witches with that sort of power end up running things?"

"Honestly, I don't know. I mean, I get it. But it seems undemocratic."

She shrugged. "It *is* undemocratic. We're not a country, we're a voluntary membership organization whose sole mis-sion is to protect and enrich member witches."

"Did you get training to rule then?"

"It's easy to be flip when you don't know anything. Yes, as a matter of fact. I've been in training since before I took my first step. I work, on average, nearly eighty hours a week."

"So do I."

She raised one brow, very slowly. "And yet, I'm not attack-ing your life. It's the other way around."

"I'm not attacking anything." Well, he supposed, it might appear that way. "Did you know your whole life you were meant to be full-council? I mean, because your mom is, you are too?"

She let him get away with his statement, but they both knew she did. "Your mother must have been as well as your father. Children born of unions between two full-council witches will be full-council. Mixed couples it's about a quarter of the time."

"It's a wonder you're not all inbred freaks." As soon as it came from his mouth he wished he hadn't said it.

"Such a way with words."

"I don't like my life and future dictated by a bunch of shit I had nothing to do with deciding."

"So don't." She shrugged and tugged free and he felt her absence acutely. "I'm not interested in forcing you to do anything, much less be with me. I want you to make that choice of your own free will. You still have it." She pushed to stand.

"I do? How's that? You walk into my club, we have this, this thing between us and now I can't get enough of you."

She sighed. "It's our chemistry. I explained that. Genetics, magick, all that is our personal stew. Yours and mine like each other." She stepped into her boots and he sat straighter, alarmed.

"What are you doing?"

"I'm going home." She held a hand out. "This is why I'm glad we didn't have sex. Stay. Think." She bent to her bag and pulled a card out. "Here. My numbers are on that. If we decide to go forward, you can try to get into my panties like everyone else. Work for it. I like opera and Thai food and steaks. You can call me for a date and we can get to know each other."

He could see the hurt on her face. "Don't go."

"No. I need to. Because you and I are at totally different places. I grew up knowing this was my path. I greet this bond between us as a wondrous thing. You view it with suspicion. And I get it. You haven't been educated about what we are and what we do."

"This doesn't mean you have to leave. Stay. Educate me."

"You don't want that right now and I can't be here this way." She picked her coat up and he moved to her.

"I want you. I like you, Meriel. But you can't expect me to just jump on the bond-mate bandwagon when I didn't even know I was a council witch until a few hours ago."

"I know and I don't. I'm happy to teach you about yourself and your history. If you want that, you know where to get hold of me."

He stood there, confused and frustrated. "Let me walk you to your car at least."

She shook her head. "No. I need to be alone right now."

She walked out and emptiness washed through him at her absence.

Chapter 7

"I can't believe you went without me last night," Gage said when she answered her phone. She'd been wallowing a little, letting herself get sucked into a thousand boring little tasks to stop wondering if Dominic was going to call. Not that it had worked.

"First things first, how are you feeling?" Food poisoning sucked. No two ways about it.

"I'm good. My mother came over and did something, heaven knows what, but I'll take it. I may even be ready to go back to work tomorrow. Are you all right? What happened?"

"He's keyed in to the font now. Took care of it myself. Still, there's a risk of exposure. I'm going to have to think on it and how I'll approach it with the council next week. For now, I think the wards will hold and do the job."

"I might pop over there just to check it out myself. Nell and I went to a club for paranormals in Las Vegas. I don't actually think it's the worst idea ever. It's nice to have a place we can all go."

"It is. Yes. But not at risk of exposure."

"Goes without saying. Okay, so, Meriel, you know I'm your friend too, right? Is there something wrong? You sound . . . off."

"I appreciate that very much. I do. I can't really talk about it right now. I'm trying to get it all straight in my head and I have a hearing in an hour so I need to focus on that."

He sighed. "Do you need me to hurt someone for you?"

She laughed. "Thank you for the offer. But no. I'll talk to you later."

"Offers of shoulders and ass kicking are open-ended. You know where I am if and when you want to talk."

She hung up and stared at her screen for a few minutes. She'd been off her stride since she first looked Dominic in the eyes the night before. She hadn't slept much, but she had to keep faith and believe he would call. The dating plan was solid, she felt. Real. And it would enable him to retain a measure of control.

A smile crept onto her face as she thought about that last bit. Dominic Bright was most definitely the kind of man who liked to be in charge. She hummed her appreciation at the naughty thoughts that had inspired.

Tossing and turning all night long hadn't helped. She was utterly sure, but he wasn't and she wasn't sure she could change that if he wouldn't listen. Who was she to mess with free will? He had to come to her of his own accord.

However, it didn't mean she wouldn't use every single tool at her disposal. *Hello*, this was a sort of contest. His wary resistance to clans against her appeal. She sat up with a smile. She had no doubt he wanted her as a woman, but he couldn't trust that and he had good reason. So the dating thing would allow regular contact and a way for them to move in a positive direction she sincerely hoped included his bed and his naked body very soon.

He was a highly sexual man. Sensual in his choice of decoration in his home and even his office. The kind of man who knew exactly what he wanted and would pursue it relentlessly. Being the thing he pursued had to be pretty awesome.

She laughed, getting up and grabbing her files. This would

be all right. They could do this, and she had no doubt they'd both enjoy it even more when they finally did end up sleeping together.

"SO repeat that." Simon sipped a cup of coffee and grabbed another biscuit.

"Told you last night, dumbass. She's my bond-mate."

"So you met this person who's like your magickal other half. She's one hot-looking woman of immense power and training and she's not here why?"

Dominic sighed. "I don't even believe in this shit, Simon. I can't just meet a woman and fall down in love with her ten minutes later. I don't care what some mystical bond thing says. It's not real. I don't like not having a choice in how I feel."

"Yeah, make believe like witches and werewolves. You're full of shit." Simon shrugged. "You won't be the only person on Earth who can key into her magick. Eventually someone else will find her and then she'll be his and no longer attracted to you. But shit, Dominic, why would you want that? You have this beautiful, magickal thing; why not accept it like a gift? I know you like to say you don't believe in fate, but I do. Sometimes you just have to let go of cynicism and let yourself believe in something."

Dominic stirred his coffee as he thought that outcome would be totally unsatisfactory. The idea of her feeling the way they had the night before with anyone else was untenable. "No matter what bond shit there is or isn't, I'm not walking away from Meriel. I just don't want to play house with her ten minutes after I met her either."

"Ten minutes? She was asking you to marry her and live in her house and have babies last night?"

"Oh fuck you, Simon, you smug asshole. You know she didn't and you know what I mean."

"No, I really don't know what you mean. Either you want her or you don't. Which is it? Also, chemistry is *always* a player between two people. She has pheromones and you have them. Some pheromones don't appeal to some people and some do. That's a fact. So right there you've got the basics of what you have with Meriel. And that's not even taking into account the fact that you cannot be a witch and still think things like bond-mates aren't real. Says who? Humans? You're not human and you should just admit it to yourself.

"You're running from it because it has clan written all over it. I say fuck that. Her foremothers built Clan Owen into a powerhouse of a clan. Nothing happens in the magickal world without their say or input. That's power and *that's hot*. She is special, Dom. Unique. Powerful and absolutely mouthwatering."

Dominic groaned and scratched his beard. "I'm not denying her appeal as a woman." He paused. "Or as a witch. Yes, yes, she's powerful and I can't lie and say I don't find that very alluring. She and I have something, I admit it. But this is sudden and this is big. I don't know if I want to be sucked into the world of these clans. All those rules and politics. She's not just an ordinary witch. There's no halfway with her. I've spent my life deliberately not engaging with them."

Simon growled as he polished off his eggs. "You want some skeeze who'll jump on your cock five minutes after you give her a free drink? Huh? 'Cause you have that already and I don't see you any happier than before. But the way you are since last night? Well, that's interesting."

"I don't have time for interesting."

"Boo-fucking-hoo. When did you become such a whiner? This is sudden? Fuck yeah. Totally sudden and life altering. My dad has a thing about those moments. Revelatory thinking. You think all this life-altering stuff happens on a schedule?"

"Doesn't mean I have to lose my mind over it."

"You told me she advised you to think on it and to call her if you wanted something with her. How is that losing your mind? You're a witch. You can pretend you aren't when it suits you, but I hasten to remind you that you don't mind being a witch when you have to set wards or use spellwork.

You can't have it both ways. Own who you are and stop whining about what you aren't. It's not going to change either way. It's just a waste of time to deny the importance of this all because you're willing to deliberately lie to yourself rather than admit freaky shit happens sometimes in the world we live in. Be grateful and grab it tight and don't fret so damned much."

"Why are you acting like Dr. Phil all the sudden?"

"Because you're going to turn your back on something for a dumb reason and someone needs to call you on it."

"I'm not turning my back on anything. I'm going to call her later and ask her to dinner as it happens. Nothing wrong with wanting to get to know her."

Simon's sigh and raised brow said he thought otherwise, but he held his tongue.

"What?"

"Nothing at all. I just don't want you to fuck this up because you were raised to be all suspicious of clans and of what you are. You're full-council, even I know what that means."

Dominic sighed. The hell of it was, he wasn't sure he himself knew.

MERIEL let out the breath she'd been holding all day when she saw his number pop up on her screen.

"Meriel Owen," she answered, sending a quick lock spell so her mother wouldn't barge in on the call.

"It's Dominic."

He paused and she paused too, waiting to see what he'd do.

"So are you free tonight? For dinner?"

"Yes, as a matter of fact I am."

Another pause. She really should help him, but he needed to do it. Needed to be in control and she understood it and let him be, even if he hadn't realized that's what he needed just yet.

"And then after, I'd like to bring you to Heart of Darkness. You know . . . we have dinner and come over here for drinks."

And it would give her a chance to know him better, for him to show her what was important to him. That appealed to her.

"All right. Do you have a pen?" She gave him her address and said she'd see him at eight.

After she hung up she had to dig through her desk, remembering the box of chocolate macadamia nut candies someone had brought back from a recent trip to Hawaii. Candy was totally necessary, but if she headed to the vending machines, it took her right past her mother's office and that was not what she wanted.

Until they performed the ascension spell, she wouldn't achieve full-council status. Such a thing would be impossible to hide. She was doubly glad they hadn't had sex the night before because her mother would have noticed the change in her energy. Hell, even right then Meriel knew her magick had ripened, thickened, rising within her and ready to join with someone else's.

After she'd eaten the fourth piece of candy, two after she'd told herself, "Only one more," she sat back and allowed herself a deep breath. He called. She smiled.

Chapter 8

SHE tried not to be annoyed when her phone rang as she was still goopy with lotion. If it was Dominic calling to cancel, she was so going to hunt him down.

But it was 401. Rodas Industries.

"Meriel Owen." She hoped she sounded commanding enough. A little difficult when standing naked and slicked up with lotion.

"Ms. Owen, my name is Arel. Gage would like us to add him into a three-way call. Would that be all right with you?"

"Yes, go on. Give me a moment, please." She put the phone down and grabbed a robe, also picking up her glasses and a notepad as she got settled in at the nearby table.

"I'm back."

"Sorry to bug you on a Friday night, but when I spoke with Arel I knew you'd want to hear this."

She sighed. "Comes with the job. What's up?"

It was Arel who spoke. "Had some excitement last evening on my side of the country. We got a call from a witch up in Boston, asking for help against some mages who'd been stalking two sisters, also witches. As a result of this call, we now have a few mages in our custody."

Unease slithered through her. "Are the witches all right? The sisters?"

"Yes. They're both fine. Took some hits. One was partially drained. She turned the draining spell around, drained the mage. Caught him off guard, but it was a great response. Still, she spent several hours puking it all out as her body had to reject all that wrong energy. Spent time with her today. She's also a shifter so it didn't hit her as hard as it would have otherwise."

She had no idea there were such a thing as witch shifters. Fascinating. "I'd like to meet her, if possible. It sounds like she's got some skills we could use."

"I explained to Arel about your desire to work with other witches to share knowledge and spellcraft," Gage said.

"I've told Kendra, that's the witch I'm referring to, about this and she's enthusiastic to meet you. Since it's all right with you, I'll make an introduction later. You should know them and they you."

She made a quick note to herself about that.

"All right. Thank you. Did she terminate the mage she turned the spell back on?"

"No. But she could have. Scared him enough to be forthcoming about what they were all up to though."

"Good to know. By in custody do you mean still drawing breath?"

"For now."

"As it should be."

Gage laughed in the background. "I told you."

"I approve of bloodthirstiness in this time and place. There are dark things on the horizon." Arel cleared his throat. "We've been watching some mages back here who'd been on the move, settling in, stalking witches, draining them and moving on."

This was what she'd been worried about.

"They're more organized than we'd assumed. And after

some rigorous questioning, I can tell you they've been work-ing with anti-Other hate groups to target witches ripe for the draining. Not only that, but working with disgruntled paranormals."

That stopped her pen. "What? How?"

"The mages had been working with a shifter, a cat. The brother-in-law of the witches attacked last night. He led them straight into the heart of their community. Set the witches up."

"Why? I don't understand this. Why would someone do that?"

"That cats handled that part, so all I know is what I've been told. This was a third brother, never going to run the jamboree. But also a little loopy and got caught up in the demon-possessed line the hate groups had been farming out."

She sighed heavily. "So we can assume they know things about us? Things that could hurt?"

"One of the collaborators was a cat shifter. It's safe to assume they understand now that shifters have their own kind of magickal energy," Gage broke in.

She chewed her lip. Her mother should know of this. At the same time, Meriel had been appointed to this exact posi-tion and her mother wouldn't really want to hear about any of this until they had more specifics. Oh and she didn't want to face her mother just yet.

"Gage, I want you and Nell to work on this when she gets back. My mother will need to be briefed." Responsible and yet still kept her out of her mother's attention for a while longer. "What do we know about them, Arel? Do they pick witches they knew? Witches who are most vulnerable?"

"It appears to be a little of both. But . . . it's only a mat-ter of time before they figure out the more powerful the witch, the sweeter the reward. Only a matter of time before some turned witch joins them and shares that."

Stuck witches were bad enough. A turned witch was one who'd damaged so much of her connection with her inherent magicks she no longer had access to them. No longer a witch, not quite a mage, a turned witch was most dangerous. Still hungry for the pleasure of the initial magickal hit but cut off from a huge part of one's existence made them all totally crazy.

"What are they doing with the energy they steal? Just using it themselves? Providing the stolen magic to stuck witches? How do these anti-Other groups feel about that?"

"I'm under the impression it has not gone far enough to be organized in anything more than a way for the mages to get the power themselves to feed their addiction. But my fear, and my belief, is that they will get more organized. This is drug dealing and manufacturing on a pretty intense scale."

"All right. Can we do anything to help?"

"At the moment, we've got it handled."

"But? We need some sort of—I don't know—a conference? Something so we can share intel."

"I'm going to leave that to you and Sadira. I have no patience for the bullshit politics."

She laughed, but there wasn't a whole lot of mirth there. She'd have to go to the council to get permission for such a conference. And she would. It had to be done. But she wanted all the information she could get first. This was a break with *how things were done* and she knew she had a big job ahead of her.

"Gage, keep open communication between you and Arel. Brief Nell when she returns. I'm going to suggest you might just check in with some of the other hunters as well. This is inter-clan so it's acceptable."

"If they start targeting the most powerful witches, you're going to be right in the crosshairs. A big target on your back." Arel's comments were correct, but they meant she had to think about something she'd been trying to ignore.

"Yes. I suppose. Good thing being more powerful also means I can kick some ass if I have to."

Gage groaned. "Let's just keep an eye out. Be extra cautious."

"Of course."

They hung up and she went back to getting ready. She sure as hell wasn't going to cancel her date. She could be sad for what the future might hold, but she wasn't going to let these mages steal another moment of her joy that day. Not if she could help it.

DESPITE how lovely she looked when she answered his knock, it was clear something was wrong.

Alarmed, he moved her into the apartment and closed the door at his back. "Is everything all right?" He looked around for a threat, ready to do harm if he had to.

"No. Not like you think. I just had a disturbing phone call. Work related. It's all right. Come in."

He stopped her, his palm at her elbow. "I don't like shadows in your eyes." He brushed his thumb over her cheek and she leaned into his touch. It wasn't a thought before she was in his arms.

"I do feel better now," she said, her voice muffled by his shirt. He leaned back a little to look into her face. "Really. It was work stuff. I can't do anything about it at this point."

He brushed his lips over hers, first as comfort. She was distressed; he wanted to make her better. Then for the pure unadulterated pleasure of her taste. Of the way she felt against him, so totally right in his arms.

She opened to him, tasting like home when his tongue danced its way across hers.

That need only she ignited with such force rolled through him. Deftly, he banded her waist and reversed their positions, backing her into a nearby wall.

The noise she made when he squeezed her luscious ass dug into him with sharp claws. A shiver raced up his arms at the way she responded to him so openly and eagerly.

She arched, stretching to expose her throat to him as he left the sweetness of her mouth and set about kissing across her jawline and over to the hollow beneath her ear.

There was nothing else in the universe but her skin against his lips. The sweet curve of her ass in his hands, the cool, soft material of her dress against his wrists.

Slowly, he used his fingertips to slide the dress upward

until he met bare skin and she groaned and then laughed. He tickled the same spot, just below the edge of her panties, where her thigh met the first rise of her butt cheek. She squirmed and he couldn't help but smile.

"Your ass is ticklish?" He stepped away or he'd be right back on her.

"Technically, it's that little place on my thigh, just beneath my butt." She tried to look stern and failed.

"We can cancel dinner if you like. We can stay here and talk."

"If I stay here alone with you for too very long, I'm going to totally let you get to at least third base and all my resolve to get to know you first will be up in smoke."

"Fine. Fine. All I'm saying is that third base would be a lovely time. I give good third base."

She moved her hair aside when he put her wrap on her shoulders. "I bet you do."

Serious after he sent her a leer, he took her shoulders to hold her in place. "It's okay then? To take you out? Is there something immediate? Are you being threatened somehow?"

"I have no reason to think there's a problem here. The call I got was from Rhode Island." But he had to admit he liked the way her face looked just then. Soft. A little befuddled pleasure.

"All right then. You will tell me about why you looked so upset when I arrived. But I'll take pity on you and let you tell me after we've had a drink and some food."

She snorted at his imperious tone, but inside there was warmth at the way he made her feel. Safe and protected. Sure, she knew Gage would protect her. Or Nell. Or frankly she was totally capable of protecting her own self. Of all the things in her life, Meriel trusted her magickal ability without question. But it was nice to have this big, slightly scary man on her side, totally willing to protect her because he wanted to.

She smiled and locked the door once they'd reached the hallway.

"How was your day?" she asked to his apparent surprise.

"I mean, what does a nightclub owner do during the daylight hours? I always imagined you'd sleep until afternoon in an apartment that would look remarkably like yours actually does."

He laughed. "And what is that then? What my apartment looks like?"

"Sleek and sexy. You have books. I notice these things. The furnishings were very high quality, well made. A media wall that gave me goose bumps. The apartment of a man who plays all night and sleeps all day." She ducked her head, blushing.

"Bear with me because I can tell you're wondering why I'm blathering and being sort of insulting and that's not what I mean. What I meant was I imagine you'd all be layabouts with naked models everywhere, but I see what you've built in that club and I can't imagine you sleep too very late or you'd never be able to handle it all."

"Not offended. Flattered in fact, so thank you. I had a late breakfast with Simon. Checked on liquor orders. Looked over a schedule for some DJs who'll be guesting in the next few months. Signed some payroll. Thought about you. A lot."

He kept a hand at the small of her back. The heat of him seemed to burn against her skin through the material of her dress. He smelled good enough without any cologne, but just then he had a hint of something on.

She leaned in and brushed her mouth against his neck when they paused at his car.

He hummed and held her a little tighter. "I like that." He helped her into the car, not surprisingly a deep blue Charger.

"Like what?" she asked as he headed for the freeway.

"Like that you feel free enough to kiss me any time you want."

She smiled, leaning back against the seat, turning to see him better. "Oh. Well, you're sort of yummy."

His lips curved up. "Just so you know the invitation to kiss or whatever you want on my body is always open."

She tried to focus on him, the details of his face, the way his magick seemed to pulse from him, like a heartbeat. In the car, in a closed space like that, it was warm and spicy, mingling with her magick, changing it, sharpening it. Interesting the way her magick changed in response to his.

"Thank you."

He didn't take his eyes from the road, but she could see surprise ghost over his features.

"For what?"

"You came to my door and you made my day better."

"Oh. Well," he sort of stammered and it charmed her. Made her wonder how often he received that sort of praise.

"I may as well ask you out for tomorrow as well. I've secured some tickets for *Turandot*."

"You did?" She grinned. "Really?"

He laughed. "I'm glad to know you like the plans."

"Can you do that? Take a Saturday night off? They do have a matinee."

"Weekends are obviously busy. And I do need to be there. But I can go after the opera. Or you could come with me. We have a manager for the human part of the club. Simon's my partner so he's there as well."

"So does he sit in that booth surrounded by women in tight dresses and their bits hanging out?"

His grin was wide and it made her want to take his hand, so she did.

"Jealous, my gorgeous witch? Don't be."

"Mmm-hmm. We'll see about that. When I come to visit do I get a harem? To match yours?"

He snorted. "I think not. And they're not a harem. Not really."

Not anymore they weren't.

HE led her through the entry of the restaurant, his hand at the small of her back. He knew, as he caught sight of the two of them in the mirrors there, that they made a striking couple. People stopped to look, and he didn't blame them. She was long, but curvy, lush. Moved with a certain kind of self-assured grace and strength. The power she had been gifted with shimmered from her, like pixie dust.

He took a deep breath, breathing it into his lungs, loving her scent all bound up with the flavor of her magick. In marked contrast to many of the dresses the other women wore, she had on a short, seventies-flavored number. Dark blue. No sleeves, but a collar that was ornamental, like a bold necklace. He was fairly sure that dress wouldn't have worked on too many other women. But Meriel Owen wasn't too many other women.

In her heels, she was as tall as he, which had proved useful when he'd leaned in for the first kiss of the evening. Ha! First kiss. If ever words did not do justice to what they'd shared in her entry, it was those. He'd had to step back to keep from pushing farther. He knew she wanted him, knew if they'd continued that kiss and grope in her hallway, they'd have ended up in bed.

And, he had to admit, this slow build, while murder on his cock, was damned sexy. Like very sensual foreplay. Because the longer he thought about what she'd said the night before, the more he not only understood her perspective, but he agreed with it.

He found himself at ease with her. So often he felt as though he had to hold back, had to stay sharp because everyone always wanted something from him. And part of that was his own fault, when you run with a bunch of criminals for years, it's not surprising when one of them screws you over.

But this was a sort of quiet ease. And he liked it.

He held her chair out and she sat, allowing him to push the chair in and circle to sit and face her. She made him want to be a better man. Made him want to take care of her. It was unsettling even as it was a good thing.

He took the menu and looked it over before setting it aside to turn his attention back to her. "I like this place. It's dark, but not so dark I can't see your face. That would be a shame, since it's so nice to look at."

Her gaze flicked up to snag with his. "Thank you. I've eaten here a few times, usually for business lunches and that sort of thing. It's quite lovely at night. Romantic even."

He'd thought so too, which is why it had been the first place that had come to his mind to bring her. "Tell me, why did you become a lawyer?"

"You might know that we run a series of design businesses. Turns out I suck at any sort of gardening or landscape and interior design. I hate math. Law was a logical choice. My father suggested it, said I could get paid to be argumentative."

Her smile brightened a little and he found himself doing the same in response. "I know I'll be taking over for my mother. It seemed logical to follow a career path where I could be active in the governance of the business. I need to be prepared."

Conversation paused as their drinks were delivered and the order was taken. A mysterious smile marked her lips when he did the ordering, but she didn't seem angry or annoyed by it.

He'd done enough research on Clan Owen to have earned a slightly fearful respect for Edwina Owen. Enough that he wondered just what a woman like her had been like as a mother. "What does she do? Your mother, I mean?" he asked once the server had retreated.

She laughed. "Edwina does everything and she does it all exceedingly well." After a sip of her drink she put it down to bring her attention back to his face. "Where did you grow up?"

"Eastern Oregon. Just outside Bend. Tom, my foster dad, heck, my dad really, he's a backcountry guide."

"Do you miss it? That sort of rural living?"

He paused, thinking. "No. It's clean and certainly far enough away to keep most kids out of too much trouble." He'd often wondered if that wasn't exactly why Tom had settled them there. It had worked. For a while anyway. "But I like the energy in cities. I like the movement and the hum and the ability to get breakfast at three in the morning."

She laughed. "Yes, I have to agree I like that too. Though I do enjoy the forest quite a bit. There's a lot of energy to draw from here. A lot of people around. But in nature I find it's often easier to work. There's less interference."

She knew a lot more about magick than he did. He might have been annoyed by this any other time, but right then, he found himself wanting her to show him her world. Maybe even to teach him about his own.

"So tell me about the call."

Casually, she looked around and he caught the movement of her lips and knew she'd done something to give them privacy.

"I've been made the liaison with other groups of witches." The look on her face told him that had been a hard-won job. "So first I got word of some witches who'd gone missing in New Mexico. We'd heard over the last eighteen months or so about some others who'd been attacked. Magically attacked. Today I spoke with the hunter of the Rodas Clan. One of the oldest and most respected clans in the country. Headquartered in Rhode Island," she explained at his blank look. "They have in their custody some mages who'd been working with some anti-paranormal hate groups to stalk and steal magick from witches."

He sat up straighter. "Do tell. Why is it they'd come to have these creatures in their hands?"

"What they know is that two witches had been targeted. One of them had been victimized over most of her life. Slowly siphoned from. The other was attacked more suddenly and recently."

"But why? Why would they do it?"

"Greed? I don't know for sure, but we have heard of these cases where witches have been targeted and then attacked."

"For what purpose though? Like feeding junkies and turned witches? What? Tom always taught me that magick with a *k* was our natural energy but what stuck witches used was magic because inherent magick can't be traded like that."

"We don't know yet. Rodas has them and they're still being questioned. Gage is working with their hunter so they'll keep us apprised. Oh, and you're correct about the differences between a witch's magick and what gets produced when it's stolen."

He had no idea they'd take people into custody. Clearly he had a lot to learn about clans.

"It's just . . . well, I'm stunned to be honest." She shook her head.

"Stunned that people would want to steal the riches you have when they have none?" He shrugged. "People are ugly, baby. They're ugly and selfish and lazy. Lazy enough to steal from someone so they don't have to do the work themselves." But if any of them came within a five-mile radius of her, he'd fuck them up.

"Well, look, I was raised to appreciate what I have. What I was born with. Of course it's stunning and horrible to know people would use pain and death to amp up their power. Power they're not supposed to have. It offends me deeply. But that's not the real issue here. My biggest concern is the existence of this cooperation between the mages stalking witches and these sick, hateful humans."

"So much for not coming out. Clearly we're not a secret like you all wish we were."

One of her brows raised and he realized he liked to spar with her. He didn't trust too many other people enough to have deep political discussions with them. Things were different with Meriel. There was an ease to their banter he only had with those close to him.

"You think we should come out?"

The appetizers arrived so the conversation halted for a few minutes.

"I think it's impossible to hide much longer. The wolves came out, the cats are out. Vampires aren't far behind. If we come out, we control it from the start. That's why the wolves did it that way and I think, considering the whole picture, they've been all right. It's not a matter of should, it will happen. So I'm in favor of being in control of the how and the when. If you let these petty thugs go unchecked, they will do it themselves. And they win."

"The wolves were forced out. It's something people toss out as if they did it on purpose. They didn't. They had the same fears we do. And now they're exposed."

"But they had a plan in place. They took it from nearly the start and made it into what they wanted." He shrugged.

"Every time we come out, or humans focus on us, we end up hunted and killed en masse. There's an active movement to make Weres register with their local governments so they can be tracked. Some counties and even a few states have passed laws restricting what jobs Weres can hold. Can you imagine what it would be like for us if humans found out that witches were real?"

He waved it away. "They do already. Pagans and Wiccans are out. People have the idea in their heads. We're halfway there as it is."

"And look at what happens to some of them! People get fired, lose business, friends and neighbors turn on them. And if this mage thing turns out to be a bigger, more organized threat? Which I think it is. What then?"

"Gonna be an issue one way or another, isn't it? The way I see it, part of the problem is that you're still closeted. Makes it easier to isolate and get away with what they're doing. Because how can you go to the cops if it's a magickal theft? The truth is they can't drown us now. We're too powerful and we'd never allow it. Isn't that why you all organized into clans to start with? United and powerful."

She smirked, but it was amused more than annoyed. "When we came west, it was one of our aims. And we are strong, yes. But we can be killed just like anyone else. My ability to protect my people shouldn't be weakened by the choices I make."

"Except you have the power to blow the doors off this place with a flick of your fingers." He'd been making an overstatement, but when she shrugged, he realized she could in fact do that.

"I don't think it would be so negative. I'm not convinced of that at all. And frankly, I just think it doesn't matter. At this point you and I both know it's only a matter of time. There are already humans who know we exist."

She leaned forward. "Yes! Yes, I do and apparently they're

hunting us down and aiding freaks to kidnap, torture and kill us. No, thank you."

"You know it's going to fall to you. You're next to run the family business." He didn't envy that task, even as he admired her for taking it on so dutifully. "It's there whether you like it or not. That's all I'm saying."

"It's all I think about," she mumbled before spearing a prawn and offering it up his way.

He leaned forward and took the proffered food, warm inside that she'd offered, at the intimacy of that moment between them. "I'm here if you want to talk. I mean, I've not been in training to be the next leader or what have you, but I'm a good listener. And"—he paused to take a drink and then to move back so the main course could be delivered—"I like to hear you talk about it all. Your world."

Her worried look faded with a smile. "Thank you for that." She paused as she ate. Emotions chased over her features as he watched. As he tipped into something far deeper than a crush or a like.

Finally her gaze locked with his again. "I'm trying to process it. Figure out all the angles. I need to understand how each variant will affect an outcome. And then I have to understand how to overcome any challenge to my clan on any front."

He waited, drinking in the sight of her there across from him. "You have doubts in your ability? Because, I'm not really seeing that. I looked you up today. I admit it. You're an incredibly successful woman. You're not the type who fails and you're certainly not the type who quits."

She closed her eyes for a few long moments. He wanted to soothe her, but he sensed she didn't need that and hoped he was right.

"No, it's not that. I don't doubt my ability to protect them. This clan has deep roots here. Our base is secure." She hesitated and he wondered what it was she wanted to add but felt conflicted over. "Suffice it to say, I can handle any sort of challenge. Just gets a little overwhelming at times.

And while we're good here, others aren't. There are places where witches don't even have an informal coven. They're pretty much alone, which makes them a target. I . . . it's more than about my clan, this is about all of us. Our whole race is at risk. We can't let that happen."

He believed her claim of being able to handle whatever was thrown at her. Made him all hard at the gleam in her eye. Yes, she was a woman who could handle it. Powerful and ruthlessly competent. But she was so much more.

He'd always imagined clan witches like Meriel to be coldhearted, ball-busting bitches who cared more about money and power than anything else. And he'd been so wrong.

This was more for her than her own skin and her own base. The only person he'd ever met with her kind of integrity was Tom.

"I'm crushing on you. So. Hard." She made him goofy, sent him reeling. It wasn't always comfortable, but he liked it just the same.

Her confusion melted into amusement and then she blushed, clearly pleased with his words. She twisted her bracelet, a little habit of hers as she thought something over. Such a delicate wrist for a woman who was so tall.

She was a mess of contradictions, which only made her more appealing. He found that juxtaposition irresistible. And he knew part of it was the bond-mate pull. But far, far more than that, he wanted Meriel Owen because she was the total package. If they'd been humans, or werewolves or whatever, they'd be hot for each other.

Chapter 9

"ENOUGH about me for a while." She waved a fork his way. "I want to know more about you. What did you do before you came here to Seattle? From what Nell and I could divine, you just sort of popped into existence."

He allowed the topic to be dropped. She'd shared a lot and he'd be satisfied with that. For now.

He grinned. "I have my skills." He paused, wondering how he could make it sound less, um, *criminal* than it was. It was important to him, probably for the first time with anyone, that she not see him as a loser.

"I'm looking forward to seeing just what those skills are."

"I keep attempting to show you but you keep telling me I have to wait."

She laughed. "Just make it really awesome when I finally give you the green light, then. How did you end up running a nightclub?"

"I ended up in New York City with a friend. We'd spent some less-than-law-abiding years together and he'd pulled his act together and started a business. I joined him and he gave me a job. I was good at it." He shrugged.

"Good at what? I don't doubt you doing a good job, but what is it that you were doing?"

"I started with cleanup." He snorted. "Took trash out during busy shifts. Kept the bars wiped down. Over time I learned how to do the books. How to get people paid. How to hire and fire staff. Marketing." Evan had let him learn every part of the job until one day Dominic had realized he knew enough to do it on his own. Which knowing Evan had been the plan from day one.

"So you came out here to steal from my font and set up your den of iniquity."

Not much sexier than a sense of humor in a woman.

"I'm all on the up and up now, aren't I? But yes, it was time for me to leave the East Coast and come back here. I stayed with Tom for a while as I searched for a good location and then eventually found the space. Simon and I had known each other awhile. He had some money and wanted to buy in. As it happened I needed both a partner and some more capital."

"Did you always know? That you were . . . *different* from the other kids in school?"

"Tom started my training relatively early." Some of his earliest memories were of being taught how to erect shields around his magick. "So I knew. But obviously there are gaps in my knowledge." Which he tried not to let bug him and managed. Not entirely, but enough. "You obviously did. Growing up in a clan and all. What was that like?"

"It was just how I grew up. I didn't know how unusual it was until I went to college. I'm going to say it was the same as not growing up in a clan but you're going to disbelieve that." She grinned. "My parents had dinner parties and friends. Those friends had kids my age. We went on vacations together, when my mother actually let go for enough time to leave, that is. Some people are foodies. Some people like the beach. My family had one major thing in common with their friends, just like other groups of people have. It was just about magick instead of NASCAR."

"Did you go to public school?"

She shook her head. "No. From kindergarten through high school graduation I attended a private school the clan runs."

"Ah, now I get the college comment. The first time you were confronted by non-magickal people?"

She shook her head again. "No. While I didn't go to school with anyone other than witches, we still had neighbors and went to the grocery store and that sort of thing. For the first time at college I had to hide what I was far more than I didn't. But it was a good lesson."

"I haven't yet been in a situation where I don't have to hide what I am more than not. Even at the club I'm having to hide everyone from the outside world."

"Which is why you support coming out so strongly? You're not in a clan; why haven't you just told people if you're bothered so much?"

"I don't think you know me well enough to say that."

"I didn't *say* anything. I asked. Big difference. If you don't want to say so, that's fine too."

"I'm sorry for snapping. I support coming out because I think it's time. I believe it will come out and soon. And I'd rather be in control from day one than have to clean up in the aftermath of someone else's behavior."

She let him process without pushing herself into the conversation. He liked that too.

"But I understand why, until now, things have been kept a secret. I get it. Which is why I respect the rules, even if I haven't been in a clan. And I agree with the reasoning. I just don't believe we have the luxury of secrecy in the age of instant information."

They continued to eat as he peppered her with questions about clan and magickal stuff. She seemed to possess an encyclopedic knowledge, which was really, really hot. Smart women really turned him on, he'd discovered, especially since Meriel Owen had swayed into his bar only the night before.

"Feels like I've known you for years." She spoke as if she'd been inside his head.

"I was just thinking that."

"Do you like gelato?" she asked as he paid the bill.

"Yes? I think. It's ice cream, right?"

She snorted. "No. It's better. Come on. There's a place near your club. I'll treat you to some." She held her hand out and he stood, bringing her with him.

"Yeah? Are you offering me sweets? Do I need to protect my honor?" he murmured, bringing her close as they left.

She laughed. "I'll protect it for you. You can totally trust me with it."

It was his turn to laugh. What an unexpected pleasure she was.

HE walked her out and she took in a deep breath once they'd reached the street. Just being able to unload her worries had made her feel a lot better. Good enough to truly enjoy this time with him.

She liked this man. A great deal. He challenged her without being patronizing. Expected her to defend her ideas. She snuck a sideways look up at his face as he waited for the car to be brought around. In charge. Big. Masculine and protective. It was beyond ridiculously hot. He stepped closer, putting an arm around her shoulders and his warmth enveloped her. She must have sighed because he looked down at her, kissed her forehead and even managed a deft pass off of a tip when the car arrived.

"Gelato first and then the club? We don't have to stay long. I just like to be there and keep an eye on things." He spoke as he weaved through Friday-night traffic on 2nd leading toward Heart of Darkness.

"Sounds fine. I don't have any plans other than this so I'm happy with whatever." She just wanted to be with him, though she didn't say it out loud.

She pointed the gelateria she meant. "It's close enough to Heart of Darkness and parking here is nuts. Why don't you park at the club and we can walk?"

He snorted. "I'm not going to make you walk. You're in heels and it's cold and raining."

"All right then." She sat straighter and focused. "Give it one more pass."

"Why?"

"Jeez, you argue over the dumbest things. I'm going to see if I can't make a parking space happen, that's why."

He made a left at a cross street and then a right to circle back. "You can do that?"

"I can do lots of things, Dominic." Pleased, she tried not to laugh.

"Teach me."

"All right. But not while you're driving." She closed her eyes and used her othersight instead. Ebb and flow. Energy swirled and broke in waves against the buildings. She found the places where the energy was disturbed and honed in. In the *should we leave now* void Meriel found, she sent a whispered yes. And when they reached the gelateria again, a spot was just opening up where a car was pulling away.

"Damn," he muttered, making a very smooth parallel job into the vacated spot. "Don't touch the door." He got out and circled the car. He moved like a predator. Like a Were. She wondered if it had come from hanging out with Simon Leviathan or if it was just part of his makeup.

"I can open a door. I'm not an idiot." He helped her out and closed the door.

"Can and should are different things. When you're alone or with other people you can open your own door. When you're with me, you'll let me take care of you because I like it and because why shouldn't you let me?"

He was so incredibly arrogant. In any other man she'd have been inspired to slap his face and huff off.

But Dominic wasn't like any other man. On him, it totally worked.

"Don't be so bossy." Still it wouldn't do to let him get cocky or take it for granted that he'd be getting his way all the time.

He laughed as he opened the door to the boutique gelateria she'd discovered just a few months prior. "Tom says it's written into my genetic code. But you're a big girl, you know how to tell me to back off if that's what needs telling."

Utterly unconcerned with that possibility though, he walked them through the crowd to the counter. "What should I get?"

"My favorite is pistachio. But it's all really good."

"Meriel, it's good to see you!"

She laughed and looked up to Dominic. "My secret's out. I come here so often they know me by sight."

He leaned down and brushed a kiss against her temple. "One look at you and who's going to forget?"

He was so good at that.

Blushing, Meriel ordered some pistachio with some chocolate malt for herself and decided on chocolate flake and vanilla malt for Dominic. He reached for his wallet and she sent him a raised brow as she opened her bag. "My treat, remember?"

He got the cutest furrow between his eyes when he was thwarted. But he shrugged. "Thank you. Will you share yours with me? Just . . . a lick or two?"

The woman behind the counter choked a little as she handed the change back. Meriel laughed. "Yes, he's really like this all the time. It's why I keep him around."

Dominic laughed at that, hugging her closer to his side. "As if you could get rid of me."

They sat in his car and shared the gelato. It pleased her that he'd liked it so much. It was such a sweet, normal moment. Still, in the air between them their chemistry sizzled and she couldn't help but imagine him naked. Ha, as if she wanted to stop that.

"I can't believe I've never had this before and it's only a few blocks from my club." He leaned in and licked her spoon, making her all dizzy and dry mouthed.

He turned enough to meet her gaze and the smirk on his lips told her he knew just exactly what he was doing to her and her hormones.

She had to swallow hard, but she did find her words enough to say, "You're very naughty."

He sat back in his seat and turned the car back on and took them to his club. "I'm trying to show you just how much, but you keep making me work for it."

She snorted. "Please. When's the last time you had to work to get a woman into bed?"

Ignoring the line of cars, he drove straight to the front, got out after giving her a look daring her to open her door on her own. He opened it and helped her out, tossing the keys to the valet. "But you're not some woman," he murmured as he escorted her through a side entrance. The same one they'd gone out the night before.

She paused in front of his office door.

"What?" He put himself in between her and the door. Good gracious, when he did stuff like that it made her all trembly and swoony.

"The warding here is off. Can I fix it?"

He opened the door and ushered her in. "Only if I can watch and you'll go slow enough so I can learn."

Dominic never failed to surprise her. Bold. Arrogant. Totally alpha-male material. But he wasn't afraid to ask questions or to learn new things.

So she walked him through the wards, showing him how to amp up the energy with some mini-feedback spells within it. "These little steps mean you won't have to use nearly as much from the font. The spell perpetuates its own strength this way."

"Can't believe I never thought of that."

Warmed by his praise, she moved through the rest of the ward, pointing out thin spots and minute errors in execution, which left the overall spell weaker and easier to pull apart.

Despite that, she had to give him credit, the work was very, very good, and she told him so.

"Thank you."

"Can I . . ." She wanted to show him how to use his othersight; it was clear he didn't really access it very well, but she didn't want to embarrass him either.

He stood very close, taking her cheeks in his hands and tipping her face up to see it better. "You can. Anything. Just say it."

She swallowed, hard. "Can I give you some tips on how to open yourself up more fully to your othersight?"

He paused and it made her nervous.

"It's just that you do it, but you're not using it to its full potential. It's a very powerful tool."

"This will make my spellwork stronger?"

"Yes. Part of the way magick works when you spellcast is you use energy to form intent. If you use your othersight better, you can manipulate and direct the energy flow more efficiently. Then your spellwork is stronger. Plus, it's a good tool in general."

"You use it all the time?"

"Yes. Most witches do. I can show you how to blend it better with your regular consciousness so it's not distracting."

"Show me. Tell me."

So she took his hands. "My mother's bond-mate was my first real magickal teacher, but it's really my father who taught me how to use my othersight effectively. He relates to his magick like it's math. And since I hate math it took him a while to get to me. But I'm thickheaded."

Dominic grinned and ducked in to give her a quick kiss.

"Essentially, your othersight is like radar. You open yourself to it, yes, but really it's about using your magick to relate to all you see around you. If you use it while you do your spellwork, you'll be better able to see the thin spots, where things are weak or the knot with another part of the spell needs to be tighter."

"But clearly you can work magick without it. I rarely use it."

"Sure you can. But an enterprising witch with a better handle on her othersight than the originator of the spell can spot all the weak points in a spell and unravel them."

"Oh. Good point."

"Your othersight is there, always. You don't have to make it, or manage it. You just need to make opening yourself up to it part of how you work your magick until it's second nature."

She walked him through it, pleased at his quick progress, delighted by his reaction to learning something new. The more he practiced, the better he'd be until it was second nature.

When they finished, he pulled her into his arms, slowly, as if they were dancing. The kiss warmed up slowly. A brush of his lips and then another quick one.

"Thank you for that. I can see exactly what you mean."

Dizzy with him, she managed a goofy smile, swallowing hard as she looked at that face of his. His eyes were her favorite feature. Thick, dark lashes framed the color, a very pale green, like spring. They were beautiful eyes. His nose was strong, not quite straight. She brushed her thumb from brow to tip.

"Broken. Three times."

She smiled and shook her head. "I'm not surprised. It suits you. Being totally perfect might offend the gods."

The sweet confused pleasure on his face made her weak in the knees.

And then his mouth was on hers again, his taste back where it belonged. Rough hands hauled her close as she opened to his tongue, groaning as he nipped her bottom lip.

The music from outside thumped against the walls, the bass line throbbing deep in her belly.

His hands were on her hips and sliding upward to cup her breasts.

Hers were on his belt, yanking at it when someone banged on the door and he broke the kiss with a snarl.

"We'll pick up where we left off later. I'm sorry." He touched his forehead to hers before easing away, but keeping her hand in his.

Simon came in and looked between the two of them. "Evening, Meriel. You look beautiful. Dom, we need to move some cash to the safe. We're at capacity. Bar's been full all night long."

"Of course." He turned to Meriel. "I need to sign some

paperwork. Would you like a drink while I do this? I'll set you up at my table; no, not the one with all the women in it from last night."

"Am I that obvious?"

He kissed her again, hard. "Bloodthirsty."

It was rather exciting to know a man like that thought her bloodthirsty.

"Let's get you settled and then I'll make very quick work out of this business to get back to you."

True to his word, he escorted her to a table in a far corner. It was tucked back into an alcove of sorts, but offered great views of the entire club. She liked to watch him change from her date into a business owner. He lost all that roguish charm and hardened his features while keeping them polite.

"Now lookie here."

She turned in her seat to take Gage in as he slid into the booth beside her a few minutes later.

"What on earth is Meriel Owen doing right here in a box that looks a little like something the owner would use?" His smirk made her laugh.

"I'm here on a date with Dominic. This is his table. He had to go sign something or whatever."

"Is this why you sounded so sad this morning?"

"This is such a long story I honestly don't have the energy to recount it all to you now."

"Nell's back tomorrow. If I can see how different your magick looks, you think she's going to miss it?"

"If I tell you, it's as my friend, not as a member of council staff."

"I would never betray your confidences, Meriel."

"He's my bond-mate." She blurted it, knowing if she didn't, she'd never get it out. "But he grew up outclan. He's not ready yet and he doesn't have to be. He needs time and I'm giving it to him."

Gage nodded, blowing out a breath. "All right. Can I help at all?"

She let out the tension from holding her breath. "You just did. Thanks for listening. Anything new on the mages?"

"And you are?" Dominic slid into the booth on Meriel's other side, getting so close he enfolded her into his side, his arm along the back of her seat.

"This is Gage. He's a friend and also runs the hunter crew for Nell. Gage, this is Dominic."

Gage gave Dominic a long up-and-down look and Meriel leaned back into Dominic, needing to soothe. Which worked because the tension in his arm lessened and he slid his fingertip in a figure eight up and down her shoulder.

"I wanted to come out here to check the place over. See where I stood on the topic of this place being allowed to remain or not. I like what I see. Strong wards. I worry about the line of entry being through a space filled with humans. But I believe we can benefit from a place all the local Others are able to hang out and be ourselves."

"*Allowed* to remain?"

She turned to look at him. "I told you exposure is a risk and that we had to assess all risks."

He interrupted before she could continue. "And you never thought to tell me any of this? About some move to shut me down? How the hell can I trust you enough to be your bondmate and all that jazz if you don't tell me everything?"

It hurt that he'd think she was capable of such a thing. "In the first place, I'm not hiding anything. I just referenced a time when I *told you* about the exposure issue being a problem. Secondly, there is no *move* to do anything. We saw you were stealing. I dealt with it. That's what the clan knows. But I'll have to give a report on this place and of course one of the chief issues is going to be how safe this place is. To ignore that would be folly. It would be irresponsible of me both as the next in line to take over Owen and as your bondmate to pretend away reality."

"So you had this guy come to spy on me here?"

"Yes, frequently when I send out my spies I have them sit and have a drink with me and introduce them, complete with a reason for their being here, to you. I'm so devious that way."

"This is totally not going in the right direction." Gage put his drink down.

Meriel held a hand up to stay Gage. "No. You don't need to explain yourself. I already did." She turned her attention back to Dominic. "And if that's not enough, we have a far bigger problem than the existence of this club."

She made to scoot out of the booth but Dominic put a hand on her wrist. Not confining, which would have resulted in an injury. "Wait."

"Meriel? Are you all right? We can go right now." Gage said it to no one but her, which allowed her to catch her breath.

The tension ramped up as the two men both sought her attention. Both protective in their own way.

Dominic leaned in, his lips at her ear. "I'm sorry. I snapped at you and made a judgment that wasn't fair. We should talk. Don't leave this way."

She hesitated. This was what she'd talked to Nell about a few times. That disconnect between what they'd grown up with and what their significant other understood and trusted. But more than that, clearly Dominic had trust issues. Which was such a cliché.

Gage waited, but looked out at the room instead of at her, giving her privacy to react.

"You're being a rude asshole," she said equally quietly.

"I know. I'm sorry. I felt broadsided. I know you told me about the exposure thing."

If she could show as much honesty when she got called out for being an asshole, she'd be proud.

"Please stay."

It would be like this from time to time. She understood that to her toes. He was a bossy, incorrigible man on many levels and she was a bossy woman who loved rules. They were bound to clash. So, she supposed, the real issue was how they got past it.

"All right."

He kissed the corner of her mouth and then turned his attention to Gage. "I apologize for my manners."

Gage nodded. "And I apologize for how I brought the subject up."

"Moving along." She squeezed Dominic's hand. "We need to talk about Rodas."

"I had to call Nell. This is too big not to relay. I caught her before they were boarding their flight home anyway. She'll be in touch when she gets back. I told her to sleep first and she was mean to me."

Meriel laughed. Oh how she'd missed her friend.

They spoke about the situation for some time. Dominic put in his opinion here and there, never in a pushy way. He had a lot of great insight about people and how they acted. He'd be so good at her side, would help her examine issues from a different perspective.

Multiple times they'd been interrupted, or rather, Dominic had been called away to deal with this or that. But it was good. It gave her a chance to watch him in action.

Gage tipped his glass in her direction. "Your mother was right to hand this over to you. There will be a time, very soon I think, where working with witches across practice and clan affiliation will be necessary to protect ourselves. You've known this for some time now. I respect the job your mother has done. But your vision is what's needed to lead the next generation."

She blushed, glad for the darkness in the club. "Thanks. I just hope we're catching this early enough to combat it."

Gage's usually amused expression went hard. "We'll take this shit out. Period. Listen, we've spent two hours talking about this. It's Friday night and you're on a date. I see a lovely woman at the bar who really appears to need some company."

She looked to see who he meant and grinned, shaking her head. "Go on then. Make her night."

Gage's mouth tipped up into a sexy grin. "He's all right. Your Dominic. Gonna be a lot to handle so it's good he's your bond-mate. Another woman might get swallowed up by a man like him." He leaned in to kiss her cheek and she knew without even looking up that Dominic's attention had been snagged and he'd be making his way back to her.

"Thanks for listening."

"I told you already, I'm your friend." He slid out and moved toward the bar, snagging the woman's awareness immediately.

"Hm. He likes touching you."

She turned to Dominic and laughed right in his face. "He likes touching me? And the eleven thousand woman who've given you an arm or chest full of mammaries as you've walked around here being all bossy and stuff? What's their excuse? Have you known them their entire lives like I have Gage?"

"No. They're meaningless and also, I never claimed to be rational when the subject is you."

Disarmed and flattered, she snorted. "You are aware that I'd never let anyone *but* you get away with this sort of thing, right?"

Grinning, he pulled her close. "Yeah. It gets me hot." He kissed her long and slow there in the dark, the music around them, the heat of all the bodies, the scent of magick and sex everywhere.

Though she'd never been the make-out-with-a-man-in-a-nightclub type, she sure was just then. Like whoa.

"We should go."

He was so close, his heat against her face. She *so* should not. Yes, they had sexual heat. No question they wanted one another. But that wasn't the issue.

He walked her to the car and once they were both inside he turned to her. "You're going to make me wait, aren't you?"

"We've known each other a few days. I keep telling you sex will make this need stronger. You're going to see me tomorrow night anyway."

He groaned and scrubbed his face with his hands. "We both know this is going to happen."

"Exactly. So why rush?"

"You're holding sex hostage."

She burst out laughing. "Is that what you think? Really? Oh, Dominic." She shook her head. "I want it as much as you do, silly. This isn't easy for me either. I'm not holding anything hostage. Such an assertion is insulting. Like I'm some dumb bimbo who has to trick you into sex."

She straightened her spine and he groaned again. Lethal, this woman. And still he smiled because she totally caught him.

"Fine, fine." He pulled away and headed back to her place. "And I don't think that, by the way. The last thing you are is dumb. It's all the backup of sperm in my system."

She laughed again, the annoyance gone from her features.

"I have to go to New York on Sunday. I'll be back Thursday unless something dire comes up. That friend I told you about? He's opening a new club and we're going to be talking about some possible joint business ventures. The rest of my group of friends will be there too." He realized he wanted her to know he'd be back.

"Oh. All right then."

He pulled up in front of her building. "Have a coffee with me?"

Chapter 10

DOMINIC was fairly sure he'd never wanted to have sex more in his entire life. And that included the year he was fourteen.

He'd picked her up at her place for the opera and she'd come to her door looking like she'd stepped from a magazine ad. Hair in a chic updo. She wore some sort of fancy dress and equally fancy shoes. No one could accuse Meriel Owen of not dressing up enough for an evening out.

She'd been elegant and beautiful on his arm. He'd never been to the opera and found himself totally falling into the story. But never enough not to be totally aware of the way she smelled. Or of the rise and fall of those ridiculously beautiful breasts heaved up at the bodice of her dress.

She'd shared a big part of herself that evening and the one before. She'd shown him some of her magick, had helped him with his. They'd debated politics both witch and human. She was a fierce opponent and their discussions had the sort of heat that only left him craving more.

They stopped by Heart of Darkness for a bit, but all he really wanted was her. All to himself. "My building has a rooftop garden. Would you like to come up and see it?"

She grinned. "Is that like asking if I want to see your etchings?"

"It is a lovely garden, even in the cold and wet. And yes, it would leave us astonishingly close to my place. Where my bed is."

She watched him, clearly wrestling with herself. He gave himself stern lectures to let her figure it out without any pressure.

"I suppose I like gardens."

"So glad to hear that," he said as he pulled her from the booth.

He was pretty sure if he didn't get inside her soon he might die. She was something else and he wanted more.

"FEELS like you can see my building from here," she said as she shivered just a little.

Nice opportunity for him to touch her though. He took his suit jacket off and put it around her shoulders and held her to his side.

"My father has a garden. Like an acre and a half of garden. Every year he takes on some new project and my mother just sighs and tells him to get on with it. He loves working in the dirt."

"Are you a gardener?"

She laughed. "No. I am a disaster with plants. I can't even keep a houseplant alive. At work my office has fake plants in it. What about you?"

"I haven't been up here in ages. I like gardens and all, but I'm not usually around during the day."

And then she turned to him, remaining in his arms. "I'd like to go inside now."

He tried to remain nonchalant but it was a chore not to drive her down to his place at a harried pace. As it was, it wasn't until he'd closed the door, locking it as he watched her toe her pretty heels off, that he allowed himself to believe it was going to happen. She turned her head, still slightly bent to get her shoe loose, a sexy smile on her face.

"I swear to you I totally am fine with whatever increased connection we gain after we have sex," he blurted and she straightened, one hand on her hip, head cocked to the side.

"I don't know if you are really. But looking at you right now, feeling the way you make me feel . . . I can't seem to find any willpower at all to make you wait. Hell, make *me* wait. I want you, Dominic. The need will grow, but I can't manage to tell you no anymore. I'm not expecting more than sex from you at this point. Feel what you're supposed to feel."

She reached up to the neck of the dress and undid something. The material slid from her body and pooled at her feet.

"Uh . . ." was all he could think to say as he looked his fill at her.

Her smile lost all its caution and he found that a good reason to get out of his shirt. He missed the buttons a few times because he couldn't take his gaze from her bare breasts. Just beautiful.

She stepped to him, gently moving his hands from the way and finishing unbuttoning his shirt and the cuffs. "I love it when a man wears French cuffs with cuff links. It's so deliciously old-school and gentlemanly."

That's always what he'd thought too. He'd watched Cary Grant in the old movies as he'd been growing up. It hadn't been a casual coincidence that he'd ended up with French cuffs and a tray full of cuff links. Each set had been a way of telling himself he'd made it. Built himself into a success.

"Your breasts look even better when you're so close I can see how tight your nipples are."

Her skin, so warm and very soft, drew his lips. He took his time, tasting and teasing. Wanting to savor her now that he had her in his bed.

Of course now that he had her here in his bed, he was totally going to keep her.

He paused at the base of her neck, feasting on her frantic pulse and the echo of her soft, sexy moans.

He heard the intake of breath when he pulled away. Liked

the way she licked her lips as she looked at him. Hungry. Loved the confident way she slid a palm from the waist of his pants, up the wall of his chest and around the back of his neck. Her nipples brushed against him and they both groaned.

"You're nearly naked. In my front hallway. It's like Christmas and my birthday all at once."

She laughed and he twirled her, drawing her back to his bedroom and his bed. They paused at the doorway where he backed her up against the jamb while he made quick work of the barely there panties she had on.

"Now I'm totally naked."

He walked her back until she landed on his bed. "You are. My favorite."

And that wasn't a lie. She was long and curvy. Her skin was pale and pretty. The only tattoo she appeared to have was the mark at her wrist, but he liked the pierced belly button. He bent to tug it with his teeth.

Everything in him wanted her. Wanted this beautiful, intelligent and strong woman all for his own.

"I'm naked," she repeated, waving her hand at him, "and you're not. You're giving me a bad case of the sads, Dominic. Why do you want that?"

Before he could answer, she sat up on the bed and pulled his belt off, unbuttoning and unzipping his pants and shoving them down his legs. "There. I did most of the work for you. Get to it."

Laughing, he kicked the clothes off and leapt on the bed to straddle her body. He couldn't recall the last time he ever laughed this much with a woman, much less one he was having sex with. Probably because he never had.

Those lush lips, glossy and swollen from his kisses, called to him again as he pulled her so she rested on top of him, close enough to touch.

"Finally," he said before taking a nipple between his teeth, "you're just where I want you."

She laughed. "Is that a compliment?"

"God, yes." He kissed his way to the other nipple, enjoying the way she squirmed.

"Okay then."

The curve of her hips called to fingertips and mouth, the dip at her waist, the swell of her thighs, velvety soft at the back of her knees. Tickled the backs of her thighs as he rolled her over. Her back was a perfect curve as he kissed up the long line of her spine, pausing to kiss each indentation at the base, right above her perfect ass.

Sweet . . . her soft shudder when he gave her a gentle edge of his teeth at the back of her neck.

"Hurry," she whispered, rolling her hips back toward him, inciting his want.

"I'm trying to take this slow. Greedy."

She turned around and grabbed his cock, giving it a gentle squeeze. "I don't want slow. Not this time."

It was his turn to swallow hard. "I don't want to hurt you. I want you so much."

"I won't break. I promise."

She dragged the head of his cock through her slick folds and he might have blacked out for a minute or two at how good it felt.

His resolve melted away and he leaned over, grabbed a condom and was ready for action.

"Still with me?"

She paused, looking up into his face. "You're very sweet." She stretched up to kiss his lips. "It undoes all my defenses."

He pressed in, counting to fifty to try not to lose it before he even got all the way inside her.

Resolve? Ha! He had none left. She'd torn it to shreds. He wanted inside, wanted to be in her as deeply as he could get and still, he knew without a doubt it wouldn't be enough.

She stretched beneath him, tightening her muscles and then wrapping herself around him.

Which took him deeper and made him forget how to count.

"So good." He kissed her lips, across her chin, down to her neck where he nuzzled, breathing her in. Her nails sank into his skin as she held on.

Her body received him and as he seated himself in her fully, he had to pause to appreciate just how amazing it felt.

He breathed deep and began to move.

Hard, she'd said. And he'd agreed. Every cell in his body had agreed as he thrust into that wet, snug heat.

He'd kept his face buried in her neck. Tenderness rushed through her, spicing the arousal. This was so much more than having sex had ever been. She'd thought she'd loved before. Had been close with those men she'd slept with. But *this* was different.

It was different because he was different. His weight against her was just right. He fit her just right. A silly sort of Goldilocks moment, but it was true nonetheless. Sweat-slicked skin slid together, the friction of it delicious. Leaving her delirious with need. Need she understood only he could fill.

That connection to him shook her. She was glad it came as he was inside her. Glad it came as his lips rested against the throbbing pulse at her throat. Possession swept over her then. She'd never been the jealous type. After all, if a man didn't want her as much as she him, it was his loss. But Dominic Bright was her man. *Hers.*

And she had zero intention of giving him back.

He angled himself, adjusting the legs she'd had wrapped around his waist. He pushed her knees up and apart, fitting into her so deeply it stole her breath. The length of him stroked over her clit over and over. The pressure hard enough that she understood he knew exactly what he was doing.

He'd moved his head; this time they were nose to nose and the intimacy of it made her nervous even as it titillated. Being seen by this man, in such a raw way, left her short of breath. Or it could have been the way her orgasm began to hover just at the edge of her vision. Waiting for that right stroke, the perfect amount of pressure for long enough.

He thrust, playing her body like a master. And she wanted more.

"More," she heard her stuttered whisper and forgot she hadn't meant to say it out loud.

Harder this time, so that her breasts bounced up each time he slammed into her all the way. He reared back and she was able to take him in better. He had tattoos on his biceps and along his belly. She'd need to investigate that further. Like with her mouth.

"Come on, gorgeous. Come," he whispered against her lips when he dipped his head down for a kiss.

Nearly there . . .

Just a little more pressure . . .

And then he moved his fingers, brushing two of them over her clit with a light but consistent touch and she flew apart with a cry of his name.

He wasn't far behind and within long, excruciatingly pleasurable moments, they'd ended up collapsed on his bed, breath heaving.

Chapter 11

"**WHY** are you here?" Nell cruised into Meriel's office.

"That's my line." She got up and moved to embrace her friend. "I'm so glad you're back. Tell me about the honeymoon."

"I'm not telling you shit here." Nell waved and her pretty diamond ring caught the light. "It's Sunday. You're at work. This is ridiculous."

"Says the woman standing in the office on Sunday lecturing me about being here on a Sunday."

"I've been having sex with my absurdly handsome husband multiple times daily for two weeks. I have the rest of my life to catch up on." Nell laughed. "Girl, I can't tell you how much I enjoyed Fiji. But that's mainly because I was too busy getting carnal with William."

"Let's get some lunch. I have so much to tell you." She squeezed Nell's hand.

"Most of it had better have nothing to do with this mage crap. I want to hear all the good stuff first. Then we'll talk about work."

"I need a reuben."

Nell looked at her carefully. "What the hell, Meriel? You only need reubens from Three Girls when you're eating your feelings."

Meriel laughed, like truly, deeply laughed because she'd missed Nell so much.

"I met my bond-mate. Guess what he does?"

Nell goggled at her. "You better mean last night. You have to since you haven't told me anything about it until right now."

Even though she knew Nell would be mad, she was still giddy over it. Both at having Nell back and being able to talk about Dominic with someone who'd understand.

"You are in such trouble." Nell looked around and grabbed Meriel's bag. "Let's go. We'll talk elsewhere. You can't be at work on a Sunday anyway."

Her friend's expression told Meriel there was no use arguing with her and she didn't want to.

They walked down to Pike Place and grabbed the aforementioned sandwiches, along with some cookies and a few lemon bars. One more quick stop for some tea and they headed over to Nell's place.

"Where's the mister?" Meriel looked around for William.

"He had to run down to Vegas for a few days to deal with work stuff. Sit down, I'm going to start the water for tea and you're going to tell me everything. Most notably why you've met your bond-mate and haven't ascended yet."

"He's the guy who runs Heart of Darkness," she said around a mouthful of her sandwich.

"Why, oh, why do we get tested with men who run night-clubs?" Nell shook her head, grinning. Her husband owned a burlesque-themed nightclub in Las Vegas and was in talks to open another locally. Nell had met him nearly two years before while investigating a woman who'd stolen money from some Owen holdings. The woman had been his ex and he and Nell had connected from the start.

"We haven't done the ascension spell yet because . . . gah, it's complicated."

"Complicated how? Is he married? With someone

already?" That happened, they both knew. The bond was perfect if one meant in the way it connected two witches and unlocked magickal potential. But people had lives and life included things like the person you're a potential bond-mate to being with someone already.

"No, not that, thank goodness. He's outclan. He didn't even know he was a council witch until I keyed him into the font and we worked our magick together."

"Good lord, so what does he think? That we have secret police and arrest people who don't give us all their worldly goods?" She stood again. "Why do we have no chips out? Falling down on the job, Meriel."

Back in moments, Nell tossed a bag of Doritos on the table between.

"I'm going to be so sick in like fifteen minutes if I keep inhaling this." Nell put her sandwich down a few minutes later. "I can't not tell you this any longer. I have no willpower and I think it might be because I'm pregnant. And, obviously I want to share that with you because it's *so totally cool!*" Nell laughed, clapping her hands and Meriel got up to give her friend a hug.

"Damn right it's cool! How long have you known?"

"Oh, you don't get to be pouty over me not telling you when you met your bond-mate and didn't even leave me a voice mail about it." Nell frowned a moment and then got back to the point when they'd sat down again.

"I was late on our wedding day. But I thought hey, stress of the wedding because as you're aware, his mother is Satan's minion on earth."

Meriel nodded, sipping her tea. This was an accepted truth.

"Anyway, I was late but it's not the first time so I'm really not thinking it's a big deal. You on the other hand have no such excuse."

"I didn't tell you because I wanted you to have your honeymoon without any intrusions. I couldn't tell you over the voice mail. I don't even . . ." She shook her head, not knowing how to say it and already on the verge of tears as it was.

"We'll get to that next." Nell gave her a brief glare. "I'm about six weeks along. We haven't told anyone but you. My parents would fuss and I'm not ready for that yet. God only knows what his mother will do, but I truly hope it means she'll stay on the other side of the country. Like forever. He's telling his brother on this trip to Vegas. It's"—she paused, smiling at Meriel—"it's the most wonderful thing I could have imagined. He's been beautiful about it. He wanted to take a picture of the stick with the two lines. The stick I'd just peed on, for heaven's sake." Nell shuddered and made a face. "So of course I vetoed it, but I'm giving him credit for being so mushy about it. And by the way, Meriel, were you aware that many resort sundry shops carry pregnancy tests? All in all, pretty much the best honeymoon a gal could ask for."

"I'm so happy for you both. This is so cool."

"It is. And you're going to be here to help me because you know how hopeless I am at this stuff. What do I know about babies?"

"Puhleeze. You'll do great. Anyway, don't look at me, I can't even keep a houseplant alive."

"You know everything. And if you don't, you know where to find the answer. I think William's more excited about that than I am. He just sold half the club to his brother. Nash will run it."

Meriel knew what a big deal that would have been. As long as William had the sole responsibility for the club, he'd never be able to live in Seattle full-time. This sale meant he was committed to life here with Nell and their baby. It was a really good day.

"I was just thinking what a good day it was."

"Yeah. I knew you'd make me feel even more excited. And you did. Now, tell me about Dominic. What's his deal?"

"He's everything I thought I didn't want. Overbearing. Bossy. Likes having his own way. Looks so damned good you know why he mostly gets it." She grinned. "He's arrogant. Just oozes testosterone. Has a mysterious past that—come on, let's face it—you know has to be dark. Wary."

She bit off the corner of the lemon bar and sighed happily.

"And he's also protective. Gentle. Sweet at times. Intelligent on several levels. He's a smart businessman. You can tell when you look at Heart of Darkness. He's got a great deal of power. He doesn't even have an idea of how much. He was raised by a foster father. He doesn't talk much about his parents, just that they'd died when he was a baby."

"What's he like in bed? What does he look like? Come on and tell me the juicy stuff."

"He's about six and a half feet or so. Big. The kind of body that tells you he works out." Meriel paused to fan herself. "He boxes. He tried to make it sound like he and his friends just met up and I don't know, punched each other a lot. And being familiar with men and the kinds of things they consider fun, I believe it. Whatever it is, his upper body is tight and muscular. It's the flattest belly I've ever seen in person."

"Damn, you scored."

She nodded. "Totally. Anyway, he's got brownish-blond hair. Just touches his collar. It's all thick and soft. He's even got one of those locks that falls forward and makes him look rakish. He's a menace. Dark lashes against these eyes. Unbelievable this color. Pale green. Dapper dresser, even his casual clothes."

She sat back and brushed the crumbs from her hands. "He's got a tattoo on his back. Giant unfurled wings in black and gray but there's a tiny bit of color here and there on the feathers. He's also got a nipple ring and around the other nipple, on his chest above his heart there are protective runes. He's actually got those in a few places. But they're not tats. It's as if they're worked into his skin and muscle. Someone wanted him protected. Probably a good thing too because he's had a broken nose on more than one occasion and he's got some scars on his side and belly that look a lot like knife wounds."

"Oh, a bad boy with a heart of gold. Those are like unicorns right? Imaginary?"

Meriel laughed. "He does appear to be of the bad-boy-with-a-possible-heart-of-gold variety. He touches me like I'm precious."

Nell's smile softened. "Yeah. That's something else, isn't it? Especially when they're all reluctant. I am sorry about that last part. Makes it all the more sweet when he finally accepts it though. I don't have a bond-mate like you do, but fate brought William to me. He was meant to be with me. I had to believe in that and do my best to make it happen. You'll do the same."

"He does admit to the bond. But he's dubious of it. Untrusting. Even without the bond he and I would have something electric. He's sexy, successful, gorgeous, funny and really, really inventive in bed." She fanned herself. "I like him. I like being around him. I want more and I can't have it because he's at a different place than I am. He's got a learning curve and while I know that—while my brain tells me this is totally normal—*I want more*. But I feel hesitant about asking for it."

She sighed.

"I'd tell you to be patient, but you already are so that's of no help at all. When do I get to meet him? And I take it you haven't told your mother about this."

"God, no! Can you imagine? She'd send you out to kidnap Dominic and then glare at him until he agreed to do the ascension. I don't want that. I want it to be his choice, totally. It's not that I think he hates me. We're good together. It's still new, but he's far more comfortable with what we have now than he was even just on Thursday."

"She wouldn't understand. Not because she doesn't love you in her own way. But because she never had to face what you're facing right now. Ron grew up knowing what he was. She grew up knowing what she was and what she'd be. She's never had to face this sort of uncertainty before. I get it. But she's going to notice. Even she can't miss that you're practically humming with magick." Nell tipped her head. "And love. I like that."

"I don't know about love. I love being with him. I love that he's my bond-mate. But love will come. As for the difference in my magick? I know. That's why I was at work. I wanted to clear some stuff off my desk so I could work from home and stay out of the office this week. That and well because I spent last night through this morning with Dominic. I don't want to get so used to him yet. He's got to go to New York for most of the week. Maybe we can get together, all four of us at the weekend?"

"When's he going?"

"He's already on his way." He'd woken her up at four and kept her up until nearly seven when he had to jump in the shower to get to the airport. "His plane left at nine."

"Stay here tonight. We'll get pizza and watch movies."

"That's a fine offer, ma'am."

ACROSS the country, Dominic had a jones for the lovely, redheaded Ms. Owen. Definitely found himself missing the warm weight of her next to him in his bed.

Funny to be used to something after only having it once. But there he was, sitting in a crowded restaurant as his financial advisor and longtime friend Trey told the table a story about a recent trip to Chicago.

All the while he thought of her.

Wondered what she was up to. The morning before he'd tried to let her sleep but failed. Every moment he'd lain there in the predawn darkness, giving himself a lecture about how she needed her rest, had been agony. Until he'd given in and touched her.

She'd come awake quickly, into his arms without hesitation. She'd even offered to drive him to the airport and reminded him to check the warding on his hotel room.

And now he'd be there in New York until Thursday night while she was back in Seattle. His bed would be empty. Damn it.

Simon had cornered him in his office on Saturday night as she'd been at the bar, conning his bartenders to show her new recipes. In a cocktail dress.

"So what's the story?"

Dominic had looked up from the papers he was signing. "Story?"

"Don't be coy, dumbass. What's the status between you and the lovely Ms. Owen?"

"You know the story."

"So you accept the bond then?"

"You're like a dog with a bone." He snorted and Simon flipped him off. "I like her. She likes me. There's a bond, I admit that too."

"Are you going to screw this up? Yes, yes, I know you'd rather I just stop bugging you over it. But though I'd deny it if asked, I've watched you searching around for something real for years now. Meriel is something real. What you have, no matter how fantastical, is real."

"I can't even think with her around. I need some distance and some perspective. I'll be in New York until Thursday. Maybe I'll come back clearer."

"What's she say about that?"

"I don't have to check all my business dealings through her. Anyway, she's got her own job; I can't imagine why she'd be upset."

"About your continued hemming and hawing."

"Look, I don't like the idea of not being in charge of my own destiny. Okay? I didn't grow up in an alternate dimension at the right hand of my dad the king or whatever. You and Meriel both had that experience." He pushed to stand. "She's not like anyone I've ever met before. I want more. That has to be enough right now until I figure out the rest. She's giving me the space I need. Every time I push her to finally have sex with me, she reminds me about how it'll only make our mutual attraction deeper."

Simon had laughed then. And laughed some more, the sound of it echoing all the way down the hall in his wake after he'd left the room.

He'd told Simon that he'd hoped the trip would give him some distance and perspective. And it had, only not in the way he'd imagined.

Yes, she was on his mind. Yes, he wanted to be with her.

But he wasn't debilitated to be so far away. It didn't affect him physically to be apart from her. He was getting work done.

What he did miss, in addition to all the sexy stuff, was her laugh. The way she indulged him and let him be bossy most of the time but pushed back when he got out of hand.

He missed the way she smelled. Hell, he even missed the way she so effortlessly used her magick. He'd learned a lot from her just by watching.

He'd come to really like her. As he sat there pushing his dinner around on his plate, he found himself making notes to tell her about this or that thing he'd seen during the day.

His pocket buzzed and he looked down at his phone to see who it was.

I think we should go see the Alien/Aliens *double feature on Saturday.*

Oh, that was me.

Meriel

He laughed and Evan sent him a questioning glance.

"No, no, it's fine. I just need to handle this."

Evan shrugged and went back to the conversation.

Charmed, he tried to ignore the warmth in his belly. She'd reached out to him. He knew she was purposely holding back, trying to give him room, which only made him want her more. Her being impulsive and texting meant she missed him just as much as he did her.

All right. Will you hold me if I get scared?

Oh, that was me—Dominic

He paused, wondering if she laughed. Hoping she had as big a smile as he did.

Only if you try to touch my boob when you put your arm around me.

It was probably right then that he fell in love with her.

I think we both know that's a given. I have a special relationship with your boobs.

He briefly considered asking her for a picture, but that was best left for when they were alone.

It wasn't long before she wrote back. *I miss you. Are you having fun?*

Right then as he texted with her he was having more fun than he had the whole day.

I am now. Good dinner. I'll bring you here when we visit. I miss you too. What are you up to?

He ordered another drink and waited for her to answer. Ray was talking about how gorgeous the beaches were in Maui in the background and Dominic imagined what it would be like to lay on the beach with her, alone and far away from the troubles of the world.

Spent the night at Nell's last night and had so much fun I'm back again. We've ordered Chinese food, looked at lots of great vacation photos, going to watch a movie in a bit.

"Dom, we're going to head out after this round."

He looked up at his friends, all in various modes of getting ready to leave. Evan, the one who spoke, owned three businesses. A nightclub in Manhattan, a wine bar upstate and the upscale martini-cum-piano bar they were headed to.

He'd told Meriel a little about his first break into nightclub work because of his friend. Evan had been someone he'd looked to as an example of how to make a success of yourself. Evan, Ray, Dominic and Trey had gotten up to a lot of trouble together in their early twenties when Dominic had left Oregon and moved to L.A.

Trey was a witch too. Dominic discovered that when they'd been a little, um, light-fingered and they'd been able to break into a door with a quick flick of Trey's fingers.

The four had sunk to various levels of lawlessness and one by one, they'd found a way out of the darkness. Evan first, when he bought a pub in Portland and nursed it back to life. He'd taken the profit from that sale and bought the first of his clubs on the East Coast.

It had been enough to convince Dominic that the path he was on was destined for jail. Or worse. Trey showed up on his doorstep, someone hot on his tail for some infraction or other and they'd said fuck it and went to New York.

Evan had hired them both. Trey went to business school and worked the bar at night and Dominic had learned to run a club.

Over three years he scrimped and saved and built up contacts and earned enough to buy the building he and Simon built Heart of Darkness in.

"Hang on a minute," he said and then called her instead of texting.

"Hey, we're getting ready to leave but I wanted to hear your voice." The talk in the background silenced and Dominic knew they all eavesdropped.

"Why, hello there, Dominic." He heard the smile in her voice. "It's really nice to hear your voice. I suppose you look rather dapper just now."

"Sweet witch, how did you know?" He did take a glance down at himself, flattered she'd noticed. And he happened to have a really nice suit on. He'd just picked it up the week before. He made a note to wear it when he took her out.

"See? You're very charming."

"Are you trying to convince me? I believe it." He laughed. "You're having a lovely time then? With your friend?"

"Yes, yes, I am. She and her husband would like us to have dinner this weekend. Or she says a lunch since you work at nights. William, that's her husband, he's selling half his interest in his club in Vegas and moving up here full-time. You'll like him. He also has good taste in clothes."

There was talking in the background and then Meriel laughed. That twinge of yearning at the sound startled him.

"Nell also says, you both have good taste in women."

He wished he was there.

"I wish I was there with you right now."

"You do say the best things. Makes my knees rubbery. Have fun with your friends and don't let the maidens get too fresh or I'll be forced to not only maim you, but perhaps make your nose five times larger and give you impotence."

"You can't do that!" He laughed, but he wasn't too sure where she was concerned.

Her laugh made him smile even though he knew he'd be interrogated the moment he hung up.

"But you'll always wonder now. My gift to you."

"I'll call you tomorrow. Any new developments in the

Rhode Island situation?" He knew it was on the other side of the country from her. Knew it probably had nothing to do with her or threatened her just then. But he hated it anyway. Made him worry.

"Nothing I can talk about on the phone. But not much more than we already knew."

"Well, regardless, take care of yourself. Keep an eye out."

"I'm with Nell. She's badass and will kick someone's face to protect me. Oh! Food's here and you have to go off and look handsome while I am here in sweats and a ratty T-shirt. Have something sufficiently glamorous in a glass for me."

Next time he came back to New York it would be with her and he'd take her to the Met. She'd dress up, he knew after they'd gone to the opera. She'd had her hair done. Her cocktail dress was classic Calvin Klein beauty. It fit her. Clean lines to highlight her body. So beautiful. Regal.

He could probably shuffle his schedule and go home early.

"Sweet dreams, Dominic Bright. I miss you."

"You too."

He slipped the phone into his pocket, missing her more than he wanted to allow.

"Sweet witch?" Trey looked him over, one brow raised.

"I'm seeing someone. Seriously."

"Come on, let's go. You can pay for the cab and I'll buy the next round," Evan called out as they left the table. "You can tell us about this mystery woman on the way."

Chapter 12

SHE did her work and cleared out by just a little after eight. Edwina showed up at nine exactly and she stayed until seven. So wedded to her schedule was she that Meriel was pretty sure she could avoid her mother for at least the next few days. Maybe the whole week if she played it right.

A court commissioner's hearing, two land use committees, a strategy meeting with a few of the attorneys Meriel used for contract work when more came up than she could handle on her own, even a trip to DDES and she found herself free and heading back to her apartment by four thirty that afternoon.

Only, as she stood in the aisle of her favorite local grocery store, unease slithered through her. Someone was watching her. Broad daylight, the place filled with people and the edge of whatever danger lurked was still sharp.

Regular sight showed her nothing. No one out of the ordinary lurking around. No obvious signs of magick being used. Aside from general annoyance and traffic grump, there were no signs of extreme emotion from anyone in the immediate area.

She paid quickly and headed to her car. No one was following her that she could see. No one looked out of the ordinary. Everyone in the lot was human and posed her no threat at all.

And yet . . .

She used her othersight and still saw nothing but a slight smudge at the very corner of her eye. Her personal protection wards were intact and hadn't risen to action so there was no direct magickal attack on her.

Her eyes told her everything was okay. Her magick told her everything was okay. But her gut didn't agree.

She went home, not taking a direct route, watching to see if she was being followed, but she wasn't as far as she could tell.

She locked the door and closed the wards and headed straight to the phone to call Nell.

"Nell, I need you to come by when you can," Meriel said as Nell picked up.

"What is it?"

Meriel gave her a brief rundown. "It's probably nothing. But my gut . . ." She shook her head. "It feels like it's something. I used my othersight, there was nothing there. But it's not that, it feels like I was blind to something. There was this thing at the very edge of my vision. Like a smudge. But I get headaches sometimes and that happens. I don't know if I'm explaining this well enough. But your eyes will be better."

"I'll be over shortly."

She needed to be busy so she began to prepare dinner and listened to her messages.

Uh-oh, one from her mother wanting to meet. She'd have to return that call when Edwina was sure to be out of the office.

More than her concern that Edwina would shove the ascension in her face, Meriel worried that her mother would make Dominic feel small. That she'd take his plusses and make them minuses.

She toyed with the idea of going to her father first. Her

father did tend to run interference for their mother. He was softer, easier with people. He adored his wife and understood her in a way most everyone else couldn't. Meriel thought it quite sweet.

On the day she graduated from law school, he'd taken her aside. *"Your mother loves you and she's proud of you. I think sometimes she's just terrified of making herself vulnerable enough to say it the way you need to hear it."*

Edwina loved her, she knew it. They just had trouble getting along. But the foundation was of mother and daughter and Meriel trusted that part would carry them through the rough times.

The sound of Nell's knock caught Meriel's attention and she opened the wards as Nell unlocked the door with her key and came in.

"So there's nothing on your car or in the garage. Gage went to the market; he says there's some odd energy there, but he doesn't recognize it."

Nell interrogated her until Meriel felt like a total wuss and that she'd overreacted. She said as much.

"We all have magickal abilities. It's what makes us witches. Your magick is intuitive in a way few others possess. If your gut told you to leave, pushed you to go, I have zero doubt there was a threat. It's your internal alarm system and that's why clan leaders stay alive. If it happens again, I want you to get the fuck out of there and call me immediately. Just what you did this time."

"Stay for dinner. Call Gage too. There's plenty."

"Cripes, I hope this shit isn't connected to that stuff on the East Coast." Nell hopped up on the stool and accepted a slice of cheese Meriel offered. "I spoke with the Rodas hunter today and he was helpful. We've set up an account where we can input information. Sort of a magickal wiki page." She snorted. "This *could* be something related to those mages. Maybe they're scouting around and found you because you're powerful. It's not like it's a really big secret who the next in line to run Owen is. But I don't want to jump to conclusions. But what they're facing is scary shit, Meriel.

If that's what we have, if these mages have sent out teams or scouts to track and stalk witches they'll target to take and drain, we need to step it up. I'm adding some personnel to do some daily sweeps of the area around the building and the residences of all the full-council witches. We'll start with that while we work out more info."

Meriel's phone rang and she looked at the screen. Dominic.

DOMINIC had been in a meeting with a group of boutique small-batch liquor companies when he'd come over feeling quite strange. A flash of energy shot up his spine and brought the hair on the back of his neck to stand.

He didn't quite know what to think at first. He wondered if he was coming down with something or if perhaps the ahi he'd had for lunch might have been off. Nervousness brought his knee to bounce until he forced himself to stop.

As he sipped icy vodka served to him on a tray held by a rather ridiculously beautiful woman who leaned enough to give him a glimpse of her body to her belly button, he couldn't relax enough to enjoy it. The pretty woman or the vodka.

It was as he'd been eating some delicious caviar that the flush he'd felt earlier moved to a full body, electric rush of heat and energy. Meriel's magick. He could smell her on the air, a phantom of her citrusy perfume.

He held it together for another few minutes, thinking he was just imagining things, willing the presentation to wrap up so he could call her. But it went on and on until he finally held a hand up.

"If you'll all excuse me for a few moments."

"Is there a problem?" Evan looked him over.

"I need to check on something. Please do go on. I'll return shortly." He said this all as he was already propelling himself from the room, his phone clearing his pocket.

"Hello, Dominic."

The smile she usually had in her voice when she said his

name wasn't there. Her cheer was slightly practiced. That's when he knew something *was* wrong. That'd he'd felt it across the country was a punch in several ways.

Dr. Neil deGrasse Tyson once said that the best thing about science was that it was true whether you believed in it or not. The bond was there and to continue to deny it seemed totally pointless when he could not only feel her upset thousands of miles away but that he wanted to be with her.

"What's wrong?"

"What do you mean? Are you all right?" Dominic heard talking in the background, a male voice and another female voice he recognized from Monday night, Nell.

"I'm sitting here in a meeting and I felt . . . weird. I hoped it would pass and it did for a while. But then it came back. This thing exploded in me. You. And for a second it was like I was with you, touching you. I could smell you, Meriel. Your magick is on my skin as if I'd just held you. What the fuck is going on?"

He fisted his free hand a few times to keep from shaking. He should be there with her right then.

"Nothing really, I don't think. I'm sorry it interrupted your meeting. I should have thought to warn you that we could feel each other sometimes."

He snorted. "Don't be sorry. Tell me what's happening."

"You're very bossy."

"I am. Now, tell me."

"I was at the grocery store and had a feeling. Just a feeling. Something wasn't right. The energy of the place shifted and it was all wrong. I just needed to get out of there. I didn't see anything. I came home and called Nell. You probably felt it because my magick rose in response to my fear. Really, I'm all right. Nell and Gage are on it. They couldn't find anything either."

He was leaving that night. Period.

"I'm coming back to Seattle."

"Because of this? Oh why? Don't do that. I'm fine. Really. Nell and Gage both are right here. I'm not a wuss, you know.

I can kick butt when I need to. Take care of your job and see your friends."

"I don't want the entire country between us when you're scared." Having Nell there was one thing, but he wasn't going to leave her protection up to anyone else. She was his and he'd protect her. Period.

"I'll be getting in long after your bedtime so I'll call you in the morning."

"Are you even listening to me?"

"Of course I am. But listening is not the same as agreeing. I appreciate your concern for my business, but I'm coming back tonight. And that is that. Don't open your door to anyone. If you get hurt, I will be pissed off."

She sighed, but when she spoke again, the smile was in her words. "All right. Call me when you get in. Or . . . come to me. I'll be here."

Chapter 13

FIVE in the morning and she stood before him, light from the nearby fireplace on her skin. He should have gone home and called her at a decent hour but she'd told him to come to her, hadn't she?

He came in and dropped his bags to the side before sweeping her into his arms. And he needed her so much it made him blind to everything but the weight of her against his body.

He struggled from his coat as she closed the wards and in a step he was on her again.

That sweet ass of hers in his hands, he picked her up and sat her on a nearby table. "Perfect height." He drew a fingertip over the swell of her bottom lip, down her chin and the long line of her neck.

Her skin was warm and soft as he continued down the slice of creamy skin revealed at the front of her robe. Naked for him beneath the silk.

He halted at the belt, sliding his finger back and forth over her belly button.

"You're not wearing anything under this."

"Nothing but my skin." Her mouth tipped up at the corner and he dipped his head to capture it.

"This is all I've thought about since the plane took off to go to New York on Sunday." Just days before but it had felt like a week he'd been away.

"I'm sorry." Her breath caught when he untied the belt and parted the silk, exposing her beauty to his gaze.

"Don't be. Nothing anywhere near as good as this in New York." He ran the backs of his knuckles across her nipples and watched as they tightened in response. He bent his head and kissed the curve of her shoulder and across her collarbone.

As he did that, her nimble fingers attacked his shirt buttons as she left a trail of kisses where she could reach on his shoulder, her hands sliding all over his chest and arms.

Heat seeped into him, need scorching his insides. She pushed him back just a little, enough to get his pants unbuttoned and unzipped.

"Now," she said right before she scraped her teeth over his nipple and it shot straight to his cock.

She shoved his boxers down and grabbed him, pumping him a few times in her fist to underline just what it was she wanted.

"Hang on a sec," he murmured as he bent to pull a condom from his pocket. But he paused to press a kiss to the seam at the back of her knee. The sound she made drove him crazy, a deep, hoarse moan.

Pushing her thighs wider, he kissed up her leg, licking along the seam where it met her body. Her grasp tightened, pulling his hair just this side of painful. He nipped the inner part of her thigh, pausing to breathe her in.

He pressed his palms against her hips to hold her just so, angle her so that he could taste every part of her. His thumbs spread all that beauty to his touch, to his mouth and his tongue.

She shivered delicately as he breathed against that hot, slick flesh. Her nails dug into his shoulder as she urged him on, the other hand still in his hair.

It seemed impossible for that elegant and ruthlessly controlled woman he knew to also be this wanton. This lush, sexy female so unabashedly taking her pleasure.

He drove her, knowing just what she needed, and it wasn't too very long before she arched hard, her muscles tightening as she came.

"I hear Portishead when your mouth is on me," she whispered, shivering as he brushed his lips against the heart of her before standing again and rolling a condom on.

He brushed the head of his cock against her and they both groaned at how good it felt. "Is this a good thing?"

He flexed his hips and pressed inside.

"Yes. Her voice is like sex. The lazy afternoon of fucking kind."

"Yes, that is a compliment. And perhaps even a mandate."

She laughed and he was so glad he'd come back.

And then he forgot about everything but the way it felt to be buried in her as deep as he could get. Wanting to come battled with his desire to never end this moment.

But she had plans, wrapping her legs around him and pulling him in deeper. She arched to sit more fully, her nipples sliding over his chest. Her nails dug into his shoulders.

But it wasn't until she licked up the side of his neck to bite his ear, tugging and whispering, *"More,"* that the driving need to fuck her, to be in her as she wrapped around him took over.

He had to have her. He stood up straighter, adjusting her as he began to thrust just like she'd begged for. He swiveled his hips as he met her body and she gasped, her inner walls gripping him even tighter.

Harder and harder as the table thumped against her wall over and over. He pulled back a little and her eyes snapped open. "What? Why?" She writhed.

"The table—"

She pulled him with her calves. "Don't stop." She canted her hips up and he slid in deeper and gave over to it again.

This time he didn't hold back and she held on, giving as

good as she got. Something fell somewhere and it didn't matter.

She was wet and hot when he worked a hand between them. She tightened around him. "You should give me another," he suggested, lips against her throat.

A few side-to-side strokes of a fingertip and she was close. Which was good because he was going to blow any minute.

A stuttered gasp a few moments later as she writhed on him, making him see stars. "Holy shit." He pressed in and fell over along with her.

He held her tight against him as they recovered. Her rapid, strong pulse against his lips at her neck reassured him. Soothed.

"Welcome home."

He smiled against her.

HE put her down so carefully it made her ache just a bit. When he slid his hands all over her again, as if to assure himself she was real and unharmed, it warmed her from the inside out.

"Go back to bed." He shuffled her toward her bedroom before ducking into the bathroom for a moment.

Back to bed. Such a funny man. She'd been awake for hours. Knowing he was on his way back to her had gotten her all keyed up. Eventually she'd given in and done some work while he got closer and closer.

She moved back out to the entry and pulled his bag out of the walkway.

It meant something that he'd come directly to her without even stopping at his place to change or drop his things off.

"If this is what I could see every day at sunrise, I might be amenable to waking up earlier." He entered the room and she turned to take him in.

"What are those marks? The protective ones?"

He paused. "Marks?"

She moved to him and traced over a few on his torso and then the one around his nipple over his heart. "These. Is this some sort of scarification or something? I've never seen anything like it."

"I . . ." He took a deep breath and shook his head before kissing her forehead. "Back to bed. We can talk after you rest."

"I've been up since three. I'm fine. You're the one who just flew across the country."

"I slept on the plane."

"All right. Would you like some breakfast while you tell me about the marks?" She bent to grab the belt to her robe and tie it closed. Her skin still smelled of him. It pleased her.

"First things first. Are you all right? Any news since we spoke last?"

"Nothing really new." She shrugged and gave in, moving to him to kiss across his back and the beautiful tattoo that marked it in shades of black and gray. "Why wings?"

"We're still talking about you. Are there any guards on you or anything?" He brought her around his body and dropped to the couch, bringing her with him and settling her in his lap.

"No guards on me. This place is warded by not just me, but my father, who is all low-key and cheerful but he's all about the mad warding skills." She smiled just thinking about him. "They didn't find anyone. I didn't see anyone either. It was a feeling and yes, I think it means something but I don't know what."

"You don't need to be physically present to scry."

She sat straight up and crawled over him to grab the phone. It was six so Nell would be awake anyway.

"Scrying."

"What? Hang on, I need to cross the street." In the background there was noise enough to let Meriel know her friend was on a run.

"Okay, now what did you say?"

"Scrying. Dominic just brought it up. If someone was scrying, I would sense it but they wouldn't be there for me to see. It might explain why I felt as if I were being examined."

"It can be done with a blood payment so you don't even need to be a witch to work it. That might be a clue. I'll look into it. Comes in handy, does your man. He's there now I take it?"

She looked at him for a moment, so relieved to have him with her. "Yes. I'm taking a personal day today, just FYI. You know, just in case she asks about me."

"She's going to notice sooner or later. You should call her, just to tell her you're away. If I was trying to duck my mother, that's what I'd do."

"I did yesterday. Left a message on her voice mail to fill her in on a few committees and to say I had a busy week ahead and that'd I'd be in touch later."

"You're better now? That he's come to you?" Nell's voice lost its teasing tone.

Meriel turned to look at this shirtless man who had her snug in his lap just like he wanted. "Yes to both."

"Are you gossiping about me?" His smile was oh so very wicked.

"I did all the really juicy stuff already. She says you're handy and we're going to look into the scrying angle." She turned her attention back to Nell. "I'm going to call down to research to see what I can find out."

"Better you than me. It's creepy down there."

"You're like a ninja. How can you be scared of them? They're all very nice."

Research was really the office of the institutional memory of the clan. Four witches representing the four directions and the four elements of magick. Two of them were siblings, Sheila and Gia Kelly and one was Sheila's husband, the last, their son, Carl. They knew what always appeared to Meriel as everything. They had great records, were computer savvy and had great connections to all the best libraries in the world.

"Gia Kelly is one of those witches who probably does know how to turn you into a frog. Plus it smells like dust and old stuff down there."

Meriel laughed. "She probably does. Anyway, when I hang up with you, I'm on it."

"I'm going to have to tell your mother about yesterday's incident."

She nearly growled, scrambling to sit upright. "What? Why? Nell, don't."

"I have to, Meriel. She's the leader of the clan! This is no small thing. Maybe if I could totally say I didn't think what happened was part of this mage thing, I could let it go. But I *do* think it's connected. Right down to my toes. She's going to want to be kept apprised. I've tried to work out ways not to tell her, but I don't think you can get around it."

She wished she could explain it so it sounded sane and not petulant.

So she sighed. "Fine. Do your report. I have to go and make this call."

"Don't be pissed off, Meriel. You know I don't have a choice. This is something she should know. And it only grants weight to your theory that we're all under attack in some way. They may have already targeted you. You're like the gold mine of witches to drain. All that power. No, I have to do it."

"I understand and I'm not pissed."

"I've known you since before you got your period. You are so pissed. Don't even try to lie. I'm pregnant and hormonal and if you're upset, it's only going to make me feel bad and I'll still have to report this."

"I'm not pissed. Also, I think you need to save that one up as an excuse or it's going to get old fast. Be more strategic." She tried to stand, needing to move away from him to have this kind of talk with Nell. But he held her in place and when she shot him a look he only responded with a raised brow.

She rolled her eyes.

"I just don't want to deal with her. That's all. Go on and be careful. Call me later."

"William's returning tonight. Ask if he's free to have dinner with us on Saturday."

"Yes." Dominic's voice rumbled through his chest.

"Eavesdropper!"

He laughed. "Of course."

Nell laughed as well. "Fine. Meet us at Dahlia Lounge at eight thirty. I'll see you two then." Nell hung up before Meriel could argue any more.

Meriel held up a finger to keep him silent as she dialed up the number for the research office and told them what she needed. Sheila promised some answers within the hour and said she'd email them.

"One last call." She rapped his wandering fingers with her phone before dialing the office and telling her secretary, ever punctual and at her desk by seven a.m., she was taking a few personal days, but should Edwina ask, she was to assure her that Meriel had taken care of anything pressing and would return to work on Monday. Kelly, bless her heart, repeated it back twice. Both times with an *are you sure you mean Monday* lilt.

And Meriel had repeated that yes, she meant Monday and that she hadn't had a vacation of longer than a day or two in three years. Which suitably calmed Kelly down and all was well again.

"Don't know why it's such a big deal. I have so much unused vacation time they get on me about it."

"That's because anyone who takes a look at you wants to get on you." He paused to allow her to kiss his nose. "And as to your earlier question about the marks. They're protective magick. Tom did them when I was a baby and a toddler. He says they keep me out of trouble. Like personal wards I guess."

She smiled. "Really?" She spun to straddle his waist and look more closely. "These are gorgeous. It must be the magickal energy that makes them visible."

"They're not visible."

Surprised, she looked into his face. "What do you mean?"

"I can see them. Not all the time, but most of it. Tom can see them because he made them. But no one else I've ever known has been able to see them."

"And how do you feel about it? That I can see them when others haven't been able to?" Nervousness ate at her.

"It's just one more example in a long line of examples. I may not be used to it, or entirely comfortable with the idea of this bond-mate thing being out of my control. But I can't deny that it's real. I may not understand it all. I may not have grown up expecting it. But how can I ignore each new thing that comes up? I'm outclan, not stupid."

She tried to hide a smile but couldn't and he laughed. "It's destiny. I don't think destiny cares much about your personal preferences."

"Simon said something similar and my friend Trey, also a witch, said I should stop whining and rejoice that you were gorgeous, talented and clearly too good for me."

So charming, this man. "You told your friends in New York about me?"

"They could tell you were someone special by the way I acted when you texted. And then when I rushed out yesterday. Of course I told them."

"I'm sorry I disrupted your work." But not sorry he was there with her.

"You needed me. I came." He shrugged and managed to look adorable, mussed and sweet all at the same time.

"How did anyone manage to tell you no growing up?"

"Believe me, people found a way. What's your plan for today?"

"I just took it off to be with you."

"You and I are going to the firing range. Then I'm taking you to lunch somewhere and there'll be more sex of course."

"The range? To shoot guns?"

"Here's how I think it should go. You've taught me a lot about my magick. I appreciate it and hope you continue to do so. In exchange, I want to help make you safer in the ways I can. Are you already an Olympic sharpshooter or anything?"

She laughed. "Me? No. Why would you think that?"

"You're good at everything. Okay then. So I'm good with a gun. Letting me teach you will make you stronger and safer. It's win-win."

"All right then."

Chapter 14

HER fantasy bubble popped two days later when Meriel and Dominic came around the corner toward her front door and found Edwina standing there, her finger steady on the bell.

"There you are. Where have you . . . ." Her gaze flicked from Meriel to Dominic, whose hand had been snagged with hers.

"Mother, come in." Meriel dug her keys from a pocket and unlocked the front door. But it was Dominic who subtly, but firmly put his body first and went in, leaving the two women in the hall for a moment before he turned and nodded. She was more than able to detect an intruder, but it was nice that he wanted to protect her anyway.

Edwina made no secret of her curiosity where Dominic was concerned, as Meriel locked the door and the wards snapped back into place.

"I'm Edwina Owen, Meriel's mother. And you are most assuredly not any run-of-the-mill boyfriend. I can see her all over your skin." She turned to Meriel. "Why have you not told me about this?"

"I wanted to get to know him first."

Edwina waved a hand and managed to make it look grace-ful. "Of course you do. You can do that after the ascension."

Clicking her teeth together, Meriel turned to him with a forced smile. "Dominic, you said you had to make a run to your place? I'll meet you at Heart of Darkness later."

"No, you won't. I'm here with you right now." He held a hand out to Edwina. "I'm Dominic Bright. I suppose you know what I am at this point."

Edwina allowed the whisper of a triumphant smile touch her lips and Dominic could see, quite clearly, where Meriel got her spine. But he sure as hell wasn't going to allow this woman, or anyone else for that matter, make Meriel feel small.

"Who are your people, Dominic?"

"Why don't we all sit and have some juice?" Meriel motioned to the table and her mother sent her a narrowed glare, which Meriel only shrugged off. Dominic stepped into the kitchen.

"Ladies, I'll get the juice. You two go on and visit. I'll be along momentarily."

"How long?" Edwina got right to the point.

"I met him last Thursday."

"As in a week ago? Or day before yesterday?"

"A week ago."

"A week you've been possibly stalked by some gang of mages bent to kidnap and drain you. You could have ascended. Been far more powerful. You've not done the spell yet. Why?" It was a demand thinly disguised as a question.

Meriel drew a deep breath and it was as if he felt it too. Just at that moment their connection glittered. Her gaze cut to his briefly. Long enough to see the gratitude in her eyes.

"He's outclan. He didn't grow up with this as a reality. He didn't even know he was full-council until Thursday. He asked for time, I gave it to him. It's entirely reasonable and it's not like there's a time limit for the ascension spell to be given. It'll be there next month or the month after."

"You can get to know him either way. Why wouldn't you do the ascension and *then* get to know each other? One doesn't have to involve the other. He's your bond-mate either way. Why you'd deny that or play semantics games is beyond me."

"Which is why I kept this to myself to begin with."

Dominic put the juice on the table and sat close to Meriel.

Edwina turned to Dominic. "Well? What do you have to say for yourself? You can do the spell and it cements the bond. It'll open up your magick and hers too. She'll ascend to the full-council and if something were to happen to me tomorrow, she could take over. Why would you rob her of this?"

Meriel interrupted, her magick washing over him and through the room. "Whoa. *No.* We will not discuss this in those terms. This is not robbing anyone of anything. This is why I didn't tell you and wasn't going to until he'd decided he was ready for the ascension. I don't want him to be pressured to do it. It should be his choice."

"So you hide from me for a week? And what's all this nonsense about choice? He's your bond-mate. He clearly enjoys you physically. You were holding hands when you came back just now so there's a romantic connection. But beside any of that, the bond is there whether you play courting for a while or not."

"Exactly. Which is precisely why I want him to make that choice himself. I lose nothing if I let him have the time and I gain the knowledge that when he comes to me for the ascension, he does it knowingly and purposefully. This is my life. This is my bond-mate. This is my heart and my soul and I won't start off my life with him with emotional manipulations and or ultimatums. If he can't come to me on his own, I'm not worthy and he sure as hell isn't."

"Do you think that sort of silliness was allowed when it happened to me? My mother didn't just say, come to your true place on the council whenever you feel like it. I had responsibilities and so do you. I—"

Meriel made a cutting motion with her hand. "But I am not you."

Dominic knew there was some difficulty between mother and daughter. Meriel had been very diplomatic when she spoke, though her jokes sometimes were sharp enough that he understood there was a lot of history there. He didn't like it at all that this woman sought to make Meriel do something she didn't believe was right. But at the same time, he knew Meriel wouldn't do anything she didn't believe was right.

And she did this for him. Because she wanted him to have that space and she'd fight off this strong woman across the table tooth and nail if she had to.

For him.

Which only made him totally sure he wanted to ascend.

HE ran a fingertip down the long, sexy line of her spine. He liked the way she looked, naked, mussed, glasses perched on her nose as she checked her email.

"I hope Edwina realizes you work pretty much all the time."

She rolled, putting her phone down on the nightstand. "I'm sorry."

She apologized to him a lot. Wondered if she saw it at all.

He kissed her quickly, still sated—for the moment—from the marathon session they'd just ended a while before.

"For what? Running the legal department of a very busy corporation? You spend the evenings with me at my business, why would I begrudge you your work?"

Her mother had left and things clearly remained tense between them. But he'd seen the love between mother and daughter even through the strain.

"I should be paying attention to you. You're far more interesting and entertaining than work."

He laughed. "Good to know. But I seem to recall some very intense concentration just a few minutes ago. My legs just got some feeling back." He pulled the sheet back enough to take a look at those breasts. "These are so amazing." He bent to kiss the tip of each nipple gently.

She raised a hand to touch him, needing that. His being there in her bed felt like a gift and one she planned to continue to appreciate. He'd stood next to her the entire time her mother had been visiting, backing Meriel up and charming Edwina. Her mother wouldn't admit it, but Meriel could see it anyway.

He *was* fairly difficult to resist. As her naked and totally boneless state could attest to. They'd spent the afternoon with

William and Nell instead of having a dinner so when her stomach growled she stretched and leaned out to kiss his shoulder. "How about we go to dinner before you go to work? Downtown? Then when we're done you can head to Heart of Darkness and I can go in to my office for a few hours to get some work done."

"Always happy to squire you around. But are you sure you have to go to the office? You work a lot, baby. Is that sustainable?" He kissed her forehead. It was nice to be worried over, made her all gooey inside.

"It's not usually this bad. I don't usually go in on weekends or at night. It's just that I've been a little . . . distracted this week."

He grinned. "Should I be sorry? Because I can't really find it in my heart to regret all the time we've stolen this week."

She traced a thumb over his cheek. "You should talk about working all the time. You work more than I do."

"Yes, but darling, my work includes bringing you along when you're indulgent enough to wear the little bits and bobs I give your way. This isn't really work."

Little bits and bobs. He spoiled her utterly with gorgeous clothes she'd never had bought for herself in a million years, but she felt like a goddess when she wore them.

"Giving me presents shouldn't be. Though you know I don't expect it."

"I find myself unable not to shower you with presents. I like making you happy."

"You do make me happy. I've never been so happy."

"Even though I haven't done the ascension?"

She took a deep breath, thinking it over. "Yes. Certainly I want that very much. But you're here with me and that's what matters most. The rest we can handle as it comes along."

"Even if it weakens your position in the clan?"

"I already told you that was my mother spinning stories. She's the only person who knows other than Nell and Gage so how can I be weakened unless she's the one doing it?"

"But will she?"

"No. I can't believe she would. Not as my mother and not as The Owen." She sat, resting against the pillows and he settled, head in her lap.

"Is that what they call her?"

"It's the official title of the leader of Clan Owen."

"It's pretty epic."

He made everything better.

It wasn't that she'd never had a relationship before. There'd been boyfriends before. But nothing like this.

"I think so too. I love your hair. So thick and soft." She began to lightly knead and scratch his scalp until he groaned and relaxed totally, eyelids sliding closed.

"Show me something," he murmured.

It delighted her the way he'd reacted to learning more about his magick.

She moved to straddle him.

"Or that. I'm always up for that. Though . . ." He paused and then grinned as he ground his reviving erection into her. "I was about to say something about how I wasn't sure if all of me was up for that. But you continue to amaze me and my cock."

"Incorrigible. I meant this." She touched his belly, the hard, flat muscle there. He was so delicious she frequently forgot what she was about to do or say when she caught sight of him.

"You look like you're about to take a big bite."

She sent a cockeyed smile and went back to his belly. "Give me your hands."

He did and she put hers around his, guiding his fingers.

"Close your eyes and take a deep breath. Slowly. Then let it go."

He obeyed.

"Your magick lives here." She drew circles with his fingertips over the spot just above his belly button and her own magick stirred within. "Sometimes mine feels like a curled-up cat. Nose to tail. Know what I mean?"

He smiled, his eyes still closed. "Yes. I see what you mean."

"You can reach out and stroke it. Coax it, bring it to the surface. Use your mind and connect with it." His breath hitched and she knew he'd caught it and brought it closer to the surface.

"When you get what we like to call a gut feeling, it's oftentimes your magick flaring up in response to a perceived need." She let go and moved back, watching him discover it himself.

"That is wicked cool." He opened his eyes, smiling up at her. "You're smart, you know that?"

She rolled off him, dipping down to kiss his lips before padding into the bathroom to brush her teeth. "The more you're familiar with your magick, the quicker it responds. And thank you."

"I imagine you're used to being told how smart you are. I'm not talking about book smarts, which you are as well, but you get your magick, you understand it. I'm envious. You're good at showing what you mean. I've learned more about my magick in the week I've known you than in years. You're patient with me."

He always knew what to say.

"You're a powerful witch. You felt it now, right? Do you see what I mean?" She was so proud of him but afraid to say it, not knowing how to give him the words that wouldn't sound patronizing or weird.

He pulled her close, her back to his front as he spoke to her reflection.

"I got the wings on my back because I was foolish enough to tell the tattoo artist to do what he thought I needed. I never understood why he decided on something so intricate."

"The ladies must dig it though."

His quick grin told her she was right.

"They may have before, but you're the only lady I want digging it from now on. But as you're my angel, maybe it was his way of telling me one day the tat would mean something more. I think we should do the ascension."

She nearly choked. "Don't you dare let her guilt you into this." She turned and he only shook his head, still smiling.

"This has nothing to do with her. Well, that's not entirely true but not in the way you think. You've given me such a gift and you don't know it. I can't tell you what it means that you never pushed. And that with her today you defended me."

"Of course I did."

He slid his thumb over her bottom lip. "I love when your bottom lip sticks out just a little when you're arguing. What I meant was, I needed the space, I was reeling and fighting what I knew was true because it freaked me out. But I can't deny this any more than I can stand here and look at you without wanting you again."

"I don't want you to think that desire is out of your control, or not your choice."

"You told her the bond would be here in a month or a year. And it will. We do have time to get to know each other. The ascension will happen and I'll still be learning you. They're not mutually exclusive. I was hung up on something and the longer I think about it, the more I believe I was looking at it incorrectly."

"How so?"

"It was sudden and I balked. You respected that and gave me some space to process something that in retrospect will probably still take the rest of my days to figure through it's so huge. And I can. I can continue to examine it and find a way to make it make sense. Baby, the fact is, we *are* connected. You're meant for me, and me for you. So I can accept that and enjoy it for all it brings to my life, or I can rail about it when I actually like it and who wins? Hm? We have this thing and it's fucking awesome. Damn. Every time you get near my system revs up. My magick rises to meet yours. You say it'll get even stronger after the ascension. Even your mother said that today. In the end, it underlines what I already know. It makes me a stronger and more powerful witch. It makes you one too. And it's a way of telling you in no uncertain terms that I accept what we have."

She blinked back tears rather unsuccessfully. He flustered her because it mattered what he thought. How he felt was important. He got it. She wanted to hug him and cry, but then she'd get tears and possibly snot all over him and that was not the memory she wanted to leave him associating with this moment.

"Don't cry. I can't stand to see you upset." He looked so helpless it made her smile.

"Good tears."

"Oh. Good. Okay then. When can we do this? The ascension I mean."

"It depends on what you want. It only takes a spell. We could do it now. But it's usually done with at least one witness each. A grounding if you like. You can have family there and do it at home or outside in a special place. Or, we can do a formal ceremony with a ritual. This would be in the presence of the entire seated full-council. You do know that even if you want to stay outclan, through me you have a seat on the governing council."

"Would that help you? Politically."

She liked that he got the politics of the situation without any prompting. So smart her man.

"Yes. I can't deny that. The more people on the dais who back my perspective the better it is for me. The stronger my position. I have no intention of shoving my mother out the door. She's good at what she does and that's good for the clan." She shrugged.

"I just realized I'm going to be bonded to the princess of witchlandia." He said this totally deadpan.

Her laugh filled her up as she tiptoed, stretching to kiss him just for the sheer pleasure of it.

"Indeed. So you do know you're like the first husband, right? I mean, you do accept that you're mine and I'm not giving you back and that's not just about the bond. It's more. I'd want you even without this bond."

She saw it come over his face and realized she'd been nervous too. She'd accepted the mechanics and science of the bond, but she'd thought long and hard about the rest. Could she be with him for the rest of her life and know it was because she loved him, plain and simple? Because of, part of, whatever relationship the bond played, she felt it and it was real and that counted.

They both let out a shaky breath. "Yes. I mean yes, I'd want you either way. I won't remain outclan. I can't play into any kind of feeling that I'm rejecting you or the clan. But I'm not like co–The Owen or whatever, am I?"

"Come on." She tugged him back into the bedroom.

"Can I pick out what you wear?"

She shook her head, rolling her eyes. "You're demented."

"Damn right I am."

"All right."

He stepped into her closet and began to look through her clothes. She liked him in there with her. It felt intimate and sexy. He had excellent taste too, which was an added bonus.

"To answer your question, no, there's one leader of the clan and that's the female firstborn of the sitting clan leader. Or a sister—that works too—and cousins. I'm totally digressing. Anyway, that's me. And before me it was Edwina. Etcetera. Not all clans do it this way."

"But Owen does and that's a big deal because Owen has a lot of power."

She turned to face him. "Yes. Why do you say it like that though?"

"Trey. My friend and my accountant. You remember me talking about him?"

"The friend from Los Angeles. He's a witch too. Clan Hayes."

"Christ, I'm really going to have to step up my game. You never forget anything."

She shrugged.

"Anyway, he said it when I told him about you. The others know I'm seriously involved with someone, but none of them are really going to get the witch stuff."

"We're a powerful force in our world. I don't deny it and I'm not ashamed of it. When you have power, people either leave you the fuck alone, or you can crush them when they do something stupid."

His smile made her tingly. "When you're this way, all in charge and ruthless? It makes me want to lick you."

She paused, flattered and flustered.

"I like that too." He tucked her hair behind her ear. "You're the genuine article, Meriel Owen."

"You make me forget everything," she whispered. "My words. Sometimes even that I have a voice. No one ever has made me like this."

"Yeah? Good to know I'm not alone." He kissed her and smoothed away that agitation.

She still felt the phantom of his touch when he finished and stepped back to look at her clothes again.

"What am I going to wear? I can't pick the proper panties and bra if I don't know what I'm wearing."

"Ah, the mystery of woman." He moved closer and her heartbeat sped again. Never, ever had any man rendered her to goo the way he did. She'd always considered herself a healthy sexual being, but if she could work a way to have sex with him four or five times a day, she'd do it.

She wanted it all the time. And he was so endlessly energetic and inventive. And really dominant. Whooo. She'd scoffed at the idea of getting off on a big alpha-male type and boy, was she wrong.

The way he shielded her with his body drove her to distraction. He was a door opener. A coat putter on-er. He gave her his total attention when they were out.

And in bed. *Mother of pearl*. He was hard and rough. Took what he wanted, but only after he'd gotten her there first a time or two.

"You're thinking about me fucking you."

She came back to herself, too late to blush or stop that one step that brought his arms around her. "It makes me so hot to know that."

"I was just . . ." She considered lying, but then realized that would be stupid. "I was, yes."

"Well, let's see what I can do about making that into a reality then, shall I?"

She nodded because he'd made her witless. Again.

Chapter 15

REMARKABLY relaxed, he leaned back against the seat and looked her over. So. Fucking. Lovely. How he'd ended up with someone like her he'd never understand, but that didn't matter because now that he'd found her, he wasn't giving her back. So it worked nicely with her declaration of the same.

That he knew the softness at the base of her throat, the subtle scent of her hair, the way she sounded as she came, well, that made him a very satisfied man.

He'd managed to take her in her closet just an hour or so before. When he'd sat up afterward, he'd seen the pretty blue dress she currently wore. He liked that extra bit of context. Every time she wore it he'd remember.

Sex addled, he'd forgotten their earlier pre-sex discussion because, well, sex.

"So, what is it you'd like? For the ascension, I mean."

She stole a spring roll and grinned. "Washington is a community property state. Just FYI that means fifty percent of your spring rolls are rightfully mine. And don't give me any of that we aren't actually married stuff because let's face it, I want that spring roll and I'm not above showing you my boobs to make that happen."

Her sense of humor had been such a lovely surprise. He hadn't really expected it.

"You may always have my spring rolls. This is my vow to you." Interestingly enough, he'd sort of been considering this ascension thing to be like marriage anyway. After all, he was binding himself to her for life. He knew that the bond wasn't always sexual or romantic, but this one sure as hell was and it pleased him she thought so too.

It was also interesting that he hadn't panicked at the thought. It was as if he'd taken one look, one deep breath of her and his entire being had honed in and said, *mine*.

"I just want you to be happy and comfortable. If you like, we can go to Tom's and do it there. It's going to depend on what you want. If you plan to join the clan as more than just the guy bound to me, then I'd suggest we do it here on Owen land. We're most powerful here, where we've lived for generations. Our magick is in the earth. Everything around us is imbued with our signature, our energy. But if we do it here, you're accepting that. It'll recognize you and accept you as well."

He'd thought about all that too. He didn't like rules and regulations. He didn't like being told what to do. But he was her bond-mate and her man and she was going to run the clan someday. What would their children think if he didn't sit with her on the governance council?

He also knew it would hurt her if he rejected the clan. It was part of her in a way that had a lot to do with her identity. He got that. And heaven help him, but he couldn't bear to hurt her.

"I'll be joining the clan. I don't have to do any more ceremonies, do I? And I don't have to like, work at your office or anything? I can keep running my club?"

"That's a whole 'nother thing. We'll get to that in a minute. Technically, once you perform the ascension you'll be a recognized member of Clan Owen. You'd normally need to come in and talk with us and learn a little about the clan's history and our expectations."

"But you've been a very helpful teacher." He couldn't

help that he leered just a little bit as he said it. She was hot and he was hot for her. And she'd taught him a lot.

"Well, I can attest that my introductions to magick and clan history have never been so interactive."

He snagged a dumpling from her plate. "Better not have been."

"You don't have to work in the business, though you'll have a seat on the full-council and as such you'd be expected to fill leadership opportunities. Committees, mentoring, that sort of thing."

"Can we do it here but not at your building?"

"Oh, of course! We don't have them there usually. I prefer my dad's garden for such things. I've always sort of imagined I'd do my ascension there."

He took her hands. "Why didn't you say so?"

Those eyes of hers locked with his. "Because I knew my path and I didn't want that to affect your decisions."

"That's what we'll have though. You know that. I'm going to want to do things sometimes just because they make you happy. And don't tell me you never thought of that because you do it all the time with me. Don't think I haven't noticed."

She smiled. "I like it when you're happy."

"If we weren't in public right now, I'd be working the zipper on the back of your dress down. I will though. Perhaps . . . in my office. Yes. On my desk." He lowered his voice. "From behind."

Her bottom lip caught briefly between her teeth and a wave of lust rolled over him.

"I sure hope this part doesn't wear off."

She dabbed her mouth with the napkin. "Me too. I can't imagine not running around all day with my head filled with all the smutty things I want you to do to me."

"What I find most delightful about you, Meriel, is that once you scratch beneath that cool and regal façade, there's a filthy, filthy woman. And she's mine."

She grinned and he relaxed, just totally happy.

And then all of the sudden her head cocked as unease slid down his spine.

"What is it?" He looked around, nonchalant.

"There's someone here who . . ." She licked her lips, clearly using her othersight. Dominic waved the server away, knowing Meriel needed the time to work her magick to check the situation out.

Without thinking, he reached across the table and took her hand. Which he'd meant as a simple thing to lend reassurance, but his magick rushed up from the pit of his belly and then through him, into her. Not draining him, which he'd sort of expected, but mixing with her energy.

Her gaze cleared moments later. "Mages."

"And we're leaving." He pulled his wallet out and tossed down some money.

"Why do you always pay? I can afford to pay sometimes."

"Are you really going to argue with me at this moment? Let's go or point him out so I can clean his clock."

Startled, her worry was replaced by a smile. "Can you please call Nell?" She pushed her phone across the table. "I'm going to see what I can find out."

He leaned in, cuffing her wrist, her pupils flared for a brief moment and he was reminded of how he'd woken her up the morning before. She scraped her teeth over her bottom lip, catching it briefly, and he nearly forgot he was pissed off.

"Are you out of your fucking mind? No, no, I can't call Nell as you scope out the area for someone who might be stalking you to do you harm. We'll call her on the way out."

"This is my town. I will not run and hide from someone who can only get his power by stealing it." She focused on him, putting her hand over the one cuffing the other wrist. "I am not weak, nor will I behave as such."

Before he could argue, she continued.

"We *made* this territory with our minds and our bodies, with our magick and our work. There is no place I'd be safer. This is our ground. Do you understand what I'm telling you?"

He realized she'd opened up her othersight and he snarled a curse as he called Nell and told her what was going on.

She'd only said, "On my way." And hung up.

"What can I do? If you're going to pull some crazy shit, at least let me help."

His magick had risen the moment she'd cocked her head and said something was wrong. But it began to spill over and into her. She took a breath, surprise on her face.

"You're doing it."

She continued to scan the immediate area. The tendrils of her magic swirled past him and he admired the control she had. He moved, subtly to keep her shielded from the room. What he really wanted to do was stand up and get her behind him and out of the restaurant.

"We take it very seriously. I guess you should know that right now. Our dominance and governance. We worked hard to get it and we won't cede even an inch."

He feigned surprise as he kept his gaze dancing around the room. He realized as he did it that he could catch magickal energies. She'd been trying to teach him how to use othersight more fully. He knew the basics, but watching her work had been like a master class. He'd been able to use his othersight, but he was pretty sure it was beyond his skill level to do that and fourteen other things like she did.

"No! Please tell me you're not a bossy, ambitious and utterly ruthless fierce bitch of a witch." He put a hand over his heart and she looked at him, laughing.

"I'm a fragile flower, Dominic. I need you to open my doors and hold the heavy stuff."

He brought her hands to his lips and kissed each wrist. "No. You don't *need* me to do it at all. You know I like to and you let me. Which is why it's so hot."

She breathed in very deep and closed her eyes upon her exhale. His energy, so attuned to hers, kicked to a higher level of alertness. He closed his eyes for just a moment and the room exploded into othersight as he saw it through her senses.

He was humbled, just then, at how much she saw, at how well she used her power and just how powerful she was to start with.

She squeezed his hands and he opened his eyes. "It's gone."

"You will stay in here. I'm going to look outside."

Not letting go of the hand she held she shook her head. "What are you going to do? We don't know who it was. I couldn't get a fix on whether it was here or outside. This is downtown Seattle, there are people everywhere outside and this building has multiple floors with multiple businesses. Traffic everywhere. It's a Friday night."

She paused, licking her lips. "Did you feel our energies mesh?"

The knot of tension in his belly eased at the memory. "Yes. I saw othersight through your perception. You're beautiful. Amazing."

She blushed and Nell strode up to the table with William Emery, her husband.

"Why the hell are you still here?" Nell demanded as William bent to kiss Meriel's cheek. Though he'd met the man who had eyes for no one but his wife, Dominic glared at his audacity.

The two sat as if they meant to stay awhile. Casual. But Dominic liked the expression on Nell's face. Intent on running her prey to ground.

"How could I have gotten that kiss if I'd left?" Meriel winked at Nell, who glowered and turned it on Dominic.

Nell turned her attention to Dominic. "And why are you allowing this? I can't be with her twenty-four-seven. I'm counting on you to keep her out of trouble."

He kept his fingers with Meriel's and looked to her before speaking. "It was important she hold her ground."

He'd done it and nearly given himself an ulcer having to sit there and not rush her from the place. And he didn't regret it when she gave him a beautiful smile.

"I know, right?" Meriel looked to Nell.

Nell, unable to hold a smile back, shook her head as she looked to Dominic. "Yeah, yeah, he's the cat's meow. What's going on?"

The two leaned in close and began to speak while William held out a hand. "Can I buy you a drink? We aren't doing much of that at home as the missus is in the family way."

Nell looked up and sighed. "I thought we agreed not to announce it to the universe for a while."

"He's your best friend's whoosit, bond thing. Of course she's going to tell him, even if it's inadvertent."

Dominic liked the energy between Meriel's friend and her husband. They clearly liked each other as well as loved. Tom hadn't really dated when Dominic had been growing up. None of his friends had gotten married yet either. He hoped the lack of exposure to working relationships wouldn't be too much of a detriment with Meriel.

"Mazel tov." Dominic raised his glass.

"We're still going to dinner tomorrow night. Just a reminder. This does not trump that." Nell sent a raised brow to her husband.

"Who am I to deny you anything?"

"Are we going to find this mage stalking Meriel? Or can I get her the hell away from here?"

Nell raised a brow his way. "Gage is here and doing his business. Meriel has given me some clues and so now I think it would be good to get up on out of here and leave."

"I think you should come to Heart of Darkness." Meriel looked to Nell and then over at William. "Nell, you can check the wards and security yourself and if it passes inspection, I can report on it next week at council."

Nell sighed and William laughed, reaching out to touch her cheek.

"Nell hates the nightlife and does not like the boogie, I'm afraid." Meriel teased.

"Even though she usually ends up having a good time." William rarely took his gaze from his wife.

"Yes, well, it's probably more fun than watching skanks rub themselves all over you like homeless cats."

Meriel looked to Dominic and winked. Did she think he was amused by all this?

"My darling Meriel," he said this silkily as he kissed her knuckles, "I don't want to go anywhere tonight with this asshole out and about. I want to get you home where you're safe."

William shifted in his chair. "Glad to know it's not just me. I agree with Dominic. We're doing dinner tomorrow, we can go afterward." He shrugged one shoulder. "I've checked out a few nightclubs in town, you know, to get the lay of the land. Maybe we can talk about that sometime."

Nell nodded. "They're right, Meriel. Not that, you know, I'm not chomping at the bit to go clubbing and all. Until we get a better handle on just what's happening, it's best for you to be extra wary. I was concerned before, now I'm convinced it's mages here looking for witches to grab. I'm putting a few more people on a team to run these mages to ground. As for Heart of Darkness, Gage has already checked the wards there, you have too. It can wait another day."

Nell turned to Dominic. "You know she'll be far stronger after the ascension."

Scandalized, Meriel whacked Nell's arm. "Shut up! I won't allow this to be used to push him into the ascension."

Nell whacked Meriel's arm right back and snorted. "Fuck you, Meriel. I'm saying what needs to be said and you're being a dumbass."

"This is my bond. This is my ascension and if I can tell Edwina to back off, I can sure say it to you. She's scarier anyway. This is about not only my bond, but about our clan and mine and Dominic's future. I won't rush. I'm not some weakling of a witch as it is, thank you very much for the confidence."

So fierce. She was so deliciously hot and fierce right then. A shiver ran through him, driving him to make her safe, to make her his.

"I've already told her I wanted to do it. We were discussing the particulars when this happened."

Nell smirked and Meriel growled. "Good. Talk some sense into her then. Go home, Meriel. Get the hell off the streets or I'll assign a guard to you full-time."

Dominic was torn about this. He wanted her protected, but he was perfectly capable of physically protecting her. They really had no idea what he'd spent most of his twenties doing.

Dominic knew the smile on his face was nearly feral, but

this was getting taken care of his way, damn it. "Why don't you two come with us to Meriel's father's garden?"

Her eyes popped open as she gaped at him. It made him laugh, even has he knew it would have been better not to show her any amusement or she'd try to get around him.

"No. Dominic—"

Chapter 16

"**SO,** Dominic and I would like to perform the ascension and we'd like to do it in your garden." Meriel stood with Dominic in her parents' living room.

Edwina's attention sharpened so taut Meriel felt the change in her magick. "When?"

"Tonight. Right now." Dominic smiled, utterly debonair but there was no disguising the rough patches. He was not Edwina's sort of witch. But he was spectacular. Standing there next to him as he charmed his way into getting what he wanted, just like he had with her earlier only reinforced her affection for him. To think she'd fought him on this, when she wanted to ascend too anyway.

"Well now." Edwina stood. "Yes, of course. Coming up on midnight in a bit." She nearly spoke again but stopped herself. "What would you like?"

Meriel grinned and gave in, hugging her mother and not being offended by the way she always sort of held herself back. "Not the entire full-council. Perhaps the quorum?" She'd explained to Dominic that the quorum was the uppermost tier of any clan's governance structure, made up of those council witches who'd ascended.

In Clan Owen it was Edwina, her magickal bond-mate, Ron, Meriel's father, Abe, his brother and bond-mate, Kent Purcell, and Sami Ellis and her bond-mate, Brenda Conrad. After the ascension, their number would include Meriel and Dominic.

"Of course. I think that's wise." She pulled Meriel along, already holding her phone and dialing. "Is he going to be joining officially? How do you want to handle that?"

"He is. But he'd like to keep that low-key. Not his affiliation, naturally. He'll be sitting on the dais with me. But the joining part itself. I'm already providing him with the education he needs."

Edwina gave a bunch of orders, hung up and turned her attention back to Meriel.

"I agree. He will receive further training with his magick." She looked to Dominic. "He's not using even a quarter of his gift right now. Don't get that look on your face, Meriel. He's your bond-mate and he grew up outclan, it's our job to help him use all his potential."

"The ascension will make him even stronger," Nell added so helpfully.

"Yes and he'll gain part of my control and my training along with that."

"I'd like to suggest that if The Owen has an idea for training she feels would benefit me, she should share that." Dominic added a tip of his head that for some reason kicked totally outrageous behavior down to sort of rakish and right then she watched her clever man charm her mother.

Calls were made as Edwina interrogated Dominic. He'd thrown down a challenge for her to make a suggestion and she was on the case. She took her job seriously and now she'd be sure to find something to fit. It amused Meriel and Dominic seemed to handle her mother perfectly.

Preparations continued as people began to show up. She'd wanted something reasonably quiet and probably with more than half an hour's planning, but at the same time it would be taken care of and things could move forward.

Satisfied that she had enough information from Dominic for the time being, Edwina dismissed him, sending him to the other side of the room where the males seemed to be keeping out of her mother's way.

Meriel looked up from her mother's yammering to watch her father with Dominic. They already had an easy way about them. She was glad about that. Her dad's opinion meant a lot. She wanted him to approve of her life choices.

He looked up, his glasses on his nose and smiled. "We're talking about you!" He waved, looking amused as he turned to pour Dominic a few fingers of Scotch.

Dominic had been such a surprise. He'd backed off enough to give her space at the restaurant. He'd not only let her remain to look for the mage, but he'd lent her his magick. He'd then turned around and dug his heels in and proceeded to seduce her with words and deeds until she found herself knocking on her mother's front door.

And then he'd held his ground with her mother when she'd gone a bit bitchy but he'd managed to charm her with his defiance instead of piss her off. It was beautiful really. He was such a con artist. She smiled as she watched him talk with her father and William. He stood there in her house and made friends with her dad. And he did it for her.

"It's funny how something so new can feel so essential." She put her head on Nell's shoulder as her mother ordered people around.

"I hear that. I like you two together. I like that he's pushing you to keep safe in the face of all this mage stuff. He's a bossy one, gonna take some maintenance."

Meriel grinned. "Yeah, that's part of the fun."

"You two stop your whispering. We have to stay on task. Say your good-byes to him for now," Edwina said, flapping an impatient hand toward Dominic. "He needs to be prepared and so do you. We're cutting it close. Brenda and Sami have arrived. Sami will help your father prepare Dominic. Nell, can you deal with that? Just show Sami to Abe and let Brenda know where we'll be doing the ritual."

Nell bustled off and Meriel, not needing any more urging, went to Dominic.

"Hey."

He pulled her into his arms and it was all right. So very all right. "You just make everything all right," she mumbled into his shirt.

He kissed the top of her head, squeezing her just a little bit tighter. "Good."

"So it's time for you to go with my dad right now. He's going to walk you through the entire process ahead of time so you know what to expect. Are you sure you don't want to wait for Tom so he can be here?"

"He's not answering his cell. I didn't think he would anyway. He's on a backcountry trip. He takes groups out all year long. He won't be back in range until Sunday night, maybe Monday."

"I hate that he's not here for you. Will he be upset?" The idea that this man who was so important to Dominic might think she excluded him or that she'd hurt his feelings really bothered her.

"We'll go down there and see him. Is that all right with you? I do want him to meet you and I'd like to show you the house and stuff. He'll be happier that way. He's not one for this kind of stuff. He'd have come because it was me, but he's not overly social."

"I'd really like that."

He bent down and took her lips tenderly, just a breath of a touch across her mouth with his lips. And yet there was so much there passing between them. He touched parts of her she'd never even known existed.

Hoo. She was so drunk off this man.

She took a step back. "See you out there in a few."

Abe, Meriel's father, raised his glass as they watched Meriel rejoin her mother and then disappear up some stairs.

"I'm so pleased to have you do this in my garden. I've

always loved to work my magick out here. Funny, you know Meriel is the worst with plants. Can't keep a houseplant alive to save her own life, even with magick! But she's loved this garden her whole life. Used to perch on the rock wall over there to watch me work and keep me company."

"She told me about your garden. She's proud of it." Dominic walked down a path, trees all around. Benches, water features, rockeries. The garden was astoundingly beautiful. Fecund. Life just dripped from every surface. He saw it clearly as he used his othersight, as Ron and Sami had suggested. Meriel had been helping him learn how to use it better and then Abe had patiently shown Dominic a new way to open himself up, a way he'd understood a little better than he had before.

And so there she was, the moon shining on her skin. Those witches Meriel had referred to as the quorum stood in a line. Meriel's dad had explained that they would form an internal circle around Meriel and Dominic, all of them protected by an outer circle Edwina and Ron would set.

Meriel stepped forward. She wore a beautiful white cape; her hair was pulled from her face, exposing her features. She held out her hand and he took it. A connection was made. Energy was conducted between them, humming.

He trusted her with everything he was.

She knelt and he followed. The quorum made their circle and Edwina set the outer circle with a snap of energy.

Edwina came forward and tied Meriel and Dominic's wrists together with red twine.

And then she stood back.

Meriel looked at him, smiled and he felt reassured. He felt like home.

"Open to me."

"Open to me," he repeated.

She spoke, sometimes in English, sometimes in what he was told was Gaelic. He repeated as she'd instructed, but there were times he added his own words to the spell they wove together. It was intuitive, and he trusted his gut. Her gaze remained steady on his as she spoke so he assumed what he was doing was all right.

He felt it like a tsunami building. Massive, rising up and up. Filling him. He never worried or feared. He just knew that as long as they stayed together they'd weather it.

Then her mouth curved up just the smallest of bits and she said, "I am open to you. I am ascended."

He repeated the words and the intent wrapped around them, strengthening their bond as what felt like raging rivers of magick knocked him off his feet and he had no choice but to hang on and trust that Meriel would keep him from drowning. Her eyes told him she had that same feeling.

And then, a while later, she leaned forward and kissed him. His knees ached from where they'd been kneeling but he didn't care. He kissed her back as someone undid their bindings.

She put her forehead to his as they both fought for air. "I'm a little dizzy right now," she said for his ears only.

"Me too. Thank God, I was hoping it wasn't just that I was a pussy."

Her gaze met his and everything clicked into place with total, utter certainty. This was right. What he should have done. He simply knew it.

He helped her to stand. "We are ascended," she announced and there was much clapping. Dominic felt part of something far bigger than he ever had before. He was part of this other person. She stood at his side, her hand in his. He tasted her magick on his tongue. Each time he breathed in it was her scent on the breeze. She was everything all at once but he never felt as if he'd lost part of himself. Just more of something else added to that. She hadn't made him whole, she'd simply snapped all the missing pieces together and in doing so he was whole.

Magick crackled around him as he looked around. His vision was altered as the othersight he'd only recently learned to open up seemed to layer with his normal vision. Meriel told him it might happen like that sometimes right after an ascension, and that he'd get used to it.

Edwina broke the circle and everyone moved back to the house where there'd be some mulled wine and light appetizers.

"Welcome to Clan Owen." Edwina bowed to him.

"Hear, hear!" Abe raised a glass in agreement.

Chapter 17

MERIEL sat and drank tea with Gia Kelly down in a bright, cozy corner. "This is pretty swank back here. I'm sorry I've never seen it before."

"We keep it a secret so people leave us alone."

Gia had called her down to talk about the scrying angle and had met Meriel with a cup of tea and the promise of cookies. Which she'd made good on. Snickerdoodles even.

"You like it that everyone's afraid to come down here." Meriel laughed, delighted.

"It's our secret. If they weren't afraid, they'd be here all the time asking us to research things *they* should do themselves."

"Kudos to you. I wish I'd have thought of that."

"Given all the information you've provided and that Nell and Gage have supplemented, we feel what you experienced was indeed someone scrying to watch you."

Meriel frowned.

"Since, in general, witches don't need to scry because they have othersight and seeking spells, it's usually something mages use."

Great.

"I'm going to guess this is connected in some way to the alert Nell sent out about mage activity on the East Coast?"

"Yes, that and more I suppose. I wanted to hope it wasn't, but it's hard to imagine why anyone would scry me except for that. How do I protect myself?"

"I was hoping you'd ask." Gia gave her a sly smile. "I have a spell that will work. It's not exactly *traditional* but it does the trick."

"I'm wary, but intrigued."

SHE got the text from Nell while meeting with Gia so Meriel headed straight upstairs to Nell's office.

"So Gia says yes, it's scrying." Meriel grabbed one of the donuts she spied upon entry. "Why do you rate donuts?"

"I'm the great and terrible Oz. People bring me things to keep me placated. Sit down and let me brief you on this mess."

"I need to be scarier if it nets me donuts."

"Don't whine, it's not cute." Nell winked. "I've been in contact with Arel. He and I are in agreement that the incidents with you being watched are connected to the mages. Gage is working with some other hunter folks from Gennessee and Rodas on putting together a database. Identifying these mages who've messed with us. Tracking them."

"Eliminating them."

"I do like the way you think. Yes, that too. We're going to need to step out of our comfort zone here. These mages are fueled by their addiction; they don't care that they're hurting and killing to do that. The only thing they're going to understand is a fist in the face."

"If you're expecting me to tell you no, you've got a long wait ahead of you."

"Good. My gut tells me they know an awful lot about us. So they've possibly tortured some of the witches they've taken for info. But I don't really think that was the goal, though I do think they may have tortured for the power of the pain they've inflicted. The missing witches we've found to be likely targets were mainly non-clan witches."

"Turned witches?" She saw red a moment.

"Given the apparent move toward snatching witches who are at the higher end of the power scale, I'm going to say yes, I think they're getting inside information from turned witches."

"Are we keeping track of them in any way?"

"No. And I should have thought of it so I apologize. Gage is on that now."

She waved it away. "Yes, so totally loserly of you not to know every single possibility ever. Anyway, in our history they've usually just burned themselves out and ended up dead within five to ten years after they get stuck. How the hell are you supposed to know they'd start working with bigots and other junkies to traffic our magick?"

"It's my job to think about every possibility."

"Make it happen and keep me apprised." She stood. "Gia taught me a spell that renders the caster invisible to scrying. She's agreed to teach it to anyone who'd like to know it."

"Good. Good. All right, I'll work with her to get my people trained and then take it outward. Be careful, Meriel. I've put a guard on you. He'll stay in the background, but your mother told me to and I agree."

"Nicely played." Meriel rolled her eyes. "Not gonna argue with it. Good to have an extra pair of eyes. It'll hopefully calm Dominic down too."

"TOM?"

Dominic had made the time to call his foster father to arrange to come down.

"Dominic! I was just thinking of you. I've actually had a few dreams about you while I was out last weekend."

It was best to just get it out quickly. "I've met someone special. I want you to meet her."

"Have you now?"

He heard the wary interest in Tom's voice and smiled. Crusty old man.

"I did. You'll like her."

"Hm."

Then he laughed. "She's nothing like any of the women I've dated before. She's a lawyer. A redhead. Gorgeous. Hyperintelligent. Works in the family business."

"Really? Well, this *is* good to hear. You know the door is always open to you. This is your home too. I'd like to meet her. What's her name?"

"Meriel." He avoided saying her last name, not wanting to get into the whole ascension/bond-mate business over the phone.

"How old is she?"

"Twenty-seven."

"She marriage material?"

"Yes."

"She one of us?" He meant a witch.

"Yes." Dominic left it at that. Once he met Meriel, Tom would feel differently and he didn't want to have her prejudged.

"All right then. Bring her down. Spend the weekend so I can get to know her. She's not fussy, is she?"

"She looks like she might be." He snorted. "But she's tough. Hard as nails. Ruthless when she has to be. She'll love the house."

They spoke for a while longer until Dominic got called away. Meriel was at an evening meeting of this or that committee. He'd gotten used to her being in the club with him and felt her absence sorely. Her schedule was the opposite of his so meshing their time would be a challenge. But one he wasn't afraid to take on.

It had been several days since the ascension and there'd been no more strange incidences with feeling watched. Nell and Gage were working with the witches down in records to figure out the scrying angle. Meriel had shown him the spell they needed to perform to render anyone invisible to a scry. At least they had that much.

He walked out of his office and headed down the long hall, away from the club. He needed to check the stock. He had staff to do this for him, but he liked to handle it himself too. No one could run the place better than he could.

As evidenced by the low number of full bottles of top-shelf tequila. It was a favorite back in the Others portion of the bar. He made a note and left it on Simon's desk.

Movement at the back door got his attention. As he moved toward it, alarm slammed into his system. Power built up in his belly and somewhere he knew she felt it too. Knew his alarm raced through her across town at her meeting. He'd have to call her when this was over just to reassure her.

"What the hell are you doing out here?" he asked the man standing near the loading dock. "No employee smoking where clientele can see you."

The icy claws of someone else's magick dug into him. A dark, oily energy that slithered through him. Poisonous. It drew his energy from his body. The pain of it like a thousand sharp pins.

Not magick, no, this was not natural at all.

The mage made a very big mistake and stepped in closer to take a better look at Dominic where he'd slumped against the door. And when he got close enough, Dominic whipped his fist out and slammed it into the mage's jaw, sending him backward, reeling down the steps and onto the asphalt below. His magick might have been crippled by the spell, but his fist hadn't been.

"You stupid motherfucker." Dominic kicked the mage in the side and then used his magick to hold him in place. "Simon, out back, now," he barked into his phone.

But even as he heard the *thomp, thomp, thomp* of Simon's boots as he ran toward them, Dominic was hit with a big blast of magic so nasty it tore at his insides.

He threw out a shield and the air stank of ozone from his energy sliding against all that wrong, dark sludge. Shoving the nearest mage back with one hand, Dominic punched him in the nose and then gave him another jab in the eye.

As expected, the fool hit the ground, holding his face. The clawing in his guts began to lessen and his head stopped throbbing. His phone buzzed in his back pocket. He knew it was Meriel and he needed to keep her far, far away from this.

A roar sounded over his left shoulder as Simon leapt over the railing from the loading dock ledge and down where Dominic was. The two injured mages managed to pull back

and erect their own shields as three human flunkies joined
them and rushed Simon and Dominic.

Simon didn't need to transform to take his wolf form. He
was powerful enough as a man and one fist the size of a
rump roast slammed into one of the thugs' belly so hard he
lost his footing.

Dominic let the haze take over. Let the violence rush up
and through him, to his fists and into his brain. This was
like homecoming. This was where he knew the lay of the
land. The law of the fists.

He showed his teeth to the human who'd been edging
toward him and rushed him, knocking him to his feet as
Dominic delivered a beating while straddling the man.

Someone, most likely the remaining human, hit him from
the side, knocking him off his prey.

The clawing began again and his head hurt so much he
could barely see. The magick rushed up through the ground
and tore from his body, draining away.

And then he knew she was coming. He felt her moving
toward where they were. Panic warred with admiration as the
well of her fury boiled the air and she was there on the landing.

Dominic managed to wrest his body up from the asphalt
of the parking lot and to standing again. Just so he could
punch the human one more time.

Still on the landing, Meriel looked like an angry goddess,
one arm out, her magick swam past him like a guided missile.

Nell ran around where Dominic managed to choke the
thug out and onto his knees. He knew just how long to hold,
watched as unconsciousness began to take hold.

"Out," he whispered and then the man went limp.

Shit. He'd just knocked the guy out with his magick?

Dominic saw Meriel moving toward him. Knew he was
yelling at her to get the fuck back. He could only hear the
drumming of his heart and briefly wondered if he was having a stroke.

She touched him and spoke, her lips against his temple
and the pain was gone. The furious pain of those claws in
his gut were gone.

"Get out of here. The mages are here," he heard himself ordering her some moments later.

"No, they're gone." She kissed his knuckles, whispered over them and the throb of the abraded skin eased back.

"It's not safe. The cops—"

"Are *so* not coming." Simon heaved himself to stand and then gently helped Meriel up and finally Dominic. "So much magick out here they won't see or hear a fucking thing. Want to fill me in on what the hell just happened?"

And then Dominic threw up.

MERIEL unbuttoned his shirt and tried not to wince at the bloom of a bruise over his left side.

Everyone had gone, leaving them alone at his apartment where she'd finally allowed herself to take a good look at the damage he'd sustained. He'd refused a doctor so he'd have to deal with the best she could do.

"I felt it." She allowed herself those three words as she gently pulled his shirt free and examined his back. He had an abrasion across his shoulders. "Hold on. You've got asphalt in there. Gravel. I have to clean it out."

"There's no magickal spell to do this?"

"You were siphoned." She said this as she stood behind him, not wanting him to see her face. Not wanting him to see how scared she was.

"What do you mean siphoned?" He hissed just a bit when she used the alcohol.

"I mean they took some of your magickal energy. That's very hard on you. A bruise will heal and I can help that along a little. This ugly thing on your back will heal, though it's going to hurt when I clean it out. I'll use a spell to numb it a little. I'll get you cleaned up and taken care of. And then I'm going to use the font to replace what you've lost."

"Is it permanent?"

She breathed out carefully and put her head on his unin-jured shoulder for a moment.

He reached up to run his fingers through her hair and she

shoved away any thoughts about what might have happened far, far away.

"No. You're probably going to have a headache for a while, but your stores will fill again. Our bond has stabilized that, closed the wound. No, not wound. Not in the sense of this on your back." She used a spell to numb his skin and muscle as she'd promised and began to clean him up to keep busy and from freaking out.

"So tell me about it. It'll keep us both calm." He put a hand on her thigh as she worked. "And thanks for whatever you did. Just now and back at the club."

She'd felt the spike in his magick, had known there was trouble and when he didn't pick up, she ended up running the seven blocks to Heart of Darkness from where she'd been. Nell had been in the building with Gage and they'd seen her dart to the elevators and had come along.

Never had she been so scared.

"You didn't need me. How many did you take out on your own?" She poked just a little too hard and felt bad when he winced.

He'd told them the story of how he'd seen the guy on the loading dock at the back doors and had gone out only to get hit by a magical attack.

"I don't know. There weren't that many."

She should have felt shame for how she'd taken him in, a full rage, fists flying, shirt torn open and bloody. She'd looked and wanted to lick him. So bad and wrong, but he was so masculine and *rawr*.

"You would have taken the mage on your own, you know. Though I shouldn't tell you because hello, how dare you have done that and endangered yourself!"

She heard the sob in her voice and it mortified her.

He turned, taking her hands after he'd made her put the tweezers down. "I'm sorry you were worried. But I'm here, and reasonably healthy apparently. I can handle my shit. It's just I didn't know much about the magick siphoning thing. Was that the clawing in my head? The oily magic?"

"Yes. I'm told that's what it feels like."

"Hurt enough to make me puke. Been a while since I've thrown up after a fight. Especially when I wasn't even drunk." He kissed the frown on her mouth. "I can handle a dustup. I've done things in my past I may not always be proud of, but it left me with the ability to fuck someone's shit up. I can protect myself and you too." He looked at her features for long moments. "And I will. What if it had been you instead of me? Damn it, I keep playing it over and over in my head."

If he kept this up, she'd cry for real. "Turn around so I can finish."

The left corner of his mouth twitched and he finally gave her a small smile before turning. "Explain it to me. What happens with this siphoning stuff. We'll both feel better when you do."

"When a mage steals magick, it tears apart your internal shields and makes a wound of sorts, like an ugly tear in the veins your magick travels through. It's not actually veins, but that's the easiest way to think on it."

He shuddered a little and she leaned in to kiss the back of his neck.

"A mage can drain you because the energies they use are . . . different than what we do. Our magick is natural, it works in certain, reliable ways. There are limits on what we can do, but our ability to do it is inborn."

"What do I need to do to stop it?"

"Funny you should ask, but Nell's been in contact with a witch who lives in Boston. She's working on some defensive magicks from across several practice paths, and she's going to work with Rodas Clan to teach their witches and then it'll move outward. Nell is sending Gage to be trained along with a few others and he'll come back here and do our trainings."

Her hands shook and she forced herself to concentrate on the wound instead of how he could have been kidnapped or tortured and murdered like some of the others.

"What's a practice path?"

"Clan witches practice a certain sort of magick. Sometimes that differs from place to place or clan to clan. Then you've got others who do things differently. There are a great many witches who use blood in their warding and some of their spellwork."

She angled the nearby desk lamp to check his back once more. "You're good. Gage left some stuff his mother made. She's a medical doctor and a magickal healer of sorts. Anyway, he uses it on his bruises." She held up the jar of bright green goo.

"I want to shower. And you need to come with me. You know, just in case I need help."

She rolled her eyes, but felt better.

"Sit." She pointed at a chair and then began to bustle around, gathering clothes and towels and getting everything ready. "Anyway, a practice path is how a witch accesses her power. But as you can imagine, there's lots of snobbery and infighting about it. So and so thinks she's better because she uses magic a certain way and you don't so you're inferior. Essentially we've lost what makes us all strong. Our ability to use our magicks in many ways for different circumstances."

She turned the water on and let it heat a moment as she walked back into the bedroom and saw him there, sitting, bruised and bloody and so unbelievably sexy it halted her steps.

"If we knew about each other's magick, we'd have a lot more defenses against these mages."

She nodded, moving to him again. "Exactly. Divided we're weak. This is magick we're talking about. A witch is a witch as long as she doesn't break the basic creed about not harming but for self-defense. These mages don't care what practice path the witches their hurting use. But they're going to expect a certain response from certain witches. I say we mess that up. If I know how other witches would react that only adds to my ability to fight back. We have to fight back."

"I agree. But you're distracting me now and I might need some help with my pants."

She went to her knees as he stood and the look on his face shot straight to her clit. Gaze on his, she reached up and unzipped his pants.

"I'm suddenly feeling a lot better, but now that I've got no blood above my waist, a little dizzy."

She pulled his pants and his boxers off and stood, but not before she placed a kiss on the head of his cock. "Later for that. Now come on. You need to shower so I can put the bruise goo on you."

He followed her into the bathroom and she then found herself in the shower stall, her back pressed against the cool tiles. "I've got some goo for you too."

It didn't do to show him how much he amused her. It would only make him think it was acceptable. But he did.

"Stop that."

His body was so close as her clothes got soaked. He made very quick work of them, leaving her as naked as he. And her shaking now had nothing to do with fear.

"You should get cleaned up."

"You're talking, baby, but not saying anything." He spoke, his lips against hers and she melted into him. She was so easy for this man. She laughed, not meaning to, but glad for it.

"Have you noticed how much time you spend getting me against walls and laying down on things?"

He laughed before drawing her back under the spray. "It's biological. If I can hem you in, I know I can talk my way past any of your excuses and right into your panties."

He underlined this by tracing his fingertips downward, over the seam of her pussy, teasing her open.

She gulped. "Seems to me, you're already there."

"I need in you." Her nipped her bottom lip.

"Yes."

He eased back, squirting some of his soap into his palm. "After I get you all clean."

He was the one who needed it. But she let him touch her, let his slick hands rove over the whole of her. She gave herself to him and he took. A circuit of energy clicked between them, heating, enticing, their attraction humming against skin where he slid over her with a covetous touch.

Around those hands, she gently soaped the blood away. Careful with the bruises, she skimmed over his hurts.

His lips brushed against her cheek and then to her mouth.

He took her in a kiss that stole her breath. His tongue swept past the seam of her lips.

"I don't want to hurt you," she whispered as he lifted her up and positioned her just where he wanted. "Don't strain yourself or you'll need stitches."

"I need you so much it'll hurt if I can't have you," he said as he circled her gate with the head of his cock.

It wasn't that she disagreed with his aims in this.

Before she could re-inquire about his bruises, he'd lifted her a little more and began to work his way inside.

And then she wasn't sure she could have remembered the words to make him careful with himself. As it was every time he touched her, she melted into him, seeking more, needing everything he wanted to give.

So hot and tight.

Dominic held the most precious thing in his world as he pressed in a little more with each thrust. He fought hard against instincts that made him want to rut. Made him want to plunge into her all the way and fuck her until they were both sated. Fuck her until the fear had gone and the panic over her safety went away.

But just then he wanted to savor all the more. He wanted to take her slowly and enjoy the tautening of their desire, that gradual build to an amazing climax. If he could hold back that part of him that wanted to own her every minute and whispered, harder, harder, more.

He knew she held back; that knowledge only made him want her more.

"Don't you dare hold back with me," he said as he kissed across her collarbone. Salt mixing with the water from the shower.

"You just got into a fistfight with four, no, five men, two of whom wanted to steal your magick and kill you and the other three who just wanted to kill you."

He heard the fear in her voice and stopped, forehead to forehead with her.

"I'm here. You're here. Let me love you."

She nodded, tears in her eyes.

He pushed in that last bit, throbbing as her inner walls embraced him.

He pressed in deep and pulled out, over and over. She kissed up his neck, stopping to nip his ear and whisper, "You feel so good in me."

Her nipples slid across his chest, slick, hard. She made small, rough sounds of need, his pretty, button-down woman. She snarled if he slowed down too much, urged him on as he kept her positioned just the way he wanted.

"You first." He kissed along her jawline. Getting one hand free, he took her wrist and put her fingers where she'd need them. "Come all around me."

He moved back to holding her ass and also thanked all the years of physical activity that he could fuck his woman up against a wall and not collapse.

She fluttered around his cock, then tightened. The muscles in her forearm corded as he knew she was making herself come. So. Fucking. Hot.

And the slow build was nearly over. Need took over as the pleasure she gave herself only made him hotter for her. Her body slickened around him as she made a soft gasp as he picked up the pace.

Faster and faster, harder and harder, until she arched and exploded around his cock and there was simply no way not to come. He bit her shoulder and pressed in hard, coming with a groan that echoed all round them in the tiled enclosure until there was no other sound but panting for breath and water hitting bodies.

He kissed her; the ability to be slow and gentle had returned, but her response was wilder than he'd expected, which he liked. A lot.

He put her down carefully and she kissed his chest over his heart, hugging him.

"Let me get your back," she said quietly.

He turned and let her minister to him as he closed his eyes and let the comfort of the bond take over as well.

Chapter 18

"ARE you certain it's the time to be making this trip, Meriel?" Edwina stopped Meriel in the hallway. She and Dominic would be heading to Bend for the next several days.

"There've been no more attacks since Tuesday. Nell has done a great job with patrols. Our people are safe. This is the man who is in every way, but biological, Dominic's father. I want to meet him and Dominic needs to tell him face-to-face about all this."

Edwina paused and took a deep breath. "You're very exposed. It makes me nervous."

Meriel smiled.

"I saw the way Dominic fights, Mother. He's just as able to protect me as Gage or another guard. I have the magick part down. You can see his magickal skills improving every day. At the rate he learns, he's going to be as easy with his magick as I am in a month or so."

Edwina nodded curtly, but it was clear she approved. "Yes, he's a very quick study. Helps that he's naturally very powerful, but he has excellent concentration. He's been a very good student. I wasn't sure how he would be. He can be irreverent at times."

After her interrogation of Dominic on the night he and Meriel ascended, Edwina had decided *she* would be the best person to teach Dominic. Whatever her mother's flaws, being a good teacher wasn't one of them. The two had clicked quickly and Dominic soaked up everything Edwina threw his way.

Surprised and amused, Meriel laughed. "Irreverent is a good way to put it."

"The two of you are clearly made for each other in that respect." Edwina sniffed. "You will call to check in. Your father worries about you and then he's out in his garden all day and I can't take him deciding to rip up more of my land for one of his projects."

Meriel's dad did have a way of dealing with his stress and worries through his *projects*. Edwina had ambition and drive. She was an intense person who ate stress for breakfast and dared it to give her a bellyache. Her father was more relaxed, but he didn't cope the way his wife did. It made them a good fit as a couple, but Meriel could see how having your spouse always ripping up and rebuilding things in the yard might get a little annoying. Then again, she imagined her dad went out there to get away from his wife's way of dealing with stress, which was to take care of things and order everyone around.

"I'll call when I get to Bend. You have my cell and I'll be sure you have Tom's home number as well."

Edwina nodded. "All right then. Tell Dominic I still expect to see him for our lessons at four on Monday." She turned and walked a few steps before pausing to turn back to Meriel. "I think having this hunter train our people is a good idea. I'm charging you to create a committee to figure out how to get our people into these classes. I put some funds for it in your budget. I want this up and running as soon as possible. I assume you'll be in contact with your aunt?"

Well. This was unexpected. Appreciated of course, but her mother had essentially just given the green light to something she'd argued against only a month before.

"Thank you. I've got some ideas on how to get started.

I'll definitely coordinate with Gennessee on how to get their people trained as well."

"I spoke with Rebecca about the attack on Dominic on Wednesday. She is similarly putting energy into this project." Edwina took a deep breath but said nothing else. Mostly likely it was that her aunt would see this as a much bigger threat than Edwina would simply because Gennessee's territory was a far different animal than Owen's was. More dangerous. Gennessee's hunter team was fierce and well trained. Nell had long wanted to bring some of the basics of what they did into Owen's structure but Edwina had resisted.

Edwina's half-sister, Rebecca, was the leader of Clan Gennessee. Meriel's grandfather had been married to Rebecca's mother, but after she died in a house fire, he'd then met and married his bond-mate, who happened to be next in line to run Owen. It was sort of *Jerry Springer* territory, but they did manage to be a family.

This cemented the dominance of the entire western United States by the same family. Gennessee started when a small group of witches, including an Owen sister, chose to stay in California when the rest of the clan headed to Seattle.

Emily Owen had taken a name from their mother's family, Gennessee, and they'd built their own branch of Clan Owen. Because of this, Owen witches would come to hold a great deal of power as the land recognized their magick and had connected with it over the generations. Owen witches, be they Gennessee or not, were the strongest in the world in their own territory and because the font included over twenty-five hundred witches, even outside their territory they were a force to be reckoned with.

Not that things weren't complicated sometimes between Gennessee and Owen. But they would always hold together against an outside force.

"I'll keep you apprised."

"Of course." Edwina nodded. "Be careful. Please."

Meriel waved at her mother's retreating back, smiling.

* * *

DRIVING south and then east toward Bend, Dominic felt freer the more miles he managed to rack up. She'd gone to work for a while, long enough to let him sleep after a late night at Heart of Darkness. Though she'd claimed otherwise. She took care of him like no one else ever had. And she'd just done it as if she always had. A little over two weeks and his life was totally different and, he couldn't deny, totally better, even with the crazy business with the mages.

She'd arrived at his apartment with hot coffee and fresh bagels. A very nice way to be woken up. She smelled good and felt right and he loved the way she looked, cool and professional in her feminine suit, her hair a soft tumble of curls held back by a pretty clip he'd given her a few days prior.

He'd lured her to bed and even now she looked sexy and sort of disheveled, though still lovely in jeans and a sweater. He'd asked, and she'd let her hair stay free. She had her boots off and he could see she wore his favorite socks.

Whimsy to balance the heavy task she would bear as she took over the clan. It made her perfect to him. Gorgeous. Intelligent. Talented and powerful witch. Uninhibited in bed, or out of it. The sex was mind-blowing. He couldn't even make up a fantasy as good as what they managed to get up to pretty much as often as they could. Well, maybe if it was a threesome with her clone. That could work.

Mmmm, yes.

"Whatever are you thinking about?" his lovely woman at his side asked, amusement in her tone.

Of course she had files on her lap and had spent the last two hours tapping away on her laptop. He'd been amazed by her capacity to work at any and all times. In the beginning anyway. Now he just accepted it as another one of her incredible gifts.

"I was thinking about a three-way with you and your clone, as it happens."

She started laughing. "Really?"

"Really."

She leaned over to kiss the side of his neck. "You're so delightfully single-minded about sex."

"I seem to recall I'm not the only one."

"Very true. And what can I say? I'm rather flattered that if you're thinking about three-ways you'd make me both women instead of adding a supermodel or something."

"None of them have a thing on you." Which wasn't a lie at all.

He wanted to show her off, he could admit it, at least in his head. He wanted to present her to Tom and have Tom see what an amazing woman he'd fallen for. Wanted Tom to approve of how he'd made his life better.

Dominic had resented the iron-fisted way he'd been raised, but now, on the other side of a really dark time in his life, it had been Tom's upbringing and his steady way of being in Dominic's life that had given him the biggest push to finally get his act together.

"It's going to be fine," she said before answering her ringing phone.

He liked that too. Her way of knowing what he needed to hear and giving it to him.

He drove as her voice soothed him in the background. And then he smiled as that tone changed.

In addition to a host of positive qualities, Meriel Owen was really, really bossy, which he admittedly had only recently come to find attractive in a woman. Watching her work was sexy and inspiring. She was effortlessly efficient. She dealt with her mother by simply letting Edwina wash uselessly around her. It puzzled Edwina, Dominic thought. She didn't understand her daughter so she provoked her, constantly trying to figure her out.

Meriel, to her great credit, did seem to understand her mother. And as much as she could, without harming her own perspective, she let her mother organize and tidy, knowing it's what Edwina did to express her affection.

With him too, Dominic supposed, Meriel understood his need to protect and lead. He loved that she could be so in charge in every aspect of her life. But with him she softened, let him be in charge. It soothed him. Not that she didn't push back when he got too bossy. She let him know when he overstepped. Which meant there'd be really smoking-hot make-up sex in store.

The scenery changed as they drove. From the lusher forests of western Washington into the warmer and drier climate of central Oregon. There'd been snow several places along the way.

Meriel, like most other Seattleites he knew, was fascinated and slightly fearful of the snow. But he'd grown up with it—with *lots* of it—his whole life. For months on end.

But he'd stopped and let her take pictures of it. She brought that into his life too. The little experiences he'd forgotten about.

She gave orders in the background as he thought about this place and wondered why Tom had settled here. He'd grown up on the East Coast, but when he'd gotten the call that the baby of one of his friends needed a home, he'd come out west and had built a home and a life for both of them.

But every summer Dominic had worked to keep his body strong and his mind clear as he'd worked with Tom on his backcountry trips. They'd canoed and white-water rafted. Hiked. Biked. Camped.

In the winter it had been skiing and sledding on the trips they'd taken. Snow camping.

It had kept him out of trouble because he was too tired to get out of line. He'd respected his body and his mind. Until he'd left and binged on all the larger world had to offer.

And now he'd come full circle.

When she hung up he touched her hand, because he could and because he wanted to. She smiled and tipped her wrist up to capture his fingers with hers. "Hey there. I'm hungry. At the risk of sounding like a kid, are we there yet?"

"We've got another three hours or so. But Tom's making a feast, he says. He's a great cook so that'll be true and believe me, you want to have plenty of space in your belly to eat. But let's stop and stretch in the next town. I'll get gas and look the other way when you drink yet another cup of coffee."

"We all have our addictions, Mr. Bright." She said it primly but the grin at the end sort of messed up that delivery.

"Damn it, I'm so glad you came into my club and gave me a stern talking-to."

Her grin softened and she brought his fingers to her lips to kiss them. "Watch the road. And me too."

Chapter 19

DOMINIC sent out silent thanks to Simon for suggesting they take his SUV for the drive. The road out to the house had been cleared, but it had started to snow and the curves would have been a lot worse had Tom not kept everything tidy and shipshape.

"Wow, is that it?" She leaned forward to get a better look through the windshield.

Tom had bought the small house on a big plot of land with a mountain view. The river was down a winding path that kept it out of harm's way when the snowmelt hit and the water levels rose. Right now it felt like home as they approached. The window glowed golden and smoke rose lazily from the chimney.

He parked out of the way. Old habit he supposed. Sometimes Tom's clients would meet him at the house and they started a trip from there so Dominic wanted to keep the drive clear just in case.

She squeezed his hand and he looked at her, just looking for long moments.

"We're here." She grinned but he saw the worry at the edges.

"We are. He's going to love you. How could he not?"
Ha.

Meriel let him open her door and help her down. She pulled her zipper up, sealing out the cold. The place was absolutely gorgeous. The house was rough hewn, but beautifully constructed. She had no doubt that the views from just about every part of the house would be fabulous.

"Come on in then," a man called from the front steps and when Meriel saw him, she looked back to Dominic and did it once more. It was when she went back for the third look that she noticed the warding.

Everywhere.

Meriel paused and turned in a slow circle. The place was a virtual impenetrable fortress. This warding was cast one on top of the next. It appeared to be crumbling and weak, but once you took a closer look any witch with a decent amount of talent would be able to see just how good they were. Tangled roots and thorny dead ends.

Tom Bright was no ordinary witch. And he sure as hell wasn't just Dominic's foster father. *Now* the fact that Dominic was full-council made sense. It was clear where the magick in his genes came from. Just what it was the man had been hiding wasn't clear. But it was big and it made her wary.

What he did, however, was look at Dominic with so much love on his face all her suspicions fell away. This man loved Dominic. There was no doubt in Meriel's mind of this fact.

"Dominic!" He came off the porch and the two men embraced. It wasn't until they stood back and Tom got a better look that he stopped and gaped. "What have you done?" Accusing eyes moved to Meriel, who startled, looked back to Dominic, who was as confused as she was.

"This is Meriel Owen. She's my bond-mate."

"You've ascended!" Tom began to pace and Meriel began to examine her surroundings better. She didn't know what was going on with the guy, but she sure as hell wanted to be able to get away if this went south.

"Why are you acting this way?" Dominic looked back

and forth between them. He looked so hurt and surprised, Meriel just took his hand and squeezed.

"Sir, is there a problem?" Meriel bent a little to see past the hands he'd put over his face.

"You need to go. Get away from here as fast as you can." He looked around, alarm on his face.

That alarm jumped straight to Meriel's belly.

"What the hell is going on?" Dominic stood taller, his hands on his hips, looking very authoritative. "You're scaring Meriel and you're really scaring me. I'm not going anywhere. Not until you tell me what's gotten you so spooked. Let me help you."

Meriel ached for him and hoped they could fix whatever it was that has spooked him the moment he saw who she was and they'd mentioned the bond.

Tom threw his hands in the air. "Get in the house. Now."

Meriel let Dominic drag her into the house as she watched Tom close the wards up tight in their wake.

The house was warm and lived in. Comfortable. Over-whelmingly male. It also smelled really good, though Meriel wasn't sure her appetite would come back after they found out what was going on.

Tom came into the house and locked the door in his wake.

She turned to Dominic. "Would you like if I went into another room so you two can talk?"

"You're not going anywhere. I don't know what's happening, but you're not leaving my sight and he's going to tell me what's going on."

"I'm just surprised I guess."

"Mr. Bright, it's more than that. These wards around your land are not simple. This is decades of magick on top of decades of magick."

"How do you know? What do you know about it? Clan witches don't have the corner on the magick market. Unaffiliated witches can do wards too."

"I'm Meriel Owen, next in line to run Clan Owen. This ward craft isn't the work of a man who doesn't know a lot about magick. It's not sophisticated, but it's very good and very strong. And the runes on his skin, those are also some serious protective magick. I'd wager you used some flesh and blood to bond them to his body."

"My flesh and blood. I didn't take it from anyone. Freely given and I've done no wrong to protect my boy." Tom spun to glare at Dominic. "Clan Owen. You bonded with the goddamn next in line to a big, giant clan?"

"Yes. So if I'm full-council, what's that make you?"

He scrubbed his hands over his face. "All right, it's time I guess. Go drop your bags in your room and wash your hands. I made chicken and dumplings for dinner and had planned a bottle of wine to go with. I'm guessing we'll need at least another bottle to get through the story."

"I apologize for his reaction," Dominic said as he pushed the door to his room open. Just as he'd left it, which always made him feel better when he came back home.

"He's scared. Let's find out why before we go getting offended or handing out apologies."

She smoothed a hand over his bedspread and he watched her take in his childhood as she walked through the room.

Leave it to her to see past the window dressing and right into the heart of the problem.

"We'll get through it. No matter what it is. He's clearly worried for you. Scared even, at a few points. But the earth here respects him. His magick is accepted by the surroundings. The earth is rarely wrong."

He hugged her tight and she hugged him back. "Thank you."

"For what?" She traded her boots for the wool-lined slippers Tom favored for use inside the house.

"For being here. For making me see past all this emotion to whatever the hell lies beneath. It feels like I can get through it because you're here."

"I'm really only here for the chicken and dumplings."

He grinned and took her hand. "You might actually mean that once you taste them."

When they got back downstairs, Dominic had calmed considerably. Meriel had been the reason for it and he'd been glad she'd been there.

The kitchen was well lit; the table dominated one entire half, sitting in front of the windows fronting the water and the mountains in the distance.

"Perfect timing. Come on and sit. Get some food into you and a few swigs of something alcoholic and I'll give you the story." Tom began dishing up the food in large bowls and sending them toward Dominic and Meriel. "I apologize for the reception I gave you." He looked up to Meriel, who nodded, accepting the apology.

"Just tell me what's going on. We'll work through it. Whatever it is."

Meriel made a soft moaning sound when she got the first spoonful of food into her mouth. "I told you," he said before digging in himself.

They ate in relative silence for a few minutes, but eventually Tom looked up from his food and sighed.

"You're my nephew."

Dominic blinked several times, surprised. "What?"

"A little over thirty years ago my brother came to my house. He had you with him. You were maybe six months old at the time. He and your mother had . . ." Tom licked his lips. "They were stuck. Worse, it was pretty clear Felix, that's your dad, was close to turning entirely."

Meriel sat straight up with a gasp.

"Yes, you've the right of it." Tom looked down to Meriel. "He brought you to me and begged me to take you and run. To raise you far away and never look back. He was in a bad way. Your dad, he was big and bold. An excellent fighter. Smart. He had a big future but she was bad for him. Your mother that is. Was. Whatever." Tom looked back to Dominic.

Meriel took his hand and squeezed.

"To be fair, Felix was bad for her too. They were all wrong together. They were so young."

"You're full-council too. What clan?" Meriel thought it might be a good idea to reach out to them.

"Not clan affiliated. We had a coven back home in Tallahassee. Our parents were active in it until they died. Anyway, he gave me some money and told me to go. He was worried about your safety. Said he was concerned about what she had planned for you. I took you and the money that very night and got out of there. I picked Bend off a map. I had some skills, used to be an Eagle Scout back in the day. Got some identification for us both and built a life."

"Why did you lie to me about all this? You said they died."

"You were about five when I got a call from your grandfather. Your dad wanted to meet. Wanted to see you. This was back in the day before caller ID or any of that stuff. I called the number he'd left and arranged to meet Felix in Chicago. He wanted me to bring you, but I wouldn't promise. I didn't trust him. Not after the way he'd left. Not after what he'd said to me. You have to understand, Dominic. If he'd turned, and I had every reason to believe he had, he'd be nothing but danger to you. I took an oath to protect you."

Dominic looked shell-shocked, but he nodded at Tom's words.

"I went but he never showed up. I waited another day, just in case. He didn't contact our parents either. But while I was there, some bodies had been found in a local park. The description of one of the victims matched Felix. It just always felt like it was him. I think anyway. But I can never know for sure. So I got out of there and came back here. Your grandparents were killed just a few months later. I never saw any of them again and I knew it was just better for you if I kept your existence a secret.

"So I raised you here and kept you suspicious of clans to keep you from the public eye."

Meriel snagged another dumpling.

"My parents' death wasn't of natural causes. It was suspicious. But I couldn't ever get there to see for myself. I believe Felix is gone, that connection we once had is empty. But Gloria? Your mother? I don't know. I couldn't take that risk."

"How can you know if she wasn't trying to find me because she'd cleaned up?" Dominic pushed from his chair and moved to go stare out the windows at the stars.

"Gloria threatened my parents multiple times. Felix had faked your death and for a while she believed it. But in the time before I went to Chicago to meet my brother, your mother came to my parents' house. She watched them. Came around later with a friend my mother insisted wasn't a witch at all, but a mage."

Dominic could hear Meriel's intake of breath at his back.

"I'd know a lot more about what I should be upset over if you hadn't raised me to hate and fear clans."

"He had to." Meriel came to him, putting her head on his shoulder. "Don't you see? He brought you out here and protected you. Changed your name and raised you to keep you away from any situation where you could be identified. If she's alive somewhere now, she might know about you. We didn't make a big deal out of the ascension, Mr. Bright. But certainly I'm next in line so I get photographed at events. My finding my bond-mate and news of the ascension would be pretty common knowledge in our world."

"If she came to the door with a mage"—Tom paused—"it could mean she was working with them to get her fix. It's not entirely unheard of."

Meriel turned to him. "Right now there's a rise across the county of magical thefts and the mages are part of it. They're working with what looks like human supremacy organizations to track us. I learned just this morning that one of their victims, a woman lucky enough to escape where they'd been keeping her and bleeding her magick dry, that the mages and some turned witches had told the humans what they were doing was exorcising the demons from their captives."

Tom blinked several times. Shock turning him pale.

"We have no reason to think my mother was one of them." Dominic went to sit.

Tom sighed heavily. "Yes, we do. I know this day has been a challenge, Dom, but we have *every* reason to believe your mother, if she's alive, is one of them. If she was on the verge of turning—as close as Felix was when I last saw him and I am sure she was—the only way she can survive is to steal magick. The only way she'd be alive today is by harming people. Pain, death, emotional torture and theft. That's how their magic works. They can't earn it like you and I do.

Turned witches have lost their connection to the earth. They have no natural power left at all."

"She could have gotten herself straight again."

Meriel took his hands and made him look her in the face. "No, she couldn't have. There's no cure once a witch turns. At the very best you can hope she's off far away and using animal blood. Or that she did indeed die at that park. She would not mean you any kindness if she's alive today."

"You don't even know her!"

"No, I don't. But I know witches and I know how this works. I'm sorry, Dominic, but your uncle was right to keep you away from them. God, what if I've put you in danger? I need to get Nell searching for your mother."

"If I'd have known any of this, we could have avoided it."

"I did what I thought was best. You're alive today. For a while I wasn't sure if you'd make it through your little phase down south. But once you got to New York I knew you'd find your way in the world and back here. I had to trust that. I couldn't risk you as a child and I don't want to risk you now either."

"There's no reason just yet to panic." Meriel turned back to Dominic. "I'm asking your permission to have Nell do some research on your parents. I want to see what we can find out."

Dominic scrubbed his hands over his face. "Fine, go ahead." He turned back to his uncle. "I had a bond-mate out there somewhere and you never told me. I could have completely missed out on this amazing connection I have with Meriel."

"I didn't come from a world of council witches. Sure, I knew of bond-mates and all that, but I had no way of knowing you'd be their equivalent of full-council. I made mistakes, Dominic. But I did everything I did for you."

Meriel remained at his side, stroking a hand up and down his back.

"I know." He went to Tom. To his uncle, and hugged him. "I know." And he did.

But he didn't know how to move forward. Didn't know what to think of all this. He was filled with a sharp longing for his parents. Anger at Tom. Love for what Tom had given up. He just couldn't let go of that ember of hope that maybe his mother wanted him and had been searching for him his whole life.

DOMINIC had been asleep for some time, but Meriel found herself restless and headed downstairs.

She nearly jumped from her skin when Tom spoke to her from the dark of the living room. "I'm sorry to startle you. Can't sleep?"

"No. Not really. He's out though." Thankfully.

"You understand." It was a simple statement. "He doesn't though. I worry he's going to entertain some idea that she can be saved despite whatever the facts might point to. He's a boy who grew up without a mother. I thought, you know, for a while I thought I might find someone. Marry. Give him a mother he so desperately needed. But I was worried about how I'd explain my past to them."

"I know he loves you like a father. I know he'll get over his anger and eventually understand what you did." It had to be hard for this man to have given everything up for his nephew. "You gave up your whole life for him. Thank you for that."

He poured her a cup of tea and followed with a healthy dollop of whiskey. She took it gratefully.

"I had a shit life anyway. Lived in my parents' basement. Had a crappy job. I liked to think I'd have gone to college but the chances are, I never would have. He gave me a direction. I love this life. It's solitary, but if I need company I can seek it out. I've been dating. Her name is Rona and she works down at the bank. I work the earth, I'm out in nature. I made mistakes with him, I know, but I don't regret this life."

"He's a good man because of his father. And that's you. I'm worried about the exposure." She explained to him about the new ideas she wanted to institute, the new training and increased communication between witches of all backgrounds and paths. Gave him more detail about the mage attacks, including the one on Dominic at his club earlier that week.

"I hope she's dead. I should feel bad about thinking it,

but I do. She poses nothing but a threat to him. She'll hurt him for fun. The only thing that'll matter to her when it comes to her biological connection to him is that it's easier to steal magick from someone you're related to by blood."

"You can? If I hook you up with one of the people in my clan, would you share all your knowledge of these mages? We don't know enough. I don't want that to hurt us."

"Of course. I only know because I felt like I had to research to keep him safe. I asked around. Spoke with my parents about it. Gloria's family was useless. They'd disowned her even before Felix showed up with Dominic. Her sister." He looked up, eyes bright. "She went missing twenty years ago. God, I wonder?"

An icy-cold finger of dread traced up her spine. "Wonder if she was drained?"

Tom nodded. "I wonder if he would stay here for a while? Keep his head down?" He shook his head. "No. He won't run."

"He's got a business. One he built on his own. He won't abandon it. And I'm going to be frank with you. This is my land. Where I stand right now is Owen land." She called energy forth and held a ball of light in her palm. The wind kicked up just a bit outside. "I am strong here. I know what they feel like. I've got their scent. I won't run and neither will he. If we can't beat them on our own ground, hiding won't help."

He sighed and sipped his tea.

"First thing we need to do is find her. If she's alive, she's a threat. If she's a threat, she needs to be neutralized."

"Even if she's your man's mother?"

"Especially if she is. She'll manipulate and hurt him. I can't allow it."

He raised his cup. "I like you. I should have known he'd end up with a woman as tough as he."

"Tell me about what he was like as a boy."

Chapter 20

"DO you want to talk about it?" Nell asked when Meriel called to check in. She'd awoken early to find a note in the kitchen from Tom saying he'd gone for a hike but would be back by nine.

She'd set herself up at the large table and spent some time just looking outside at the world as she'd jotted notes down.

"I don't know what to think just yet. I feel terrible for them both. His love for Dominic is written all over him. You should see it here. Pictures of him growing up, the odd misshapen mug made by a grade-schooler. Whatever his flaws, he didn't do this to hurt Dominic. He did it to protect him. I know Dominic is reeling. I feel . . ." She rubbed her eyes, knowing it was bad but she couldn't help it. "This is all stuff I brought into his life."

On the other end of the line Nell sighed. "You didn't bring it. Fate brought you together right now for a reason. These are dark days. He needs you. You need him. And you had nothing to do with his uncle or his mother. I understand you're upset for him, but this isn't anything you're respon-sible for. Speaking of which, are you ready to hear it?"

"Am I going to need to add whiskey to my coffee?"
Another plus in the Tom category was that he'd left a carafe
of hot coffee out should anyone wake early and want some.

"You're going to just need to forget the coffee and go for
the whiskey. I got on this last night after we talked and by
the time I'd gotten up this morning I had an array of shit
waiting for me. Gloria Ochoa, that's her name, grew up in
Tallahassee. Multiple arrests. Closed juvenile record."

Meriel waited, knowing a little thing like a closed record
wasn't going to stop Nell.

"Her taste for illegal substances started early on. Busted
for possession seven times. Many trips to juvie. Ran through
caseworkers like cookies, this one. Removed from parents
home by their request. She was sixteen. Went to live with
relatives. The sister disappeared after school twenty-three
years ago. No one ever saw her or heard from her again. No
history like her big sister. Family is closed up tight about it
but shortly after that they moved out of state."

"Wow."

"Yeah well, don't feel too bad for her. Some people are
just fucked up and awful. Meriel, you have to harden your
heart. If she's alive now, she's turned. You know that. If
she's turned, she'll be a danger to her son until she's not
alive anymore. And if the stuff Tom said about her working
with mages is true, she could very well be part of this now.
If it's easier to steal magick from a blood relative, and Gia
says it is, imagine what a big yummy snack Dominic would
be. And I don't mean in the fun way."

"I know!" She traced a fingertip along the rim of her mug.
"I hate this. I want it to be happy for him."

"You can't fix this. I'm sorry. You can't make her into a
good mother. I've got CPS records here."

"CPS? Wow, you're really getting good if you grabbed
those. And in less than twenty-four hours? Genius."

Nell snorted. "Of course I'm good. Also, this is about
you. I made it happen. That's what your best friend does.
CPS was called twice. Infant had been left alone the first
time. According to records Mom said she just went to the

store while the baby was sleeping. Police interviews indicate the baby had been heard crying for hours until a neighbor called the cops and the landlord let them in. Mom didn't return for six hours after that."

Meriel sighed. Edwina hadn't been the warmest of mothers, but she'd been there.

"Christ."

"Second time was after a visit from a health worker. The baby seemed listless, ashen. He wasn't gaining weight. They enrolled Mom and Dad in parenting classes. He was five months old at the time."

"That was right before his father gave Dominic to Tom."

"I doubt it was failure to thrive. I gotta tell you, if she is alive, I hope she lives long enough for me to punch her in the face a few times for that."

It had to be hard for Nell, Meriel knew, pregnant herself, to read about all this stuff. But this was Meriel's man and she had plenty of her own outrage.

"Get in line."

"It would appear the dad staged an accident. Made it look like Dominic, whose name was Eduardo then, had died. Swept away in a river when Dad's car skidded off a road. They never found the body but they did declare the kid dead. Mom was looked at for a while by the cops, Dad too. But they were never charged. They moved three months later. Fell off the map for a long time."

If she thought he was dead, maybe they could keep it that way. At least until they found her and neutralized any threat she posed.

"And then what?"

"Nothing for a while. I have some Jane Doe hits I've got staff looking into."

"Is she dead?"

"No. I don't think she is. The dad is though. His body was found about five years after Tom left."

A chill worked through her. "In Chicago?"

"Yes. How'd you know?"

"I'll tell you in a minute. Give me the details."

"He'd been in jail for assault. No identification but eventually they managed to get it. From his physical description I'm thinking he was seriously turned. The victim claimed she met him a local bar and she took him back to her place where he'd stayed for a week. She accused him of drugging her. She said she felt weak all the time and had woken up with him above her. She claims he was sucking her oxygen out."

"Why would the cops arrest on that? I mean, obviously you and I know what it means, but stealing oxygen as assault?"

"Because he then choked her out for it. They arrested him for that."

"Choked her out when she woke up and tried to get away, thus halting his fix."

Her stomach hurt. She wanted it to be true that he'd come to Chicago to meet Tom and see his son.

"He died in jail?"

"No. He was released until trial. Someone fronted his bail money. They found his body in a park not even a day later."

"Tom told me a story about the last time he'd heard from Felix." Meriel repeated it to Nell.

"They found a woman's body too. Police report dated it older than Felix. One of the notes says her skin was like rice paper. The vic was Asian though. That's not our Gloria."

"Damn it. No." Tom had described Gloria Ochoa as tall with dark hair and big brown eyes. Had said she was beautiful back in the day. "Nell, if she's alive . . ." Meriel looked at a framed picture of Dominic at about eight or nine, holding a fishing pole, looking up into the camera with a huge gap-toothed grin. "He looks a lot like his uncle. I can't believe he never really realized that. But if I see the resemblance, what if she recognizes him? What if because of me, she sees Dominic's picture and comes after him?"

"Life's full of what-if moments, Meriel. We'll create contingencies for as many as we can. He's tough. He's full-council and ascended to you. The bond will only make him stronger. The magick of Owen will shield him. Whatever happens, we'll keep him safe."

"And what if she decides Meriel is the target?" Tom came into the kitchen, followed by a cat, who deigned to let Meriel scratch behind his ears before he sashayed off to go settle in a window.

"Better me than Dominic." She looked to him and then focused back on Nell. "What else?"

"We've got our own version of an APB out on her. I'm tapped into different federal and state systems to keep an eye out for any hits of arrests with women fitting her description. 'Cause you know, there just aren't many dark haired women in their fifties who get picked up without ID. Ha. Anyway, she's turned and given what you've told me about her appearance with the mage at her in-laws' door, we've got reason to believe she could be with mages now. Even the ones in our neck of the woods."

"I've written up an account of the whole conversation and emailed it to you right before you called."

Nell snorted. "Should have known. Perfect. Okay, so I'm going to focus in those states we've seen the mage activity in. And I'll expand to the areas around it. But not too far. She won't be going into Gennessee or Owen territory unless she's desperate. The West Coast is far afield for her."

Meriel's stomach clenched. "Someone has."

"Yes, but those mages aren't necessarily tied to her. I just don't think she'd have survived for thirty years turned if she wasn't being somewhat smart."

"Get back to me."

"You stay safe. You use all your magick if this bitch rolls up on you. Or any of them. Do not think you can talk sense into these people."

Meriel knew the stakes.

"I know. We'll be back tomorrow night late. Call me if you find anything else."

She hung up and turned her gaze back to the windows, but her mind was a million miles away.

* * *

DOMINIC came down to find his gorgeous woman having a rather intense discussion with a cat. He grinned when Ernie finally gave in and jumped down from her lap.

"He's a snob. He likes Tom and that's about it." Dominic paused for a kiss but she stood and wrapped herself around him, which was even better. "You should be honored he sat in your lap."

"We were just fine with that. But he drools *and* he has sharp claws he likes to use when he's getting pets. We can't agree on whether this is acceptable behavior or not." She glanced at the cat, currently washing his face with his paw. "Good morning." She kissed Dominic.

"It is now."

Laughing, she pointed at the carafe on the counter. "Coffee there. Tom has promised a big farm breakfast and I graciously accepted his very fine offer. I promise I was even going to wake you up in time. After I filled my own plate first, of course."

"He'll make enough for fifteen people anyway. That's why the cat's so fat."

Ernie looked up at Dominic with one green eye and one blue eye. Neither was that impressed. He did stretch his head out to get a scratch though, so Dominic complied and was rewarded with a throaty purr.

"How'd you sleep?" Tom asked as he came into the room with an armful of food.

"It was hard to get used to the quiet, but after about thirty minutes my mind let go." Despite all his emotional upheaval, it had been a deep and dreamless sleep. He'd needed that. Needed to wake up to the quiet of the house and Meriel's scent on his skin and the sheets. He'd lain in bed, staring up at the naked beams above, just thinking.

Of course all the thinking had only made him itchy. Uncomfortable and off balance again.

"Tonight will be the one you really conk out. You should

stay an extra day or two." Tom began to pull out bowls and pots. Dominic automatically moved to help.

"If you two won't miss my helping hands, I'm going to grab a shower."

He turned to find her near the doorway, the sunlight on her hair, backlighting her like an angel. He saw her worry and it comforted. She cared about him, worried over him. She'd probably been up four hours already and had most likely been in contact with Nell about this business with his parents. He wished . . . wished she could take his side in this. Understood she had to protect her people, *their* people he supposed. But he wanted her to believe with him that his mother wasn't a lost cause.

"We've got it handled. Breakfast will be ready in about half an hour so you've got some time." He moved to her, meeting her halfway. He wanted to join her, but that wasn't the time. He needed the alone time with Tom and she knew that too.

She said nothing else, but tiptoed up to kiss him quickly and then left.

"I like her. She's a lot like your grandmother, your Meriel. I've got a lot of things I've held back for you, for the time when you finally learned the truth. Pictures, that sort of thing. So you can know your grandparents too."

Dominic rejoined Tom at the kitchen island. Automatically, he began to peel potatoes. "I can't believe you never told me any of this."

"I know you're angry at me."

"I'm angry, period. What if she's been looking for me?"

"You're a smart man. You were a smart boy too. Too smart to hold fantasies as reality. She's not a fairy princess, boy, she's a turned witch working with mages to hurt her own people to get a fix. Don't forget it. If she has been looking for you, let's all say a prayer of thanks she never found you. Gloria is nothing but bad news for you."

"You had no right to make that decision for me."

Tom slammed his fist on the counter and spun to face him. "Bullshit. I have *every* right to make that decision. I adored my brother. Idolized him. He was everything I wanted to be. He was good at everything. Sports, academics, women, my god, the women. But our parents didn't know how to keep that channeled in a positive direction. In college he met Gloria and that was it. I'd hoped they would be good for each other, but they weren't. She encouraged his reck-lessness and he doted on her. She needed a man who'd help her get her act together, but he wasn't that man. He needed a woman who'd have given him a reason to finally stop fucking around and build a life as an adult. She wasn't that woman.

"And then you came along about six months after they married and we'd all hoped that would finally do the trick. It didn't. So he came to me, on the verge of losing it. The last time I saw Felix, he stood in my living room and begged me to kill him if I ever saw him again. He gave his child to me to raise and protect and you'd damn well better know that's what I did. I don't have the right? Fuck. You."

Tom turned again and went back to slicing the bacon as Dominic peeled potatoes.

Both men worked silently. Tom was slow to anger and usually quick to get over it. Dominic thought about his life. He thought about the way he'd been raised. Physically hale, fed intellectually and emotionally. The very firm way Tom dealt with him and any infractions made sense on a whole new level. He'd done it to keep Dominic from turning out like his own dad.

And Dominic didn't quite know how to process it. It had been a long time since he'd felt so out of sorts. He hadn't missed it.

"Did you hate him? Or me?" Dominic poured oil into the cast-iron skillet and waited for it to heat while he grabbed some onion and green pepper to go with the potatoes.

"Never you. I was young when I came out here. Having you . . . well, it gave me a direction. One I didn't really have. I suppose you saved my life in a lot of ways."

Dominic waited for more as he slid everything into the hot skillet. Tom would say more when he was ready.

"I grew up with a larger-than-life big brother. He took me with him sometimes when he'd go with his friends. Seeing what he'd become . . . I was disappointed, but more than that, I was angry. He had everything, including a baby, and it wasn't enough."

Dominic looked around the kitchen. At the cabinets they'd made and installed themselves.

"Did you know I made extra money when I was in L.A. by doing carpentry?"

"Yeah? Good. You have a good hand with it. But you're better at running things. This club of yours. Meriel told me about it last night. She invited me to Seattle to stay whenever I like. I want to see what you've built. If you'll have me in your life, that is."

Dominic turned to face the man who was his father in every way that was important. "I'm pissed off at you. But that doesn't change that I love you. Of course I want you in my life. Why do you think I'm still here?"

Tom turned the bacon. "Put the biscuits in the oven please."

Dominic did.

"Maybe you're only here to get more info on your mother."

Dominic turned the potatoes, satisfied with how golden they'd gotten. "Really? You think that?"

"No. Not really. Leastwise that's not how you were raised."

"I know I haven't been much for thank-yous and stuff. But I get it now."

"What's that?"

"All the limits I used to think were so severe, so much more strict than others. You did it to keep me from being him."

Tom snorted. "Partly I suppose. You're headstrong. He was too. But so am I. Headstrong isn't a bad thing. I just wanted you to have a sense that you could do anything you set your mind to. That inner strength and confidence your father lacked in the end. And then you ran off to Los Angeles and I worried so much. I just had to hope you'd snap out of it. And you did. You've built a good life, Dominic. You and Meriel will have a good relationship. And one day you'll have babies and I can teach them how to fish and camp too."

Dominic had needed to hear that. He hadn't realized it until that very moment just how much.

"Meriel can see the marks. The protective ones on my body."

Tom's brows rose for a moment. "Really? Your magick works together well then? I didn't grow up in a clan. And then once you came along I wanted to get you away from any group of witches where you might be discovered. I know the rules I was raised with, but you'll have to teach me about your life now."

Dominic realized no matter what else, he and Tom would get past this.

"When I first met Meriel we had this sort of . . . potential. Major attraction. The clans are run by full-council witches, as you know. But they're like junior partners until they meet and do the ascension spell with their bond-mate."

"So you were compelled to be with her? So she could take over a corner office?"

Dominic grinned. "I felt that way at first. I didn't trust any of it, but I can't deny the appeal. Anyway, it's not so rare it's only one person in the world or whatever. I could have walked away. She gave me space, gave me time as I worked it through. But I don't want to."

"So you're one of them now?"

"Yes. What I choose to do is up to me. Meriel is obviously very involved. They have committees and they own several floors of a building in downtown. They have businesses and it's all to benefit the entire clan. They're like a giant corporation but also maybe some of the mafia too."

It was Tom's turn to laugh. "When you're hiding from those who want to harm you and yours, the rules change."

"Exactly. Anyway, not all bond-mates are romantic or sexual. Sometimes it's just a person you're magickally connected to. Meriel's mother's bond-mate is like that."

"So what's the catch? I mean, the bond is voluntary you said. What happens next to ascend?"

"This is how it was explained to me and I've found it pretty accurate. Each of us has natural defenses—barriers around our magicks. Not all witches, but a small percentage the clan witches call full-council have a way to unlock it via another person. You have to *choose* to let those down and marry your energy with your bond-mate. The ascension spell unlocks those walls and, well, the best way to put it is that the magick of each person works as one unit. The spell throws all the walls around our latent magick wide open. Essentially an ascended witch is operating at full capacity because there are no reserves waiting for the balance of a partner. The bond-mate is a stabilizing element to channeling all that magick. Like the third leg on a stool. I've got my magick, Meriel hers and then there's our magick."

Meriel came into the room and he turned to smile. He liked the way she looked, her hair loose, face clean of makeup.

"Am I interrupting anything?" She looked worried and he wanted to fix that.

"I was just explaining how the bond works. I was about to say that the spellwork we do together is even stronger than anything we do individually. It's harder to break down with unraveling spells. You should see the warding she helped me do at Heart of Darkness."

She smiled up at him.

"Can you get these potatoes on the table? I'm going to do the eggs. Scrambled okay?"

"Yes, please." She took the potatoes and set the table, getting coffee and juice for everyone.

Chapter 21

"SO do you want to talk about it?" Meriel looked up from her meal and across the table. He'd been moody and a little distant since they'd returned from Bend. He'd thrown himself into his work, making excuses to stay at his place instead of staying with her.

He'd been fine when they were still at Tom's. A little pouty here and there. Snippy, but he hadn't really distanced himself until he'd pulled up at her place and said he had a lot of work to catch up on and left.

He hadn't asked her to stay with him and she'd felt like he needed the space so she gave it to him. She'd given him a few days, knowing he was upset about his parents and probably needed a little time to process by himself without the pressure of her or Tom's presence.

But this had gone on long enough and she was done. They had a life together and it was time to remind him that she was part of it.

"About what?"

"Really?" She sent him a raised brow.

"Look, it's over and done with. The past is the past."

"Really?"

He sighed. "I don't want to do this."

"Hm. Too bad. I do. You can't just pretend you're not upset about all you learned when we were at Tom's. I get it. How can you not be? I'm not going to judge you for your feelings. I just want you to talk to me so we can work our way around it."

"I can't emote on demand."

"I'm not asking you to. I'm asking you to *share* yourself with me. I'm not looking for tears or rages, unless that's how you feel and you want to do that. But you've avoided me for four days. If you're angry at me, let's talk about it so we can work it out."

"It doesn't matter. You think what you think about her and I think what I think. Anyway, just because we're bonded doesn't mean I have to vomit all my feelings at all times for your amusement."

She stood and grabbed her purse, clamping down on her own hurt. "You're right. You can't. And if sharing with me makes you feel that way, there's nothing more for me to say. I'll be away until Friday. I'll call you when I get back."

She'd hoped he would come after her, but he remained seated so she took her coat and left Heart of Darkness, running into Simon on the way to the door.

"Meriel. It's good to see your pretty face." He bent to hug her. And then when he pulled back he took a good look. "Don't tell me he's still locked up."

"He doesn't want to share with me and I can't make him. But I can't sit here knowing he's upset and that he won't open up even a little. I know it's still new between us, but I can't feel this way and I don't think it's helping him either. Keep an eye on him please. I'm going to San Francisco. I'll be back Friday."

"Give him a chance. He's never had anything even remotely like what he's got with you. It makes him vulnerable to share. He doesn't know how to do it right."

"I know. I'm not walking out on our relationship. Just this moment in time. I brought him dinner. I try to talk to him. He ignores me. He hasn't slept over in a few days. He's shutting me out of his life so until he's ready to let me in, I have to be patient." But it hurt too much to stay around just then. She wanted him to come to her and share. Understood why he hadn't yet, but it left a lump in her throat and hurt her stomach.

"He's been working too much. I think he slept here last night. Though I did notice he's got one of your T-shirts as a pillowcase, so he's not as tough as he tries to come off. Will you be safe? I mean, away from here when all this stuff is happening?"

"Yes. I'll be on Owen land with other Owen witches. Life goes on. I can be there for him, and I am, but I can't experience his grief and his guilt. I have to go. Please watch him. If anyone suspicious comes around, will you let me know?"

"If that bitch comes around, I'll make sure she never can again. And you be careful too. I don't like you being away right now with all this mess."

"I can't be here right now, Simon. I've given him space. I've not shown him just how upset I am. But I have feelings too. And I have a job. I have a clan to run. This meeting is important and so I'll go. It's two days."

And all she could do, she thought as she drove home, was hope he felt it when she was gone.

"YOU'RE being a grumpy fuck who is going to have my fist in his eye in about five seconds." Simon growled at Dominic from across the table.

Dominic slumped, looking around for the eight-millionth time, hoping to see Meriel and then remembering she was gone. And then he'd start missing her again. Even more than he had an hour before.

"You miss her."

He sighed. "When she said she was going I didn't think she meant it. I went to her house yesterday morning and she was gone. I had no chance to apologize or to even say good-bye." He should have followed her when she'd left Heart of Darkness that night. He'd let pride keep him glued to his seat as she walked away.

"Do you even know if she got there safely?"

"She sent me a text when she got to San Francisco giving me her hotel and room number."

"You haven't called her yet? What the hell is wrong with you? I know you understand the magickal stuff now, I've seen how much stronger you are. The wards on the club, all the diversions and glamours between the back room and the front of the house are seamless. Gage's idea of changing the overall flow of traffic between Other and human entrances was helpful too. You're better now. With her in your life. You're stronger. You don't lose your cool at all. It's like you've finally calmed down enough to know you're doing just fuckin' fine, thankyouverymuch."

Dominic laughed at that description. "Pretty much from a short time after we met until this fight, we've gotten along. Sure we bicker. She's a very vexing woman sometimes." He said that with a big smile. "I came up on this thing and when we were in Bend, we had this unity and closeness. She'd been supportive and helpful. She left me and Tom alone enough to work through our stuff, but not long enough for us to start fighting.

"The way she is stuns me. She's got this effortless intuitiveness about what I need. I took that. But I got back here and we sort of fell back into our schedules and I guess I fell back into my old patterns. I didn't have this person to share with and turn to before her. I sure didn't have a person I was metaphysically attached to, who shared my life in such a breathtakingly intimate way. And I was pissed off. Scared too probably, that she gets to me the way she does. I didn't want her to be right about my mother and I resented that she was."

"Why aren't you telling *her* this?"

"I thought I could hold out until she got back. Give us both time to get past the anger and hurt. Be a little further from it. I'd show up at her place with flowers and some sea salt caramels and a lot of groveling, that we could get to makeup sex within an hour or two." He covered his face. "I know. God. I've never run after a woman before. I let that get to me and then I've suffered for it just like she knows I will."

Simon laughed. "That's tough love, man. But it's either

deal with it now and at least get some relief from this suffering and then you can get to the sex part way faster when you get back. Or you can wait till she gets back after you've suffered for another day and then still have to apologize and admit you were being a jerk." He tipped a beer in Dominic's direction. "She's a ruthless, canny bitch. I really love that."

Indeed. He did too apparently.

"So I talked to Nell earlier. They got some possible hits on my mom."

His friend looked around and then shook his head. "Get your head out of your ass. Damn it, Dominic. You are one of the smartest guys I know. Street smarts, business smarts. You are a survivor for a reason and that's because you are fearless when it comes to the truth. Except for now. Why you holdin' on to some fantasy that this witch is anything but a cancer? You don't need to find a witch like her unless you got plans to remove her from your enemies list."

"Why does everyone judge her? You don't even know her."

"Fuck you, Dom. Neither do you. And that's a fact. What I know is as much as what you know. It's as much as what Meriel knows. Tom knows even more. You're the only one who looks at all this evidence and decides to just ignore the facts. That's not you, man. Think about this woman."

"She's my mother."

"So what? Huh? She gave birth to you and then abandoned you a time or two, oh and then maybe was even stealing your life force to get high. Brava. We know she's turned. We know there's no cure once you turn. She's a turned witch who will kidnap, torture and maybe even kill, most likely kill, to get her fix. She is not whoever she was when she met your dad. She is not even a witch anymore. Her ties to her own magick are dead. She's cut herself off from her gifts. When even nature won't recognize you, you are not a cat people want at Thanksgiving dinner."

Dominic chewed his bottom lip a moment.

"You're my brother as assuredly as any of the ones back home who turn furry and have claws. I can't allow you to lie to yourself. She can't either. Meriel is exactly what you need. She won't take your shit and she'd take a bullet for you. Don't go fucking that up for some junkie who means you nothing but heartache. Don't be dumb and lose everything real and good for this dream of yours."

Shit.

MERIEL'S phone buzzed and a text from Dominic came onto her screen.

I want to hear your voice. Can I call you?

She smiled.

Yes please

Moments later the phone rang and she picked up. "Hey there."

"Hey there yourself. I miss you. I'm an asshole too. I'm sorry."

"I know you're having a hard time with all this. I understand that. And I understand that you're feeling exposed and raw and that maybe a lot of what you'd thought was your past was all just made up.

"And I'm sorry. I'm sorry it happened to you. I'm sorry you're hurting. But you wouldn't let me in. You were so open with me at Tom's but when we got back you dropped me at my apartment and went home. You made an excuse the next night too. I brought you dinner and you wouldn't even look at me. You owe it to me to look me in the eye if you don't want me around. It's not fair for you to hurt me to get me to leave." That had been the worst part.

"I know. I'm sorry. I am. I was a dick. And I was scared and all off balance and I shoved you back even when I knew you would make it better. That you would help me find a way to give it all some meaning, so that it made sense somehow. And I knew I'd hurt your feelings when you left and I didn't come after you, even when I knew you were upset. I came to you yesterday morning and you were gone. I miss you. I need you to help me make sense."

Meriel wiped her eyes with the back of her hand and tried not to sniffle where he could hear it. "You didn't come after me. I wanted you to and you didn't." That's when the tears leaked from her voice and she cringed, not wanting to make him feel bad.

She heard his intake of breath. "I'm sorry. God. I'm sorry. I hurt you and it was totally my being a dick. I'll come for you. Always from now on I will come for you."

She believed it. "You'd better. And how are you then?"

"I haven't slept much. I talked to Nell about some information that came up about my mother, Gloria, whatever. Simon yelled at me, but I think he set me straight. I guess I'm lucky to have a friend who'll totally take me to school."

"He did? What for?" Good heavens, did they regularly get into fistfights? For fun? "I can't believe that gets me hot."

He paused for a moment and then laughed. "God, I've missed you. We talked about the whole thing with my family. He just reminded me of who I was. I want to talk to you about all this face-to-face."

"I'll be home tomorrow morning. Eleven thirty. You can pick me up from the airport. Call Gage and tell him."

By the time they hung up she felt a lot better.

HE was there where the gates dumped passengers. A huge bouquet of red roses in one hand. He looked so good she sighed.

Many women paused as they passed him, taking a long look, trying to get his attention but he had nothing for any of them. He looked at no one and nothing but Meriel. And when she reached him, he put his free arm around her and hauled her up to her toes to receive the kind of kiss she'd missed so very much.

"You're back."

She nodded.

"Are you free for the day or do I have to share you with work?"

"I'm all yours."

"Yeah. I'm a lucky guy that way."

She took the bouquet and buried her face in the silk of

the blooms, breathing in deep. He had no idea but she loved getting flowers.

He got her settled in the car and she relaxed for probably the first time since he'd dropped her at her door on Sunday night.

"So I talked with Nell earlier today."

She nodded. "Yeah, me too." In the time since they'd learned about Gloria Ochoa's existence, Meriel had come to believe that the only way to exorcise her from Dominic's mind and heart was to find her and get rid of her. Nell had suggested, and Meriel agreed, that Gloria would probably be amenable to a cash inducement. But the next in line and the part of her that was Dominic's woman was pretty sure there was only one way to deal with Gloria. She hoped it wouldn't come to that, but it if did, Gloria would deserve it. Besides, Nell was only tossing that out because Meriel had demanded some nonlethal remedies as well as the numerous violence-filled ones.

Nell had found someone who might just be Gloria. She'd been living in Canada for several years, but had recently shown up in Michigan. Coincidentally, they'd recently gotten a report of a witch in Detroit who'd been attacked and drained. Someone had approached mid-attack and they'd left the witch for dead. It was a silly thing, but Meriel was totally sure Gloria also had something to do with the recent attacks in Seattle.

"You think she's part of the attack." He said it flatly, totally able to read her.

"Yes. I do. And the ones here as well. I have no reason to believe anything else. Given her history, it's clear to me that if she's in the same place as an attack against a witch or the site of some sort of ugly ritual, she's part of it. I'm sorry for that. But I can't pretend it's not true. Even to make you happy."

He was quiet awhile as he drove. "I don't want to write her off entirely."

She was quiet, just listening to him process as the miles passed.

"Simon didn't actually punch me in the face. He just threatened to," he said suddenly.

"I know. He told me." She didn't want to keep that communication between them secret. Dominic needed to know that he had people around him who cared enough to make him upset if that's what it took to get him to face the truth.

"He was right. You're right."

She took his hand and he squeezed. "I'm sorry I'm right. I wish I wasn't."

"Yeah well, me too. Nell yelled at me."

That was a surprise. Nell hadn't mentioned it. "She did? I didn't know."

"She told me I made you cry."

"She had no right."

"Don't get mad. She was right to make me see what a dick I was being. I just wanted to believe she wanted me. Not Nell," he added quickly, "my mother."

Meriel wanted to laugh at that, but he was so sad. "I want you. Tom wants you. Edwina is charmed silly by you. My dad thinks you're wonderful. If Nell yelled at you, it means she likes you, just sayin'. I know this is hard. But this is about what *she's* missing. Not what you're lacking. She had a gorgeous little boy and she hurt you. What she is repudiates all of what we are. What we stand for. And that people like her are joining with humans who want to erase us from the face of the earth makes it even worse. She's a threat to me and mine. You're mine. I won't let her hurt you again. Are we clear on that?"

He sighed. "I don't know how you manage to always say what I need to hear, but thank you. However, I don't want you going to meet her on your own. If this is her and you manage to track her down, let Nell and her people take care of this."

Meriel said nothing.

This was personal. This woman had used and abused Dominic. She'd left a swath of pain in her wake and that had to be answered. Meriel wanted this bitch to understand just what she was dealing with and that was best done face-to-face.

"Meriel, I can hear the gears turning in your head."

"Dominic, I need to confess something to you."

"Do you? Crap, Meriel, are you going to tell me you have to? I really think you don't need to go there."

She raised one brow and waited until he got himself calm again. "I'm aware that many believe I'm too mellow to run a clan. I'm efficient, yes; they trust my brain and even my magick. But they don't know if I'm tough enough. Mainly because really, unless I started going Godzilla and tearing cities apart, how can I outdo my mother in that department?"

He laughed.

"In any case, in general, I prefer to avoid conflict when I can. Not because I'm afraid of it or because I'm too weak to fight back. But because conflict eats up your time. It is exhaustive in terms of energy you have to expend to be involved in it. More if you mean to win, and I'd never do it if I didn't mean to win. I'd rather spend my time on other things and in general, most people aren't worth that much of my time and energy.

"But sometimes, well, sometimes we need to show and not tell. If you get my meaning. This woman has harmed the people I love. The people I'm honor bound to protect. I will be involved in whatever it takes to eradicate any threat she may pose."

He was silent a long time as they approached her building.

"I agree, that we are honor bound to protect Owen witches." He touched her face. "And each other."

"I can hear the unspoken *but* at the end of that sentence." He took her bags and escorted her upstairs.

"Before we continue this discussion, let's try something. I learned something in San Francisco. Use your othersight." She took his hand and opened her own. "You can see how everything here has an energy signature. Plants look a certain way, inanimate things like benches or walls have that flat, opaque feel."

He nodded.

"Just beneath that there's another kind of signature. But I didn't know what to even look for until one of the witches I met day before yesterday showed me something."

Meriel drew the sigils in the air. This sort of magick was older than spoken spellwork and varied all across the world.

The witch in San Francisco had learned it while she'd been in Tibet.

"Do you see how it all works together?" she asked Dominic, indicating the symbols she'd drawn in the air.

"It's like calculus. Holy shit, this is beautiful and really old." He looked at it and added something and then adjusted a symbol earlier on in the spell. Their intent made it real and suddenly the hallway to her apartment exploded into a wash of colors. Of ebbs and flows of the kinds of energies lining the place.

"How did you know how to do that?" Whatever he'd done to adjust the spell, it made everything else fade into the background, enabling her to focus on these energy swirls.

"I aced calculus." He shrugged. "You told me to let my gut have its say. It seemed right to fix it the way I did."

"That was awesome."

Surprise washed over his face. He dipped to kiss her. "Thank you."

"So you can get a general idea of what this hallway looks like. Lots of that sort of soft wash of blue there. Humans obviously. But you can see deeper now. Now you can see the sorts of energies they expel. Weres have that vibrant green, but it's got this sort of verdant feel on this level. Vampires are red, obviously. But you can see if they're using darker energies and hurting people. With witches . . ." She paused and saw it.

"Witches are the brilliant blue. You can see a lot of it near my door. But mages, or anyone who uses unnatural energies has a sort of sickly gray smudge." Just like the one in the hallway ahead.

His mouth flattened into a hard line and he grabbed her upper arm, marching her back toward the elevators. "We're leaving."

"No, we're not. You can see that it didn't get close to my door. My wards are holding just fine. We just know someone who's doing something bad has been here. We don't know enough to panic."

She moved to her front door and unlocked it.

He went inside first and she followed closing up behind herself. "We're fine in here. No one has been inside since I left. I need to tell Nell, but this doesn't necessarily mean they know where I am."

"Oh, so a random mage was just walking down your hallway and stopped near your door. Just because."

She called Nell, who gave a similar lecture.

"Go stay at Dominic's or come here, but you need to move to a place where you're defended better."

"I'm just fine here."

"Shut up. Put Dominic on the phone."

"No."

"I can hear the entire conversation anyway, Meriel. I already had an appointment for us to look at an apartment in my building and one across the street. I planned to grovel and then suggest it. This obviously pushes my timeline forward. Let's get some of your bags. We can come back tomorrow and get more."

"Pushy much?"

"You know it. Don't test me on this. I'll bring this to the quorum if I have to. You should let me keep you safe. Plus my building is close to the office and it's close to Heart of Darkness. We can be together and you can be taken care of."

"How do you know I'm safer anywhere else?"

"What I know," Nell barked into her ear, "is that you've got a mage lurking around your hallway. If Dominic doesn't have one, that makes his place safer. Plus you'll draw even better being so close to the font. You won't win this one so let it go. Anyway, his place is closer to mine."

"She's right." Dominic raised a brow as he shoved her clothes into a bag.

"Hey! You're going to wrinkle that."

"Yell at me later. I want up and out of here. I have a bad feeling."

Chapter 22

HE stalked her as she walked through his place. She sent him the side-eye but he wasn't deterred. He *liked* having her in his apartment. Which was sort of funny given that he'd never, ever seriously considered living with a woman. Now though? This woman? He wanted her with him all the time.

She would be safer, no doubt. He'd be around. She'd be closer to her job and he wouldn't have to run back and forth across the lake to see her.

"You're making me nervous."

"No, I'm not. Very little makes you nervous." He smiled and she huffed and went back to putting her clothes away.

"I missed you when you were gone."

She must have gotten a pedicure when she was in San Francisco. Her toes were different. A deep, dark red. Like every other part of her, her feet were sexy.

She looked up at him, suspicion on her face. "Mmm-hmm."

"Why you gotta be this way?" He added a little bit of a purr, just for her.

"What way is that?"

"How was San Francisco?"

"Useful."

"Are you going to remain prickly so that I have no other choice but to seduce a good mood back into you?"

"You're pretty bold for a guy who's still in the doghouse."

He stood and moved to her. "But you know my general feelings about being challenged."

She held a hand out, trying not to smile but failing. "Stop that. I have to unpack and do laundry."

He shook his head. "Your clothes are already in the washing machine. Laundry—check. Your stuff is hanging in the closet—check."

"Are you in charge of my schedule now?"

"Or maybe you need your own stress relief. Orgasms are good for you. And maybe, maybe I'll do it just because I can." He got closer and she moved around the bed.

"Maybe you'll be bloody by the end."

He shook his head. "Maybe. But that's part of the fun of fucking you, Meriel Owen. A man needs to be kept on his toes. You never let me slack."

Her smile broke free and she threw a pillow at him. "I have stuff to do."

"Yes, yes, you do."

He pounced, bringing her to the bed with him. Laughing, he rained small, sweet kisses across her forehead and the bridge of her nose. "How can I want you so much?"

"Because I'm fabulous?"

"Well, yes. Certainly your body is fabulous. You're gorgeous. You're tight and hot and wet every time I get near you." He slid his palm down her belly, stopping to cup her sex.

Her soft gasp echoed through his system. Pounding at him like the blood in his veins.

"It's more than that. I can't quite believe you're mine." He eased her shirt open, exposing one of those pretty bras she favored. "And I'm greedy for you." Deftly, he popped the catch between her breasts and freed them. "For these."

He pressed a kiss between her breasts as he unbuttoned and unzipped the pants, easing them down.

"You're astoundingly good at getting my clothes off."

"It's my favorite pastime. Well, my second favorite." He leered and meant it.

"Who am I to stand between a boy and his favorite sport?"

But she gave as good as she got. Rearing up, she pulled his shirt off and kissed over his chest, rubbing her cheek against him like a cat.

And then her hand was down his pants and she was gripping his cock, a definite look of challenge on her face.

"Show me what you got, then."

His pants were off, followed by his boxers. As much as he loved the way she looked partially clothed and disheveled, he preferred naked. So off came her shirt and bra, the pants and a pair of teeny red panties.

"I've got a witch naked in my bed. A pretty flush on her skin. Nipples hard and dark." To underline this, he bent and licked across one and then the other until she yanked on his hair to get his attention.

"Yes, mistress?" he teased.

She grabbed him again, thrusting a few times to underline her urgency.

They hadn't been together since Sunday morning. He'd missed this thing between them—the urgency to take her and to feel the trembling of her muscles as he made her come, the easy familiarity they'd had since the first time he touched her.

He'd run from that and it hadn't worked. He didn't feel better without her. He missed her and her voice. The way she was so orderly and in charge but once it was just Meriel and Dominic, she'd softened and given herself to him. To them.

Why he'd ever imagined running from her would fix the ache in his heart he didn't know. She made everything better. Even as she laid him bare and saw him down to the bone, she accepted him.

This intimacy they had drove him to possess her, to touch and kiss every part of her skin he could. The sweetness of her lips drew him back time and again. He wanted to take it slow, give her pleasure for the entire afternoon.

She writhed as he slid himself against her. But before he could get any further, she wrapped her legs around him and rolled over, straddling him. "You're going too slow. I need you now."

He didn't ask where she got the condom she held up. It was one of his; she'd probably found it in his nightstand. It didn't matter, only that she had it and wanted to use it.

"Will you miss your lady parts buffet now that I'm around and would naturally cut anyone who tried to show you her bits?"

And he put her on her back again, kissing down her belly until he ended up where he wanted. "These are the only bits I want." He breathed over her, smiling again when she stuttered a breath.

Her taste wended through him. Drove him. He wanted more. Always wanted more. Loved the way her inner-thigh muscles bunched and strained under his palm where he held her open to him. Loved the way she arched to get more. Loved the way she exploded all because of him. He brought her pleasure and she knew who did it.

It made him smug. Made him feel like a king.

Even better, while she was still catching her breath from her orgasm to slide in deep, to catch the surprised gaze as her lids flew open, and then her eyes blurred with pleasure.

MERIEL had zero plans to move. She lay there on his bed, his body wrapped around her as he caught his breath.

"It's been far too long since I've been this tingly and slightly sore."

She didn't open her eyes, but she didn't need to be looking at him to know he laughed.

"I've neglected you, terribly. I apologize. For what it's worth, I've been un-tingly and not sore at all since Sunday too. Though I did get a little sore after I worked out this whole week. But that's not the same." He pulled the comforter up and over them. "Not that same as having you make me tingly and sore."

"All right, that's pretty good."

She turned and opened her eyes to look at him.

"Tell me about San Francisco." He kissed her forehead.

"It was dramatic, as it tends to be when we all get together. I have an official report to make tomorrow for the council. This mage issue was one we were not alone in bringing up. Several other clans and covens have had problems. We traded some ideas. We'll be doing a lot of cross-training over the next year I think. Nell's already on this with some of the other hunters or lawkeepers for the smaller groups. I learned that nifty othersight trick. I'll need to send out the changes you made. I think you really amped up the spell and cut out the background interference."

"I should have gone too. I'm sorry."

"You have a business to run, Dominic. You can't come to all these meetings. I have them all the time. It's part of my job. But I would like it if you'd help with something."

"You know you only have to ask and I'll do it."

"You're full of shit. I ask you to do all sorts of things and you do your own thing anyway."

"I love when you're vulgar. How about this—what I mean is, professionally. Ask and if it's not something I think is dumb like letting you continue to live in a place the mages know about and have stalked you in—I'll do it."

"You already had appointments set up to look at apartments. Don't pretend you didn't jump on this to get what you wanted."

He laughed. "Of course I did. Do you think I'd merit a woman like you if I was easily led or if I didn't take full advantage of every situation to get my way?" One of his brows rose and she snorted.

"Don't snort, Meriel, my love. You're naked in my bed, still mussed from my attentions." He winked. "Exhibit A."

"I'm truly afraid of what our children will be like."

"Yeah, me too. But you can handle me just fine. You'll be great. They'll adore you like I do."

She rolled her eyes but snuggled into him. "I'm afraid this mage thing isn't going to go away without a lot of work and most likely more people hurt and killed."

And his mother was a part of it. Meriel had spoken to Nell about this and with Sadira Rodas, the leader of Rodas Clan. Sadira had told Meriel what they'd discovered when they were able to capture some of these mages, was that they'd been part of an organized movement to hunt and use witches for their magick.

And as they'd suspected, there were several witches helping the mages. Mainly by giving them information, critical information that only a witch could help them with. Where witches would likely congregate, what practice path they used so they could defend against anything a witch threw their way. And now it appeared they knew about the hierarchy in clans and were targeting council witches to steal magick from.

Now that their secrets had been exposed, it put them all at greater risk. This was a threat to their entire race. She could not shake the gut feeling that Gloria Ochoa was involved. They had a lot of circumstantial evidence on this fact already. It was really only a matter of time before they knew for certain.

"Having bands of roving mages out to stalk and kidnap us sounds like a plot from a novel. Humans have to deal with this fear. I guess I should too. But I hate the idea of it! I hate that these mages are hunting us like animals and will use us up and toss us to the side. I can't abide it."

He smirked. "Of course you can't. We'll do what we can."

"Will you help me with this?"

"With what, baby?"

"I need to reach out to witches who aren't in clans, unaffiliated witches, coven witches, outclan, all that. I have some ideas, but my mother has charged me with this and I'm already getting started. I'd like you with me, helping me."

He nodded. "Of course. I have some ideas too. You and I can make a difference. Tell me what you need and when you need it, I'm in. You know, your mother told me yesterday that this issue would make your place in Owen history. She's proud of you."

"She hated this stuff just six months ago. Told me it had

nothing to do with our world, that if the mongrels wanted to kill each other, they would."

"Edwina can admit when she's wrong. She believes in the strength of the clan."

"So do I." Meriel sat and grabbed her shirt. "But we're targets too. The rep from Rodas has interrogated these mages. They have more info than any of us and what was shared was enough to convince me that if we don't work together and strengthen ourselves, it'll be open season on us."

"Mages can be taken out. Your mother showed me a great new spell. It's a feedback spell. You can probably do it while multitasking about forty-five other things. But I think if it's used at the right time during a mage attack, it can cascade into the mage, draining him until there's nothing. At the very least it should give the witch being attacked some time to get out of there."

"She's never taught me that spell." But she was flattered, nonetheless, that he thought she was so competent.

"Really? Well, it's handy. She probably thinks you already know it. I'll show it to you."

This was entirely possible. "Nell's mother was the hunter before Nell. Within Owen, it's almost always been a Hunter. Yes, that's Nell's real family name. Back then you know you were named what you did a lot. Smith, Baker, all that. So it's been a Hunter or a Garrity. That's Gage's family by the way, only his mother is a healer and it's his father who was in our hunter team until just three years ago. Anyway, I'm tangenting. Nell's mother taught me all my defensive magick. Though I've certainly learned a lot from my mother too. I'd love for you to show it to me."

"Is it all right with you?" He pulled on his boxers and jeans but stayed shirtless and she stared for long moments at him. Big. Imposing. Those wide shoulders of his leading down to a flat belly and a narrower waist. A waist showcased even better with low-slung jeans hanging from them.

"You're going to end up right back in bed if you keep looking at me that way."

She laughed and walked from the room.

"To answer your question," she said as she began to make a pot of coffee, "I like that you're learning from Edwina. She's hands down the finest spellcaster I've ever seen. It's good to learn from her. She never takes shortcuts, which means you'll learn how to do everything the long way. And it's easy to change a long spell to adjust it for all sorts of uses. But learning her way, you get the mechanics of the spell, which is important."

"And she likes me. She didn't want to at first. But she does now." He grinned.

"She does. But I can understand that very well. I like you too. You're very charming."

"So glad you think so. I'm clearly going to have to buy more coffee if we'll be living together." He hopped up on a stool to watch her, pleased and smug.

Oh, back to that. "Why do you want to look at the other places?"

"The one here is on a higher floor and has a private elevator. Keycards only. So it's less access. Safer. And the view will be better. And it's bigger. A three bedroom. That way you can work from home and we'll still have a spare room for people to stay if they like. Simon does from time to time, for instance."

"Well, I'd actually just meant why you wanted to jump to actually renting a new place when we both have apartments already. But I think the point about a bigger place with better views and the safety issue makes sense."

"I think it's silly to pretend to take this slow at this point. Don't you?"

"Have you ever lived with anyone before?"

"Other guys as roommates. Not a woman. I always figured it would happen when I found the right woman. And look. I was right."

She'd never admit it to him, but his utter self-assuredness was so attractive.

"I'm bitchy. I hate it when you leave beard hairs in my sink. I need space and time when I work. I work a lot. Edwina will stop by to check in because that's what she does. Nell will be over all the time too. I'll fill your fridge with goat cheese and salami. I drink coffee all day long and I'm not going to hide my tampons when the dot comes calling."

He laughed. "Is this supposed to deter me? You think I haven't ever seen a tampon before? I like Nell and William so her being here won't bug me. I'll ignore the goat cheese and remind you occasionally that salami is bad for you and that you drink too much coffee. I want you with me, Meriel. Tampons and coffee habit included."

He moved her. With just the smallest things, he made her feel desired and understood. Maybe this moving in thing could work. Her current lease was up in a month anyway. They'd sent her a note about signing a new agreement and she hadn't gotten around to it yet.

"Let me get dressed and we'll go look at the other place."

"I'll watch."

Chapter 23

MERIEL laid it all out for the governing council. The deaths, the disappearances, the intelligence they'd gathered.

She went item by item and laid it all out carefully. Knowing it was important to give them a sense of just how serious the entire situation was.

"To cap—we've got an organized group of Other-hating human separatists working with mages whose numbers also include turned witches. These mages are taking intel the witches give them and then they both manipulate the bigot humans to help them find us and kidnap us. There are incidents all over North America and it's not hard to imagine the numbers being far higher than we think now because plenty of people just up and leave town. If they were loners, who'd notice that they left and call the cops? And even then, we may not note this as an attack against a witch because that's not how any of the victims are being classified by the authorities."

"How many of these people are out there? What's the threat to us, really?" Sami asked.

It was a fair question. "There's no real reason to believe they're a contagion. Most witches don't turn. Most mages wouldn't be stupid enough to join with the very humans who'd turn on them if they knew their true nature. This isn't a DEFCON One sort of situation. Not yet."

"Weak prey is attractive prey." Dominic spoke up, looking ever so handsome in a three-piece pinstripe suit that made Meriel want to lick him. Well, to be fair, she just liked to lick him in general. But the suit worked.

"Are you saying we're prey?" Meriel knew it was Sami who had to be convinced. She came from a very long line of full-council witches. Being very powerful, she had little idea of what it felt like to be attacked or in fear. She believed in Clan Owen and thought any witch who chose to live outside a clan was foolhardy.

She was also intelligent and if Meriel could hit the right notes with her and win her support it would go a long way with others who might be sitting on the fence.

"So what's your plan then?" Abe asked, cutting through the chatter and urging everyone to stay on track.

"I've been working on opening up some diplomatic relations of a sort, with other groups of witches. It is my belief that having guests come here to learn defensive magickal techniques and having our witches go to other clan territories will help bring us all together."

"We have standards; I don't see why we should lower them simply to protect witches who've rejected what we are." Sami shrugged.

"I don't think it lowers our standards to combine forces against an enemy who has been hunting us. I'm not suggesting we break the clan. I'm suggesting we stop pretending other witches don't exist if they cast bones instead of working spells in other ways. I don't see how that can do anything but strengthen us."

"Why should we help anyone outside a clan?"

Meriel looked around the table and then back to Sami. "For me, the answer is very simple. But you'll have to ask and answer that yourself. We were born with these gifts. We are powerful and united. A clan makes us even stronger. The very land we tread on protects us. This is important.

It's why I don't fear for our witches the same way I do for others. But I think ignoring our brothers and sisters outside the clans is a repudiation of what we stand for just as certainly as those who mean us harm. And I think it's a bad idea to let them develop a taste for our magick any more than they have. I'm not willing to accept the constant threat of these mages showing up to harm our people."

Dominic nodded. "I grew up outside a clan. This isn't a secret. I've learned more about my magick since I've been with Meriel than in my entire life before I met her. Meriel didn't make me join. She shared her knowledge with me and brought me into this clan because of that. I saw the value. I saw the importance of what she was doing. And if you turn your back on outclan witches, you're only underlining that clans only care for themselves and would coerce instead of seek those new members who join freely. Show them how you are. Open your doors, let them get training, listen to what they might teach you and *everyone* is safer. It doesn't degrade what you are to lead. It's part of why Owen holds so much power. Isn't it? I think the real question, Sami, is why *shouldn't* we help all witches by offering to teach them?"

"If I may speak." Nell stood, waiting for permission to say anything else.

Edwina granted it.

"Gage just returned from Rhode Island where he was given access to all files about these mages who were caught as well as taught several defensive magicks that would do everything from repel an attack to striking down a foe. We benefit from that already, don't we? Meriel and her committee have arranged training courses on a monthly basis. Gage has taught me these spells, and yes, one of them includes blood, but it's the caster's blood and it's not mandatory to learn if this is a problem for any witch personally. In turn I've already taught my entire staff. They'll be teachers now."

Meriel nodded. "We can teach and be taught. We can keep ourselves safe but also offer that safety to others. And if they come to us, that makes us stronger. If they decide to create a clan of their own, this also makes us all stronger.

Even if they continue along alone, we've made them safer and they'll remember that."

Nell smoothly came back into the discussion. "Training of all Owen witches has begun. Gennessee will be sending some of their people as well. I met with Lark this week. She's already putting a plan in place."

Edwina took notes for a few moments and looked up again. "We'll be seeing this training go live when?"

"As Nell touched on, we've begun training already with our own witches. The first two classes filled up within a day. The training isn't overly difficult. It's just old-school defensive arts we haven't used in a very long time. We can do this pretty quickly and pretty efficiently and then, if it works like I hope, I'd propose that we begin teaching our youth as part of their catechism. If we make this a normal part of our array of spellwork, we won't need all these workshops on more than occasional level. As you know, we're giving workshops for our investigative and lawkeeping staff. Essentially most of us will have more tools for defense in a relatively short time. And it'll be part of our system, which makes it automatic.

"Just to be totally up front, it's my aim to equip all our witches from the earliest ages to defend and repel an attack by these mages. We either live in fear or learn how to deal with the threats ourselves. If we do it enough, they'll leave most of us alone. That won't protect everyone, but it's easier to protect a smaller group."

The council took a vote and unanimously decided to support the trainings and the cross-training with other groups on a trial basis. Meriel would be in charge of making sure nothing any outsider was exposed to was of a clan-only nature.

"I've another matter," Dominic spoke as Meriel was putting her cap back on her pen.

"Yes?" Edwina made a continue motion with her hand.

"Some of you may have heard that my biological mother may be involved with some of these mages. I wanted you to feel free to ask me any questions you might have to address anything you might be bothered by."

Of course if anyone gave him any trouble, she'd take care

of that right away. Not that she was biased or protective or anything.

A few people asked but thankfully no one accused or seemed to view him with suspicion. Probably in large part because Edwina had so publically thrown her support behind Dominic. Meriel would never forget that.

As the meeting had adjourned, Nell stopped Meriel. "I think I found her."

"I should call her myself." Dominic groused.

Meriel took a deep breath and looked to Nell. Nell had found a phone number that may or may not belong to Gloria Ochoa. Between what Rodas told them and her own investigative work, Nell had compiled quite the dossier on the woman.

"Don't look at me." Nell shrugged.

"I should call her myself," he repeated. "This is my mother."

"Do you still hold out hope she's innocent in all this?" Meriel tried to keep the question neutral.

"No. I don't. I think she's part of it. How much I don't know, but it looks pretty damning for her."

"Why don't you call her on your own? I mean, you can do it here and now, but as Dominic her son." Nell sipped her tea.

"Because I'm not just speaking as her son. This is my clan too. Shit." He burst from his chair and began to pace. "I don't need my woman to do my dirty work."

Meriel only looked at him, letting him get it all out.

"Why don't we go home? Hm? You have to be at Heart of Darkness in a few hours. You haven't had dinner yet."

He paused and sighed, knowing she was soothing him but not caring. "You're coddling me."

She shrugged.

"All right. Call her. You call her now and we'll go home. I'll call her too if I decide to."

Meriel waited for him to change his mind but he didn't.

She dialed the number and got the voice mail. Logically, she knew it wasn't necessarily Gloria. But she didn't need that. Her magick was going off in her belly like sparks.

When the brief message ended, Meriel began to speak. "I'm calling for Gloria Ochoa. My name is Meriel Owen and I believe you and I have a little problem. It seems you might be under the misapprehension that you're allowed to come onto our earth and harm my family. This is, of course, untrue. In fact, I'd like to have a discussion with you about these issues." She gave her number for callback and hung up.

Nell snorted. "I know it was foolish to hope she'd have a voice mail recording that identified her as Gloria Ochoa. You did well. If it's her, she'll call back. She'll use this number and I have an awesome new spell to work with the trace program. It unravels confusion spells. Arel, the hunter at Rodas, showed Gage. It's awesome."

Meriel nodded. "Good."

"You didn't tell her you and I were bonded," Dominic pointed out.

"I don't know if she knows you're dead or alive and I have no plans to aid her in figuring it out."

"You don't think she's going to stay away, anyway. Do you?"

"No. I think your mother knows you're alive. And I think it was her in my building."

It was Nell's turn to explode from her chair. "What? What? Why didn't you tell me this before? How do you know?"

"William will kill me if you get all worked up and you go home to him all grouchy. Sit down. When we used that spell to boost our othersight in my building yesterday, it stripped back some of the other things we see in regular othersight. I can see Dominic's energy right now. Yours too and the baby. In addition to marking you as witches, there are marks, you know what I mean. Little things that identify the person. I missed it when we were there yesterday since everyone got so excited. But when I went back over there today I used normal othersight at first, just without thinking. And the smudge in my hallway had a lot of the same markers Dominic has. What are the odds it's not her? It's just a feeling."

"That's not just a feeling. You have some reason to feel it." Nell ran her fingers through her hair, making it stand on end. Automatically, Meriel reached out to pat it down and the two women paused to grin at each other.

"If you two ever feel the need to kiss, you know just to get on with the friend thing, you should feel free." Dominic winked and Meriel laughed. "As for the other? I think Nell's right. It could be a coincidence. But how many coincidences can there be before we just accept what's going on? Also, I'm really pissed you didn't tell me."

"I didn't connect it right away. It wasn't until about half an hour ago that it clicked. It was bothering me, but I didn't know why. Sometimes I do that, you know. My brain sort of takes over thinking about stuff in the background and I don't notice until the lightbulb moment. And I still don't know. Not for sure."

"If that's her, she'll call back. Especially if that was her in your building. She'll have to, just to rub your nose in it. I say we don't need to mention the Dominic-is-your-son thing unless she already knows. Why should we expose Dom to that if he doesn't have to be? Also, it might make her worse."

Meriel liked that Nell was protective of Dominic, that they'd all made friends. It would have sucked if one of them hadn't liked the other's man.

"Well, you guys go on. I've got your building on our watch list. My staff does a drive-by several times a day. Sometimes at random they'll go in and check things out. Now that we've got this new othersight Meriel learned, we'll add that. It should help a lot. And of course you'll still be accompanied by a guard when you're at work and out and about."

Meriel hugged Nell before kissing her cheek. "You doing all right?"

"So far so good. No morning sickness for a week or two. I sleep a lot but that's okay. When I wake up, William is there with a cup of tea and some snuggles. He takes care of me." She blushed, shrugging.

"Of course he does. Why don't we all go out together? We'll walk you to your car."

Dominic held two elbows out, Meriel took one and Nell the other.

Chapter 24

DOMINIC watched the bar. Something wasn't right and it didn't set well with him. It was most likely all this business with his mother had put him on edge. Simon prowled around keeping the women entertained. Which was nice as obviously he couldn't anymore, even if he wanted to. Meriel was not the kind of woman who'd find it cute that he let anyone rub up on him. She'd probably maim him for it.

He grinned.

She'd taken to stopping in on the weekend nights and hanging out with him. He knew she wasn't much for club hopping and she was also an early riser, but it pleased him that she made room in her life for him and what made him happy too. He liked seeing her at his table with her laptop. Yes, she even did work there. Or enjoyed a drink with Simon or their friends.

He just liked that she wanted to be with him and that she did it in a way that felt natural. He was lucky. Despite all the nonsense with the mages, he was lucky to have this woman in his life.

Dominic examined the wards again and then opened up

his othersight to take the room in. So much magick here.
Others packed the place nightly. It was more than a nightclub;
it had turned into a sort of general hangout and meeting
place. He liked that too. Profits were up and he didn't have
the stress of thinking about what the clan would do when
they found him lifting from their font. He was proud. Heart
of Darkness felt like his in a way it hadn't until then.

He didn't need the extra help now. Between him and
Meriel, the warding was fine-tuned and powerful. He had
no need to borrow magick now that he knew how to use his
own. Admittedly he got a kick out of that.

The place continued to fill up as the evening wore on.
There were the usual problems. He had to threaten a table
of Weres to behave or be barred.

It was a waste of his time to have to stalk around to keep
people in line. He gave them this place and they couldn't
just act like they had some sense?

"Why is it so hot in here? Fix that," he barked at one of
the servers, who scampered off to take care of it.

He slugged back a few drinks and then switched to water.
His head hurt. He needed more sleep. But he wanted to be
with Meriel when he could. There were always others who'd
take up her time if he didn't claim it. Always someone who
couldn't seem to do it themselves so Meriel had to do it. Like
she was their mother. Stupid.

Dominic made a move to go back to his office but Simon
hailed him with a wave.

"There a problem?"

"It's hot. The DJ is fucking things up with this crap. I
know I told him I didn't want trance back here. Gets the
vampires all worked up. Plus it annoys me. Don't know why
I have to say things a hundred times to get it taken care of."

Simon looked at him closely. "Wards holding up?"

"Far as I can see. I used othersight and everything looks
okay there too. We've got some pissed-off Weres near the
bar, but I already told them they'd be barred if they didn't
keep it together. I can't have all this fighting here. That's

worse than worrying over this mage bullshit. Last thing I need are bar fights back here."

"You're on edge. I trust that. Something doesn't feel right."

And then she walked in, scanning the room until she found him. Her smile made his head feel a little better. But he didn't like the way men always looked at her.

"She's a pretty woman, you know that? Fresh and lovely. Always smells good. That witchy—"

"Do you think I want to hear you wax rhapsodic about my woman's smell?"

"Whatever. She smells good whether I tell you that or not."

"Simon!" She approached and patted Simon's arm. "I love that suit. You're looking very handsome."

"Me?"

Meriel turned to him. "You're handsome too."

He pulled her to his body and kissed her. He wanted everyone to see it and know she was spoken for.

Simon cocked his head. "Hey, I need to talk to you two. Office?"

Once the door was closed Simon turned, his arms crossed. "Someone is fucking with you."

Meriel nodded. "I agree."

"What?"

"You're on edge. Prowling around like a shifter. You're hyperaggressive. The magick is pouring off you."

Dominic only felt rage. "What the fuck? You saying I'm so weak I'd be manipulated by some spell?"

Meriel looked him up and down. "I can feel it. Through the bond. It has to be outside the club because I'd feel it if it was happening in here. The wards would sound with that kind of spell."

"You too?"

With an indignant sniff, she turned, kicked her shoes off and her hands began to dance as she spoke under her breath. Magick filled the room, made his own rise in response to join hers. That's when it felt like she grabbed a string and unraveled him. His stomach went into freefall and he held back a gag.

And then things got really weird.

She raised her voice, this time speaking aloud as she wove the spell. She tapped the font and shoved it all into Dominic so that he gagged with it. He held a hand out but she didn't stop. Instead she took it and squeezed.

Latin, yes, she was speaking Latin. He realized this as he warred to keep his consciousness and failed several times.

And then she was on her knees and his ears popped and he could hear clearly again.

He saw the red. "Blood?" He tried to stand, but dizziness made him stumble. Simon braced him and eased him into a chair.

"It's not yours. It's Meriel's."

His gaze shot to her and he found her pressing one of his handkerchiefs against her arm. "Did I hurt you?" He wanted to vomit.

Concern filled her eyes then and she came to him, kneeling and taking his hand. "No. Do you think you ever could? Really?"

"I don't know. Baby, Christ, what happened?"

"It was a possession spell. Someone was riding in your consciousness and trying to affect your behavior."

"Something was in me? And cut you?"

"I needed the blood to cast it out. It was ugly and powerful and not mage magic. It was darker than that."

"You cut yourself for me? How could you do that? You are not to put yourself in danger like that."

She waved it away. "I'll do what I need to and you can't stop me from protecting what's mine. Anyway, it's locked out. My blood mixed with the spell. The way is blocked."

"How can this have happened? I thought my magick was locked, that you can't be possessed . . . like demon possessed? Is that what the Latin was? Meriel, did you fucking exorcise me?" Sickness clawed at his insides.

"In a manner of speaking, yes. See what I mean about how we can learn from other kinds of practitioners?"

"Faith as magick?" Simon asked, handing her a bottle of water and then one to Dominic.

"Negative energy, no matter what you want to call it, can be affected by belief. The words hold power. I gave them intent."

"But I can't be demon possessed. I've done a lot of bad shit, but never dark magicks. Ever."

Her face washed into a blank mask and he knew it before she even spoke. "If someone is of your blood, they can do it if they're close enough. Siblings. Parents."

"You're telling me my mother just called a fucking demon into me? Like the guys who watch my front doors here?"

"No, not a demon. More precisely, I'm saying your mother was the bridge to let a very dark energy ride into you. It's not like you think. Your head won't go round three hundred and sixty degrees or anything. No levitating. But this dark chaos she let in can eat away at your foundations. At your boundaries and filters. Over time she could use you to be violent or other such things. She used her flesh-and-blood connection with you to let it in."

"Get it out of me. Now. Or take me to the middle of the forest and leave me. I can't be around you if I can't trust myself."

He felt unclean. What sort of people had he come from?

"Let's go home. I'm going to ask Gage's mother to come over. She's a healer of sorts and can help you flush the darkness out."

"No. Are you listening to me? Simon, take her to her parents' house right now."

"She can't get in again." Meriel got in his face, his shirt gripped in her hand. "Listen to me, Dominic. She *can't*. Nothing and no one else can. I'm there now. I cut off that bond to her. I cut it off and cauterized it and then I put my own energy there. She can't get in. You're not going to go anywhere but home with me."

"How do you know?" God, he couldn't bear it, couldn't bear to think on hurting her. How could she ever trust him again? Would she be scared of him forever?

"Because it's my spell and your mother is a punk-ass bitch in the magick department. Oh, that's right." Meriel was pissed off, he realized. Not upset with him, not afraid of him at all. But murderously pissed off at Gloria Ochoa.

Simon eased back and sat on the corner of the desk as they settled in to watch Meriel.

"I got her number. She's a fucking amateur wearing a costume of a powerful witch. She will not get in because you are mine and that is that. She can't best me. Not ever. I am badass, Dominic. I know most people don't know it, but you better believe it. I will tear her apart when I find her. You can bet on that. I. Am. Not. Having. This."

He exhaled long and hard and took her in.

Magnificent.

Glorious.

Righteous.

"I am stupid in love with you." He moved to her, putting his arms around her. Their magick flared and flowed into the room again. It felt good to be back in synch.

Her rage faded as she smiled sort of crookedly at him. "You love me?"

"Ah, I should go now." Simon stood.

Startled into remembering Simon's presence, she straightened. "We're going to go home." Meriel pulled her phone out and called Gage's mother about coming over.

The way she gave orders was ruthlessly precise. She was putting a plan together. She might wear novelty socks and know all the words to *Grease*, but she did things with a purpose. Gloria had issued a challenge. And Meriel would answer that. But she'd do so only after she had considered every option and mapped out every single factor. His woman would understand and be prepared to beat every possible attack.

"You all right?" Simon asked.

"Yeah. I just . . . she made it okay. It was like I was far

away and then she was there pulling me back to shore. Watching her right now, I'm just struck by how truly lucky I am."

"She's right, you know. Gloria can't get in again. You were out of it for a while when Meriel was doing the spell. I've never seen magick like that. She reflected what your mother was putting out to keep the bridge open and then she stole it. Like yanked it out of her. Whipcrack. And it's over. Epic witchery. I am impressed as hell."

"I wish I'd have seen it. Nell's going to ask me about it, so can I have her call you so you can describe what Meriel did?"

"Sure."

Meriel approached and tucked her hand in his. "Come on. She's on her way. Nell's coming here. My mother will most likely also be at our apartment too." She put her head on his shoulder.

"You need to go home. She's right. I'm just fine here on my own. You've already been here most of the night." He turned to Meriel. "Will you call me to check in once he's settled?"

"Of course. Thanks for your help tonight."

"Anytime, sweetheart. You were indeed badass. Now let's get you to your car. I'll feel better if I go with you. Unless you think there's going to be a problem here?" He looked to Meriel again.

"The club'll be fine. She didn't break the wards; her magick came in another way. I was stupid to not have thought of it. But she can't get in again. This is her way of testing to see if her hunch was true. If her son was alive, she'd be able to test that. One way or another she'd know. And now she does."

"What a vicious bitch." Simon walked them to the back where her car was waiting.

"Yes. Watch your back, Simon. Any hit at all on the wards and you go to safe mode." They had contingencies for all kinds of potential problems. Safe mode would alert the security company. Only it was a special kind of security company made up of Others. Usually witches working with Weres. Nice to have the magick and the muscles.

Meriel got him up to their apartment. Gage's mom was waiting, along with her parents and Gage. She nearly lost it when she saw them, but managed to hold it back.

"Let's get him cleaned up first." Gage's mother got right to work, rolling up her sleeves. "I have some soap in my bag." She thrust it at Meriel. "Use it on him from head to toe. I'll get the bedroom ready."

Her father smiled and patted Dominic on the back. "You look damned good. My girl protected you." He kissed Meriel's cheek. "You did well."

"I'm going to go over these wards again," Edwina called out. "Do you want Gage to take him in, Meriel? He's got to be heavy. It won't do if one of you slips and falls."

Meriel choked back a sob and nodded quickly, clearing her throat. "I'm fine. He's steady on his feet. I'll yell if we need help."

She pointed at the toilet where she'd just put the seat down. "Sit."

A knock sounded on the door and Gage handed Dominic a mug of something. "Hold your nose and drink it fast. It'll be over soon and you'll feel better."

"You speak from experience?" Dominic, amused, asked Gage.

"Enough to know how to keep from gagging on it. This is a system cleanse of sorts. It's got all kinds of crap she grows and picks and then says spells over. It works, if that helps at all."

Meriel had had that crap when she was in high school. They'd been in a car accident and the smoke had been horrible. They'd been relatively uninjured but the smoke from the car fire had blown in their faces as they'd waited for the cops and aid cars. That stuff had cleared the gunk out, but she felt every damned minute of it. Blech. But it did really work, she agreed with Gage.

He drank it and she caught the shudder.

"He didn't lie."

She laughed. It was brittle. She heard it herself. Quickly, she stripped him down and then herself and took him into the shower. The goop smelled good. Clean and right. She had to stretch to reach him all, but he bent and let her get his hair. She let go for the moment, just reveling in being able to touch him that way. The water pounded on him and she kneaded and caressed, scrubbed and stroked from head to toe. Her magick had softened and warmed. It flowed from her and around him. Healing. Loving. Connecting.

The block of fear she'd been choking on since she'd left Heart of Darkness and began to really think about how much they could have lost began to melt away. Helpless in the face of the love she felt for this man. She hadn't told him she loved him back when they'd been at Heart of Darkness; the situation had shifted and it hadn't felt like the right time with Simon there.

But here between them she could show him.

"Wow," he murmured as he stepped out some minutes later. "That was amazing. I feel so good. Taken care of. But that doesn't really do it justice. You make me feel like I can come home and be safe. Be loved. Thank you for being my safe place. Tonight it was you, Meriel. You snapped me out of it. You fought some sort of major magickal battle with my mother and a dark spirit and you haven't broken a sweat."

"I love you too." She leaned in to press her face to his neck. Warm and vibrant. He was alive and he was fine and everything would be all right. Gloria couldn't have him. She'd see to that.

"I might have sweated a little bit. But that'll be our secret."

Chapter 25

HOURS later, she closed the door after the last visitor left. Dominic had been tucked into bed under a very deep sleep spell her mother had cast. He needed the rest so his system could heal.

She tossed herself on the couch next to Nell. "You need to go home."

"William is coming to pick me up. Gage has my car. Anyway, I need to talk to you. Are you all right?"

Finally, after everyone had gone it was finally safe to let it go so she just turned and buried her face in her hands and let it go. Nell rubbed a hand up and down her back, not saying anything, just letting Meriel get all the tears out.

She cried until she got the hiccups and then slowly pulled herself back together again.

"She knows he's alive. I think we should be expecting a call very soon." Meriel tapped her knee. "But the good news is, she's weak. Her magic is hollow, brittle in places. I don't know how she's made it this far. But I will make sure she doesn't do it again."

"We'll make sure. Leave the hunting to the hunter please.

And don't assume she's the only turned witch working with these mages either. You're what they call a high-value target, Meriel, don't forget that. You're like the big bank job or whatever."

"Pfft. She tried to take him from me. She tried to take his will."

"We'll get her."

"He thinks he was weak because of what happened. But he was so strong. What she did would have taken over a weak man inside ten minutes. From what I can tell it had been cast at least two hours and all it had really done was make him aggressive. His defensive magick was working even though he had no idea. I'm the one who was weak. I didn't even think about possession. It's my job and I failed."

"Really? Well, forgive me for thinking you saved him. I'm sorry you seem to think you need to be omniscient. Even Edwina isn't all knowing, sister."

"It's my job to know."

"You did your job. You can't possibly think of every single outcome of every single thing. Even *you* can't do it. No one can. Anyway, are you going to let this low-rent bitch ruffle you? Girl, you beat her. Over and over."

This made her feel infinitely better, as she knew would happen when she laid it all out for Nell. "I have her taste now. I *know* Gloria Ochoa. That was a big mistake on her part. Now I can find her easier and remove this problem for good."

"She's gonna be calling you. You know that, right?"

"Looking forward to it. My best guess is she'll be on my phone at work bright and early. And I'll be waiting."

"Good. There's my girl." Nell's grin was vicious. "Calls will ring in here like we talked about. I talked to Simon. He told me you were amazing with Dom, said your skills were off the charts. You used the Latin exorcism rites? That's pretty Hollywood."

"Once I got inside him I could see what it was. It just came to me to try it. Seemed to me that sometimes holy men and women are shamans in a sense, their rites and rituals have meaning too, so I gave them intent. Worked out." She let out a long breath.

She could do this. She *would* do this.

William showed up at the door. He gave Meriel a hug and went to Nell. "I'm here to collect my wife."

Nell smiled up at him. "Hello there."

He shook his head. "Is everything all right?"

"It is. I was just giving Meriel an update. Dominic is sleeping. He'll be fine. No lasting effects. In fact he'll come out of this stronger, Meriel's mother said."

William helped Nell into her coat and they headed out. "I'll be back tomorrow morning. First thing. You can work from here, I get that. But I want to be here if she calls."

"Fine. Just please rest. If she calls before you get here, you're only a few minutes away."

DOMINIC woke feeling better than he had in a few days. Refreshed even.

Her side of the bed was still warm and the scent of coffee filled the air. Meriel was there and awake. He rolled to stand and stretch and when he turned, she was standing in the doorway, smiling.

"How are you feeling this morning?"

"Better now." He pulled her into a hug. "Damn, you feel good."

She tipped her head up to look him in the face. "Coffee and some breakfast can be had if you're up to it."

"I figured I'd have to scrub the goop off. But it's gone."

"Gage's mom said it would soak into the skin. You smell good. Clean and fresh."

"Well, that's a plus to having your friend's mom rubbing goo all over you. Don't know that I'll be looking her in the eye anytime soon."

She laughed. "Come on out then. I'll make you something to eat."

"Meriel?" He caught her hand in his.

"Mm?"

"I love you."

Her smile widened. "I love you too."

He followed her out and settled in at the table. "So tell me. Fill me in."

"You sure you want that first thing? Before you even eat?"

"I can do both. Do you mean to tell me you went to bed right when I did and only woke up five minutes ago?" He looked toward the spare room where she'd set up her office.

"My body clock wakes me up at five. No matter how much I try to sleep in. She's going to call today. I want to be ready." She began to pull a breakfast together and he watched, content to have her there.

"Nell will be by in about half an hour so you'll need pants or she might die from how sexy you look with no shirt and those snug boxer briefs hugging your butt and your package."

"I'm flattered that you think she'd notice any man but William."

"Puhleeze. He's handsome and sexy and all that. But he's no Dominic Bright. Also, a girl can look. Doesn't mean she's gonna touch."

"You'd break her fingers if she did."

Her smile brightened as she put some toast and eggs in front of him. "Yes, and other parts of you if I thought you enjoyed it."

"Come sit with me, my pretty, vicious witch."

She kissed him before putting the Tabasco out and sitting with him.

"I'm going to work from here today. My phone will be forwarded here. Nell has the hardware already set up so when the call comes in a trace will start. She's also got that spell to break through any confusion spells Gloria tries to use." She looked at her watch. "And once we've got that, Nell will plan to bring her in. She's a possible way into this group of mages here in Seattle. Let's hope she's a weak enough link to lead us straight to them. We've got her in my hallway and in the same cities where witches have disappeared. She's with them, I know it."

"I want to say up front that even before last night I knew

Gloria was too far gone. It's not just what she did to me, it's the way you were risked too. Don't think I didn't hear your mother ask you all those questions."

Edwina had interrogated Meriel while searching her for any signs of damage. Plunging into someone's magick while they were being possessed was dangerous in and of itself.

"Then you heard her say I was just fine."

"No. I heard her say she was proud of you and that she thought you showed cunning and skill."

Meriel blushed. "Yeah. That part was cool." She hugged her cup and then looked to him. "I will always risk everything to save you."

He let out a long breath. "Yeah. Right back atcha."

He took a shower and did some of his own work. Nell showed up and gave him an impromptu magick lesson, which he appreciated. And, he had to admit, it made him feel totally that he was all right. Nell wouldn't have trusted him to learn anything from her if she thought he was weak or tainted in some way.

So much pent-up energy was the impetus to working out at home. He usually liked to go to the gym, just to get away, but he didn't want to miss it when Gloria called.

MOUTH suddenly dry, Meriel sat at the desk, body turned sideways so she could watch Dominic do pull-ups in the door frame across the hall. Wide, muscular shoulders gleaming with sweat, muscles trembling with exertion. His tattoo looked nearly alive as he moved.

She'd work from home a lot more often if this was what her view would be.

And then it came in.

Nell walked in calmly, talking to Gage back at the office. Dominic, moved to her side, pulling a T-shirt on and sitting on the corner of the desk. When Nell gave Meriel the thumbs-up, she answered.

"Meriel Owen."

"Ah, my daughter-in-law." Which answered the question as to whether or not Gloria knew about Dominic.

She knew her lip curled at the sound of Gloria's voice. "Cut the shit." Meriel wanted to punch this woman's face.

"Oh, the manners on young people today. Is my son around?"

"You should know the answer to that after your ass was handed to you last night."

"I'd say I didn't know what you were talking about, but now you understand I'm not to be trifled with."

"Fuck you, lady. I'm going to explain this to you once. And I'm only giving you this because you're responsible for making the man I love and he's the best thing you'll ever do. I know who you are. I know what you do. And I will end you."

"And what does my son think about this?"

"You don't get to talk about him as if you had anything more to do with his existence than gestating him. Lucky for him he was raised far away from the likes of you."

Dominic put his hand on her knee and she calmed a little.

"I can easily move my business elsewhere. Given some incentive of course, because moving costs money. So, here's what you're going to do. You're going to be sure to deposit two hundred thousand dollars into my account by midnight tonight. And then you'll be sure I receive the same sum quarterly. *And* you'll give me access to your font."

She laughed, but there was no mirth there. "Even if I wanted to do that, it wouldn't work. The font wouldn't recognize an abomination like you. You're not a witch anymore. You're cut off from your gifts. You can't tap the font. Are you really so stupid you never knew this?"

Silence from the other end as Gloria thought. Of course it occurred to Meriel she'd just given them information they hadn't had. Then again, it would solve at least the problem of them thinking they could take the font over.

Nell rolled her eyes, but made the *keep-it-going* motion with her hand.

"How can I trust what you're saying is true? If you let us access the font, we'd have to . . . *supplement* our diet far less."

"The font only recognizes a connection from a witch, dumbass. And you're not. You've been turned for a long time. As for how you know I'm not lying? Well, first, I'm not you."

"Fine. Then make it three hundred thousand a quarter."

"No. I don't pay the trash to be taken out. I take it out myself."

"You can pay me to keep my mouth shut. Or, you can take your chances and hope I'm not feeling talkative and find the need to go to the press to tell them about this world you've all been hiding for so very long."

"If you think you'd make it long enough to do that, go on ahead."

Nell looked up, holding out three fingers. Just keep her on longer.

"Or maybe I'll come to visit my son. See about mending some fences. Boys need a mother. I can't imagine why you'd try to keep us apart. Does he know this about you? You're very jealous. He's handsome, my boy. Without the bond, would he even have looked at you twice?"

Dominic's gaze narrowed, his handsome face hardening. He shook his head and reached for the phone but she patted his hand and shook her head right back. As if she'd believe that crap anyway.

Meriel laughed because she couldn't help it. "You're dialing the wrong number. And it doesn't matter anyway. I'd protect him no matter what. He's everything to me. My people are everything to me. You can't have them, or Dominic. It's your biggest mistake that you tried. All you're going to get from me and my clan is misery. You declared war on us last night when you played with dark forces and used them on one of my witches. You clearly have a lot to learn about clans. I'm going to enjoy teaching you."

"You sound almost strong enough to do it. But I've been around the block a few times."

"I bet. But this isn't a contest to see who aged worse, is it?"

"Oh, you think you're so clever. We'll see how clever you

are when I drain you. When your magick keeps my belly full. With my son at my side, imagine the feast I'll have. I'll destroy your precious clan witch by witch. You'll keep me fed for a long time."

She was making such a mistake to peg Meriel as an easy mark. But fine, that would only serve Meriel in the end.

"Being turned makes you crazy too, I see. You have nothing. You are no one. You don't scare me. I *know* you, Gloria. Do you know what that means? Last night I saw into the heart of your power and you are a shell. Empty. You work with stolen power. Stolen power won't ever be stronger than what I've got in my belly. I tasted what you're made of. I'm not impressed."

Dominic sighed and raised a brow at her.

"You and your precious font and your clan. What do you know about struggling? About working for anything?"

"Focus, Gloria. Why is it you're mad again?"

"We'll see how smug you are when I go to the press and expose you."

Dominic leaned forward. "And how will your friends the human-only separatists feel when they know you're a paranormal too? If you do that, you only expose yourself . . . Gloria."

His voice was wrapped with so much violence it sent a shiver through her. They hadn't known for absolute sure Gloria *was* working with the humans. Simply taunting Gloria into revealing all her plans seemed too easy, but Gloria wasn't working on all cylinders and had already given them more information than Meriel had thought she'd expose.

Nell held out five fingers. Just a bit more to go.

But she didn't deny it. Which answered that question. "Oh, is that you, Eduardo? My baby boy."

"I'm not your baby boy. And my name is Dominic. My father gave it to me. He says hey."

"I don't think he can."

Meriel felt sick. Gloria meant Felix, who she obviously knew was dead. Because she'd helped kill him. Not that he'd been anything less than a villain by that point too.

Dominic laughed and it made the hair on the back of Meriel's neck stand up.

"I said my *father* gave it to me. Not my biological donor. The man who raised me. But back to your threat about going public and your buddies the human separatists. I'm not sure who's worse, but I know they'd get a fairer shake in the court of public opinion than an old, shot-out hag of a turned witch with no power and a giant drug habit. You think you can control them when this gets out?"

"They're stupid, but useful."

Nell's gaze darkened, her mouth hardened. Gloria had just admitted she was part of this plan.

Meriel decided to poke at her some more. "I imagine they'd be more useful if you had a *plan* instead of just rolling into town draining a few witches and going away."

Nell nodded, giving her the keep going with that motion of her hand.

"You don't know who you're dealing with. Until a few years ago, they were uselessly attacking Others. The odd hunting and killing of a Were. Vampire stakings. And then there was a story about how one of these silly groups had caught themselves a witch and wanted to kill her. I was nearby and stopped in."

The phone was silent for a few moments and Meriel wondered if she'd hung up. But no, she came back on the line. Talkative woman, Gloria Ochoa. Meriel would be pleased to use that against her.

"Sorry about that interruption. I'll tell you more when we meet. Then I can teach you my lovely ritual and introduce you to some mages who'd love to play with you awhile. Some of them even have bounties on the heads of clans. I'll be sure to point them in your direction. You can't win. I'm too powerful."

She would eat this bitch for breakfast. And she'd smile as she did it.

"First I'll kill your mother. She's the icing on the cake. Oh, I'll be so powerful after that. Then I'll let them drain you partially, but I have better plans for you. A ritual I've found to be very effective."

"Oh, I'd pay money to see that." Meriel laughed. "Not in a million years are you half the powerhouse my mother is. But I'd love to see her rip you to shreds and then curl her lip at the mess on her shoes. But I'm growing super bored with this back-and-forth smack talk. I have a job, so if you're done?"

"I'll drain you slow. Feast on your fear and pain. And then I'll kill you. Afterward, I'll take Dominic. Maybe I'll keep him around if he's useful. Pretty bait for witches I'd wager."

She also didn't seem to understand just what a bond was. Which was good too.

Nell gave her the thumbs-up that they'd unraveled the confusion spell and had traced the call. They knew where she was.

"You've been warned, Gloria Ochoa. There is a warrant for your death in all our territories. You can't have Dominic."

Meriel hung up.

Chapter 26

NELL had left and Meriel came back inside to find Dominic hanging up the phone. "We can move into the new place at the beginning of the month."

They'd chosen the apartment open in this building. Ron had already volunteered to help with the warding, not just of the apartment but of the hallways too.

"But I turned it down."

"What? Why?"

"I think we need a house. I want a house. I like it here in downtown, but being at Tom's reminded me how much I like living near water. I want to buy a house with you. I don't want to worry about how loud I'm being and I don't want to hear people walking above me all the time."

"You want roots? With me?"

He moved to her and swept her up into his arms. "Yes. I want to build a life here with you. In our house where we'll raise our family. What do you think?"

"I think I can manage to like that. I think I can suffer through waking up next to you for the next six decades or so."

"When I'm with you like this, I can sort of see the appeal

of a magick addiction. You make me drunk on your magick."
He breathed in deep at her neck and walked her backward
until her back met the door.

"Here I am again, Dominic, backed against a door while
you have your way with me."

He kissed her just behind her jaw and if she hadn't been
pinned to the wall like a butterfly in a case, her knees would
have buckled at the shocking pleasure of the heat of his
tongue and the scrape of his teeth where her skin was so
achingly sensitive.

He was so good to her. Every touch telegraphed just how
much he wanted her. Rough, yes. Hard, yes. But his touch
never hurt, was never aimed to harm her in any way.

He needed her so much she often saw the strain in how
he held back. It filled her up in the best kind of way, this man.

This man she wanted as much as she wanted him in return.
She managed to break free and fall to her knees, looking up
at him while she unzipped his jeans and pulled his cock out.

Dominic groaned at the sight of her there, so raw and
carnal, on her knees, a hand on his cock as she licked her lips.

It was he who had to lean against the wall for a change
as he placed his palms against the door and looked down at
her. At this beauty who'd come into his life without warning
and had turned everything he knew upside down.

He groaned when she took him into her mouth and then
was lost to her and the way she knew what he needed and
how he needed it. There was no ugliness between them and
what was around them they'd overcome.

So close, she took him so close with the heat and wet of
her mouth. He had other plans though, so he had to force
himself to pull her back as he got so very close to the edge.
"Couch. Bend over it. Panties down."

Her eyes widened and a flush rose up her neck. He
couldn't resist such a response and cupped the back of her
neck to take her mouth again.

Her hum of satisfaction was sweet and spicy all at once.
But her squeal of surprise when he got them to the couch and
spun her, bending her forward, shot through his system like a

pinball. When she made those sounds, when she gave herself over to him and his pleasure the way she did, it undid him.

His usually chic and elegant woman was bent over a couch. Bare-assed. Her normally tidy hairdo had come loose, freed to tousle around her face.

Her beautiful face he caught glimpses of as he began to thrust. The curve of her cheek, or the pink of her lip caught against her teeth.

This was no long, sensual lovemaking session. He needed her with an intense greed. Needed to reconnect with her on this level. His system screamed for more, faster, harder, more more more. And when he reached around her body to touch her clit and drive her toward climax, she squirmed back against him in entreaty.

And he gave her what she wanted. And took what he needed as they both hurtled into climax.

This was part of what they were together. Meriel made his blood sing, made his magick rise, made him hard and short of breath.

This was everything.

MERIEL got into the office later that afternoon feeling remarkably relaxed despite three hours' sleep, a harrowing experience with a turned witch and a lot of anger and heartache aimed in their general direction.

And yet she was totally certain that she and Dominic would be all right.

Her mother tapped on Meriel's door an hour or so after she'd arrived. "I trust you're well?"

She nodded. "Dominic is good. He's hanging out with Tom, who showed up on our doorstep about half an hour before I came here. Thank you. For last night. I appreciate that you came over and that you looked over our wards too. And I'm sorry for letting you down. I didn't do my job."

Edwina came in and closed the door before sitting down. "What is it you mean?"

"I should have known and been prepared for that possession. It was an amateur mistake. You expect better from me."

"I didn't think of it either. It's far outside the norm. You didn't anticipate some sort of arcane dark arts. You're not perfect." Edwina raised a shoulder. "You've shown true leadership during this whole thing. *You* brought the issue of these mages to me. *You* brought the issue of sharing information between other groups of witches. You sensed a need and moved to fill it even before things became so much clearer. That's leadership, Meriel. I won't hear you denigrate my judgment. And as my judgment finds you worthy, you must do the same."

She sat back and pulled a flick of lint from her skirt and dared Meriel to argue.

Edwina started to speak several times and then would fall silent again. Finally she took a deep breath. "I may not have been the best mother in the world, but what she did to him yesterday—what she's done her whole life is not acceptable. We will take care of this because he's our witch, and your man. But, I'd like to counsel you to let Dominic take the lead when it comes to dispatching her. He needs to do this to exorcise any doubts he might have that she could still get in."

Meriel twisted her bracelets as she thought on it. Her mother was right. Dominic was a guy used to handling his own business and Gloria wanted to destroy that.

"He's already told me this. But thank you for saying it. Aside from putting this ghost to rest, he's a tough guy. This is his arena more than it's mine." She trusted his skills and she'd be there in the background if he needed the help or if there was some unforeseen problem. But it would be his to deal with.

"Good. Nell briefed me on the call as well. Vile, vile woman. I heard the recording. Thank you for your defense of my skills." Her mother smiled.

"Well, really, did she think I'd let my boyfriend's mom talk bad about you?"

Edwina stood. "Yes. Well. If she comes at me and Dominic isn't around, it will be my great pleasure to underline everything you said. This is our clan and you're doing all you're supposed to and more to protect it. I believe that. The quorum believes that. Your witches believe that. When you take over, you'll do it with everyone knowing how powerful and capable you are."

She opened the door. "Keep me apprised. By the way, you are forbidden to hare off after this woman if she contacts you. She's got mages with her and these humans too. You can best her magic, but a bullet can kill you either way. Don't risk yourself. You have more important things in your future."

Well. Okay then.

TOM answered the phone at the house when she called to check in on Dominic.

She smiled though it was a phone call and he couldn't see it anyway. "Hey there. You settling in all right?"

"Yes, thanks. I'm making dinner. Pot roast okay with you?"

"Is that a trick question?"

He laughed. "Good to know you like it. If you're looking for Dominic, he went over to Heart of Darkness to handle deliveries."

She frowned. "He was all right to do that?"

"He's a strong man, Meriel. A strong witch. He needs to do this. He's been attacked *twice* in his business. That's his ground. He has to claim it."

Boys.

"All right. I have to run. I just wanted to check in. Do you need me to bring anything home? Does Ernie need food?" Tom brought the cat with him.

"Nah, we're good. I brought some along. I don't know how long I'll be here. It's just . . . my gut said to come and after that call about Dominic last night, I knew it's what I needed to do."

She breathed out. "I'm going to be a happy camper when this is over and I can go back to my normal level of insanity. I'll see you in a while."

*   *   *

DOMINIC walked all over Heart of Darkness. Both floors of the human club, up and over the catwalk. Down and through the back. Behind the bar. Under tables, over the stage. Down the back hall and through his office and Simon's. The walk-in coolers and the supply room. Even through the kitchen and out back on the loading dock and the lot back there.

Everything was exactly the way it should have been. The place was locked down tight against any magick but his, Meriel's and Nell's. Nell had done some sort of limiting spell for other kinds of magick; apparently it was whatever this club in Las Vegas had done and from what Dominic could see, it would work just fine. Nell had explained it was the same sort of spell Arel and the people from Rodas used in their cells to keep the witches and mages they had in custody from using any magick or magic at all. Not to escape or try to harm anyone. A sort of nullification spell. She'd promised to show him how to use it when all this mess had ended.

He set up in the center of the club. Placing everything he'd need carefully nearby so he'd get to it easily when he needed it. On his knees in the circle he'd invoked, he began the rite. Purification of soul and of heart. Purification of this place. He needed to make it his again. He'd gone through the archives available online and thanked the folks down in research for being so good at their jobs.

The magick flowed through him as he worked and he felt each part of Heart of Darkness respond to him. This wasn't just his place of business, this was his future and a big middle finger to his past. This was *his* place and no one was going to take it from him.

When he stood and blew out the candle he felt a connection to the physical space around him that he hadn't before. The magick of the club, all the energy it was filled with nightly was a sort of lifeblood and it responded to Dominic's magick and his will.

By the time he finished up and started home, he felt not only better but completely in charge again.

Tom had of course cooked an amazing meal. The smell when he opened the front door made his stomach growl immediately.

TOM peeked around the corner, a book in his hand. "It's you. I was wondering who'd get home first."

"Meriel's not back yet?" He looked at his watch.

"She said she'd be home a little after six. Dinner'll be ready at seven or so. I figured that'd give everyone a chance to get home and clean up."

"She's a machine. I'll call her."

She was all right. One of the things he liked best about the bond was that he could feel it when she was upset or very angry or scared. Right now things were calm. She got caught up in a meeting of one type or another, he was sure.

He dialed her number.

"I just stopped to pick up a bottle of wine. I'm on my way home right now," she said as she answered. "I know. I know. I had to mediate something. It's fine. I'll see you in a few."

He smiled. Of course she knew he would call to check in on her.

"Excuse me," he heard her say. "Sir. Hey!"

The phone hit the ground. Dominic heard the clatter and he was moving to the door before he'd even thought about it.

"Meriel? Meriel?"

"Let's go." Tom was next to him and they hurried out, the phone still pressed to Dominic's ear.

Dominic continued to listen, his heart pounding so hard he was light-headed.

"I have a message from your mother-in-law."

"You should let go."

"Witch, you have no power over me."

"You're so wrong there."

"Ouch! Here, she wanted you to . . ." A snarl and a loud cry of alarm.

"Yeah? Tell her that's from me." Meriel picked up her phone and spoke to Dominic again. "I'm here."

"What is going on?" he demanded.

"Just a little messenger. I took care of it."

"Where are you?"

"An alley at 2nd and Bell. I'm not that far. I'll be back shortly. I'm all right."

He cursed the slow elevator and headed for the stairs instead, talking them three at a time. "Stay here, Tom. I'll call if there's a problem," he called back over his shoulder.

By the time he hit the sidewalk outside she was already making her way up the block.

She waved to him like it was totally normal to scare the shit out of him on a daily basis.

"I told you I'd be home soon."

Her skirt was dirty, an oily smudge along her thigh, and her blouse was ripped.

Rage bubbled through him.

"Who did this to you?"

She looked up at him. "It was a friend of Gloria's. A human one. He's a lot more fragile than he thought he was. I punched him in the nose and my hand hurts. I hate punching. And I kicked him in the junk too." She had the audacity to look proud of this.

He started to move past her and she grabbed his arm. "No. He's gone and I want to go home."

"Why are you smiling?" Annoyed, he turned away and escorted her home.

"Because you're ridiculously hot when you get protective."

"It's not a joke."

"No, it isn't. She sent a human, Dominic. She knew I'd flay her or any mages alive, so she sent him knowing I most likely wouldn't kill him. But this messenger of hers told me she wanted to meet me and gave me a piece of paper with an address on it."

"He gave you something of himself?" If that was the case, he clearly knew nothing of witchcraft or he'd be shitting himself. A strong witch could use that paper to trace the item back to its owner.

She shrugged. "I don't trust it. Doesn't matter anyway. When I popped him in the balls, I also managed to attach a fun little homing spell of my own. Also, Nell called when I was getting the wine too. We have a location for Gloria."

So fucking smart. He wanted to haul her up and kiss her silly, but he wasn't sure how hurt she was and so he put an arm around her and steered them into the building.

Tom was waiting near the elevator and when he saw Meriel, his face darkened. It made Dominic feel a lot better to see it.

"Come inside."

"I'll be right back. I need to clean up." She tried to move past him, but Dominic put an arm around her.

"We'll be right back. I want to check you over so don't argue with me. Where's the paper?"

Meriel handed it to him. "I disabled a homing charm."

He grinned. "Despite how you're destined to kill me by the time I turn forty with all this business, you sure are smart."

"Not hard to be smarter than some dumb bigot human." She shrugged.

As gentle as he could be, he stripped off her clothes and examined her for any use of magick or any sort of physical harm. She had a bruise on her thigh, where the smear of oil had been.

"He pushed me into a wall. Dumb, I know. But I wasn't expecting it. The bruise will be a good reminder."

"Sometimes, Meriel, I really wonder what it was like to be you growing up when you say stuff like that." He held out her favorite pair of lounge pants and then a soft, long sleeved shirt.

"All the best lessons in life are those learned the hard way. If I don't take them as lessons, then I take them as failures. I prefer the former."

"I prefer for my woman not to get assaulted in the middle of a crowded city at rush hour."

"Me too."

Chapter 27

"I'VE got something." Nell walked into Meriel's office.

"Really now? Can you clear it up with a cream?"

Nell's serious face fell and she snorted. "Ha! Thank God William used a rubber before me. No creams needed, though dude, my mother happily informed me yesterday that I'm going to leak. *Super* glad I told her I was pregnant."

Meriel moved back. "Like how?"

Nell laughed. "Thank God for you, Meriel Owen. Milk. From my boobs. Though you can leak amniotic fluid. Which, ew."

"Have you been watching those baby delivery shows on cable again? You cried the last time. We agreed you weren't to do that anymore."

"I cry a lot. Especially when my mother tells me my breasts will leak dairy products."

"This is what happens when you let the boys go too far, Nell. I would have thought you'd know that by now."

Nell socked her.

"Enough baby talking. I know where your human is. Your homing spell worked perfectly. I also sent some people to go check the address on the paper. In entirely predictable news, it's a warehouse complex in North Seattle. Lots of empty space there. Only two tenants left and I think she's one of them."

"WELL, let's search a little, shall we?" Meriel moved to her computer and began to search. They'd already done a search on the address. It was a commercial property run by a management company. The management company had come up clean. But that didn't mean there was a dead end.

"How are the individual warehouses numbered?"

"They're lettered. A through F. B and E are occupied. Tool and dye shop in B. Has been there in that location for nineteen years. Owners are a local family. Not a witch in the bunch that I could find."

Meriel was busily verifying this herself. "No liens against anyone in the family. No criminal records." She continued clicking. "The business pays on time, the owners too." She looked at pictures on their website. "They're established. She's not there. This isn't about them at all."

"I agree. E is a smaller warehouse. Current business has been there three years. They make specialty trailers to pull luxury cars. I shit you not. I've seen these trailers, they're really amazing and cost a crapton of money too." Nell's love of cars was clear on her face.

"These people aren't as well known. One of the owners' sons has a record for assault. Also for writing bad checks."

"I already got that part. Sheesh. I can handle the police record stuff."

She glanced to Nell. "They're mortgaged to the gills though. But, that's not unusual right now. Many people are hurting."

"I don't think she's in the occupied warehouses."

"Why'd she not say which one if I'm supposed to meet her?"

"I'm sure she planned to have you wander around and then get the drop on you."

Meriel rolled her eyes. "She's dumb."

"Totally. So your boy is interestingly enough in the vicinity. Want to take a pass with me? I'm not going in or even getting close. I just want to see it for myself."

"That little shit who ripped my blouse yesterday is at the warehouse facility?"

Nell nodded.

She got back on the computer and began to look for the origins of the building and then the land it sat on.

"Do you think she knows enough to choose a powerful place?"

"No. I would of course. But she's been turned for thirty years. She didn't grow up in a clan at all. What she knows about us, hell about herself, is all superficial. She never bothered to hone her own spellwork, that much is clear. Her laziness is what got her stuck to start with."

"And it's going to help us take care of her once and for all."

"I can't go without telling Dominic. He made me promise."

"I like that he worries. Call him then. Or is he still sleeping?" Nell winked.

"Tom is staying with us. So they had plans to go to breakfast. Dom took him to Heart of Darkness last night and they had a great time. I'm glad he's here. Dominic needed it." Needed to know that just because the woman who gave birth to him could have killed him just a few nights before didn't mean a damned thing because he had a father. Tom loved him and Dominic loved him right back. It was a good thing, made Meriel happy to see them together the way they were.

She called him. "Hey you."

"What's up?" Meriel heard talking in the background. Simon's low bass tones and Tom's smoother voice.

"I'm sorry to bug you. I know you're busy."

"Never too busy for you. What do you need?"

"I'm going on a scouting mission with Nell and I promised I'd tell you when I was going to do anything having to do with Gloria."

"Meriel."

She tried not to laugh.

"Yes?"

"A scouting mission? And what does this entail?" His

voice had lowered and gone all silky. She knew he was honed in on her and pissed off too. But it was hot and she was crazy because she loved it.

"You know what that voice does to me."

He sighed and she knew he was searching for patience and trying not to be amused. "Why do you need to go? Why don't you let me go?"

"I need to go because it's part of my job. You don't need to go because you're busy with something and you don't work for the clan. I'm calling because I promised to. It's not a commando mission. We're just going to cruise by the place the homing spell pinged for, which also happens to be the address Gloria gave me. This isn't an episode of *I Love Lucy*. Nell is a smart woman who is very good at her job."

He groaned. "Why don't I come along?"

"Say hello to everyone for me. If you like, I'll text you when we're out so you know what's going on. Oh and hold dinner for tomorrow open on your schedule, please. Some of the witches from Rodas are coming out, including the hunter."

"I didn't agree to this plan with you and Nell."

"I never said you had to. I promised to call you and tell you and I did. Now, I love you. Have fun and I'll text you in a bit."

"If you get hurt, I will kick your ass."

"Same goes, buster." She hung up, still smiling.

"YOU think you can do a covert look at the warehouse with this car?"

"Look, you, this is my biz. I know how to do it." Nell rolled her eyes.

"I never thought it was possible, but you're even bitchier now that you're knocked up like a dirty whore."

Nell burst out laughing. "You're going to make me have to pee. Stop. Anyway, this is not *that* unusual a car and given that this place has a specialty car service, I can't think anyone's going to look twice. Well, other than the fact that this car is bitchin' and all."

"Good point. I have been properly schooled on the matter of covert investigation. Also, you were what? Five when the word bitchin' was en vogue?"

"I see how you are." Nell slowed down a little and Meriel opened up her othersight. And then exhaled.

"Turn there."

Nell obeyed.

"She's been here. In the last warehouse, the one with the blue doors. Keep driving."

On the way back to the office Meriel texted Dominic that she was fine and then turned to face Nell. "There are a lot of them in there. At least six different signatures."

"Six mages? Arel said his group had been working as a unit of about eight mages using the humans to locate the witches. Maybe that's their organizational structure or something. Seems unbelievable to me that six mages would come onto Owen land and think they can get away with it. But they could be stupid like Gloria. Other than the attacks on you and Dominic, we've heard nothing from anyone else. All our witches are accounted for."

"Not six mages. Some of them were human. Two appeared to be like Gloria. Turned. They had a sort of grayish smear to their signature. One or two mages and if I'm correct, they're the same two from Heart of Darkness."

A sore subject because they'd managed to get away after their first attack on Dominic and Nell blamed herself.

Nell sighed heavily. "All right then. I'll get my people together and we'll formulate a plan. I'll let you know what we decide and report when I finish up."

"First of all, the road back to work doesn't go this way. It does, however, pass Red Mill. What a coincidence. And second, I will be part of this. I'm not a magick commando or anything, but this is personal."

"We'll talk over rings." She found a place in the always-packed parking lot.

Meriel got out and motioned back to Nell. "Sit. There's a line out the door. I'll get it to go."

* * *

DOMINIC knew she was trouble from the first moment he saw her and yet the moment she walked through the door with several bags of what he could smell contained several Red Mill bacon burgers, he couldn't help but smile.

"This is going to be good."

She laughed. "Dominic, whatever are you insinuating? I brought you bacon burgers and rings and you doubt me?" She fluttered her lashes and Simon groaned.

"I brought some for you too." She handed out bags and he steered her into the bedroom, closing the door behind them.

"What are you going to ask me to do?"

"Geez. Just eat your burger and rings and I'll tell you. Unless you think you can nail me really fast, we should go back out there so people won't think we're quarrelling."

He took the remaining bag from her and tore into the burger. "I'm waiting."

When she finished telling him, he simply goggled at her. "Why on earth would you think I'd back this? Let Nell and her people handle this."

"She already agreed I could come. If you came too. She says she doesn't want you pissed off. Imagine. I'm her best friend and, I might add to all you haters in the room, I am also a really excellent witch. Arguably better than anyone else who'd be there. So of *course* I should go. Gloria has a lot of stolen magick. If they walk into a room full of mages and turned witches with some angry humans too, I'll be needed. And lastly, she wants to meet with me, not Nell. They need me in more ways than one."

She pulled her shirt up and then peeked at him. "Does that help things?"

He burst out laughing and put the food down. "You're going to kill me, Meriel Owen. But you have great tits and you're partially right about how much you're needed. But I'm going with you."

She pulled her shirt down and got herself in order again. "Good. Now let's go eat and have a nice night."

Chapter 28

MERIEL looked up to find her mother standing on her doorstep. "Have you been waiting long? I'm sorry, I had to run in to the office."

"No, I just got here a minute ago." She followed Meriel into the apartment. "Did I catch you at a bad time? Or, well, I guess that's a silly question. May I have a bit of your time?"

She took her mother's coat and motioned her to the couch. "I'll make some tea."

Edwina followed Meriel into the kitchen and sat there instead. Meriel looked her mother over closely. "Are you all right? Is someone sick?"

"I know I've had very high expectations of you. I know I've driven you to succeed and I made mistakes sometimes in how I did it. Holding the leadership of Owen is an immense challenge. A burden at times. A burden so heavy you wonder if you'll survive it."

Meriel made the tea automatically.

"And other times it's the most amazing thrill I've ever experienced. When you take on my seat, your magick will grow. You're powerful now, the most powerful witch I know other than me and Ron. When you take over, the clan will reside in you. Their magick enhances yours."

"Get out! Really?" Meriel set the tea out and remembered she had shortbread cookies and added them.

"Really, Meriel, you're such a bright girl, why do you talk the way you do?" But her sniff was more amused than indignant. "But to answer the question, yes really. When you take my seat, you'll be, well, you'll be strong enough to handle whatever this woman has to throw at you. It'll strengthen the bond exponentially as well. It's too much power for one witch to hold, that's why full-council holds leadership. Only a bonded, ascended witch could hold the leadership. You and Dominic both will ground all the extra magick running through you."

This was a total trip. "Mother—"

"Don't interrupt. Now, as I was saying. I have been harder on you than I should have at times, but it was because I knew you'd need to be ready when the time came. I've watched and I've waited and now is the time." She paused to put sugar and milk in her tea.

"I can't let you give me the leadership of this clan because you want me to win a fight. That's not how it's supposed to work."

Edwina made a distinct pffft. "Of course that's how it works. Meriel, my mother transferred to me when I was twenty-three years old. Her health had been in decline and I'd ascended the year before. So she told me the things I'm telling you."

"I think I need to get the Thin Mints out of the freezer for this conversation." Meriel grabbed a whole sleeve and headed back. Edwina looked at her suspiciously, but went on.

"The clan is supposed to transfer whenever the next in line would better protect the clan from a threat than the current leader. That is you right now. This isn't about a mother helping her child, though I'd do that too. This seat holds the clan and the clan holds it. It is a weapon and a shield. It has been my duty and my honor to hold it for nearly forty years and now I'm passing it to you, where it will do the most."

Edwina paused and looked at Meriel, horrified. "Whatever are you doing? You don't dunk cookies like you're a monkey. For goodness sake!"

Meriel dug a fresh one out of the sleeve and handed it over. "Try it. Come on. I won't tell anyone."

"If I don't, I expect you'll just pester me." She barely dipped but Meriel reached out and pushed her mother's wrist down, holding it for a long moment.

She tried to look disinterested as her mother tried it, holding a napkin strategically over her clothes like Meriel should be doing.

"It's fabulously too much, isn't it? Just nod your head and dunk your cookie. We'll never speak of it again." She pushed the cookies to the center of the table and dunked her own a few times.

"The clan is under threat. My time is up. Owen needs a new direction and new leadership. You've consistently shown me how prepared you are. You think on your feet. Dominic has loosened you up a little. He has that effect. My goodness, he's a charmer."

"Imagine what it's like when he's at Heart of Darkness and the women see him in the mood lighting." But inside she was jumping up and down whooping it up that her mother had just paid her all those compliments.

"I can believe it. He's good for you. And you're definitely good for him. He's been ill used by this creature who bore him. And you'll be protecting him as well as the rest of Owen."

Meriel blinked fast and looked up at the ceiling to keep from crying.

"I need to discuss this with Dominic."

"Yes, of course. He'll need to be here as well. When you take the font, it'll fill him too. He needs to be here with you." And as if she hadn't just thrown a curveball, Edwina eyed the cookies. "You go on ahead. I'll continue to enjoy my tea and perhaps have a few more cookies while we wait for him to arrive."

"You mean you want to do this right exactly now?"

"Whenever else would it be? You're going out there tonight. It won't take very long. I can continue on as CEO if you like, or you can take over. I would argue that I'm a better choice for the position. I have more experience and I think you running the legal department is your strength."

She nodded. "Yes, stay on. You can take more clients for design work now if you like. I'm happy in legal and I really can't believe we're having this discussion. I'm honored, Mother, that you would find me worthy." And she was. Her heart was full of love. And pride.

Edwina paused, clearly moved. "Oh, Meriel, that was perhaps the loveliest compliment I've ever received."

Knowing her mother would be uncomfortable, Meriel got up and took her phone. "I'll be right back." She ducked around the corner and called Dominic.

"Is everything all right? I'm three blocks away."

"I look forward to the day when we don't answer all our phone calls that way."

"Me too."

"My mother wants to transfer the leadership to me."

"Well, sure, that's been the plan, right?"

"Today. Now." She explained to him about how it would make her stronger and that it would affect him too.

"Wow. This is . . . wow."

"I know. What do you think?"

She heard him take a deep breath, knew he was thinking it over. If she could only have seen his face and his body language right then. She could read him so well, even after such a short time together, she'd have known how he felt.

But she didn't have that and so she waited.

"I think you're exactly where you're supposed to be. I'll be home in five minutes. This is what's supposed to happen."

She wanted to believe that was true. It certainly *felt* true. And so she decided to ignore that little voice and believe.

When she came back out she and her mother cleared the tea and put everything away while they waited for Dominic.

He came in and walked directly to her. "What do I need to do?"

She explained the rite briefly before Edwina set the circle. Dominic wasn't part of the rite, but he would receive the font. He'd be with her there when it hit.

Edwina held out her hands and Meriel took them. "I will offer you the seat and you must accept or deny it. It's rather simple, as I said."

Meriel had a sinking suspicion that it would also be painful.

Edwina set the circle and turned to face Meriel again, clasped hands again. The power between them hummed, like to like.

"Let the seat pass to the next in line, new holder of the font. May the ground at her feet always recognize her power."

"I accept and pray the ground at my feet always recognizes the power of the clan."

Edwina smiled. "It is your turn." And pulled her hands away.

The ground at Meriel's feet dropped away as vertigo hit. Around her it swirled. So much magick and energy she breathed it, it pumped through her veins. She turned to look at Dominic, who reached out and took her hand and the bond snapped into place, fighting to equalize all the input, trying to make sense and process all the power rushing through them both.

It hurt her teeth and the backs of her eyes and her skin heated as she began to sweat. Of course Dominic looked cool as a cucumber.

The roar of it, so much electricity, energy, intent all tied up into one massive whoosh of white noise.

Her back bowed and her skin felt as if it would burst.

And then it eased back as the bond regulated itself. She opened her eyes to find Dominic looking at her.

"Wow."

"No kidding. I feel like I feel every Thanksgiving when I have one too many pieces of pie."

"Such a poet." He laughed and pulled her in for a kiss.

"JUST for the record, superpowers aside, I do not like you being here."

He knew in his heart and mind that Gloria Ochoa was a turned witch who meant to harm him and his woman. His clan and his family. And she was right there inside that building. Coiled like a snake.

Which is why he didn't want Meriel anywhere near her. Something very bad might happen when they moved in to capture Gloria and he wanted Meriel away.

She leaned over and kissed him. "I love you. This'll be over soon. And then we can get on with our lives."

He let out a long sigh, reaching out and connecting his magick with hers. He surprised her. "I love you."

She lit up, thrusting her magick back into him and they were suddenly so connected and strong. They'd fully opened their bond. "That never gets old," she said lazily, pausing for a moment.

She charmed him with all her ferocity.

He held a hand out. "It's time to go meet Nell."

She took it and hugged him tight. "We're stronger than she is and she can't send anything into you. No matter what she says she can't get past me."

He grinned as they headed out. "Yeah, I know."

MERIEL rode beside him as they drove to Nell's. She was now the leader of Clan Owen. Their lives would change again as they got used to that. She could do it, he was totally sure.

Her magick seemed to shimmer against her skin.

He knew he'd do anything to protect her.

Chapter 29

THE dark was very quiet. Every single small shuffle or step felt as if it was deafeningly loud. They'd dropped off the cars a few blocks away and crept in behind the motel next door. Dominic's blending spell would make sure no one saw them. And he was able to broadcast it in a new way courtesy of a spell Edwina had shown him at their last lesson.

They approached from the side and soon they'd split up to flank the warehouse. He shielded her from his body for as long as they could. Wishing, again, that she was home and very far away from this mess.

Meriel would go in as bait. They'd all agreed though Dominic had argued he was just as good. He'd been over-ruled and wanted to punch someone, but she'd talked him down.

He turned to her when they reached the spot where she'd split off from the rest of the group and approach the warehouse directly, in plain view.

"You will be careful. I mean it, Meriel. I love you."

"I love you too. Watch your ass. I'm going to need rescuing soon." She kissed him quickly and waited for the time they'd need to get into place before she came out into full view and began to approach the warehouse.

MERIEL knew she should have been afraid. But she wasn't. It would be over soon and she'd walk away the winner.

"Hold it there," someone called out from the shadows. She could see the sickness in him from where she stood, though she wasn't sure if it was so visible because he was so stuck, or because she was so much stronger now that she held the seat.

"I am Clan Owen, come to send you from our land." Somewhere out there in the dark, she knew Nell was grinning at that one. She'd made up the line and dared Meriel to use it. It sounded good so she did. "You are outlaw and in violation of Owen rules. You have five minutes to vacate or your lives are forfeit. That means I get to kill you if you don't leave, just in case I wasn't clear."

"Bring her in and let's get this over with."

Not Gloria. This had to be the other turned witch. He was stronger, not as far gone as his partner.

She walked forward and through the doors but they remained opened, though two humans at her back tried in vain to close them.

"Just close them for her!" Gloria's shrill voice sounded as she stomped into view.

Meriel took a long look and was not impressed. She turned to the male who'd had her brought in to start with. "Let me guess, that shot-out bitch over there with the big bags under her eyes and three inches of roots must be Gloria. I feel as if I should say something witty. But I'm too pissed off."

Someone tried to drain her; she felt the tendrils of that dark sludge getting closer, but she reflected it back. "You have really bad manners. Now, time's a-tickin'. You all need to be scurrying away."

"Says who? The woman who actually showed up alone

to a meeting with someone like Gloria?" One of the mages sneered.

She raised her hand and the human who'd been running at her was blown backward against the wall. "And just so you know, I get to defend myself against humans who try to harm me." He got up, limping a little. "Now we don't have to worry about any misunderstandings."

"She said you were strong. I can see that. I hope the knowledge that you're going to be feeding me, and her, for some time will be of a comfort."

She'd been so focused on the magickal attacks she hadn't been ready for the physical one. The crack sounded and then she listed sideways a little and fell to her knees.

Meriel just looked at him for long moments. "Ouch! You shot me!"

And then a roar behind her as Dominic stormed in and the human who'd shot her crumpled to the ground.

"You all right?" Dominic called to her as he avoided a magical attack. Mages, any non-witch in general, could build up and use magic. Magic did not come from the person wielding it. It was often stolen or dark rites were used to gain more. It was easily used and spent just as quickly.

Witches had magick, an energy that was part of their compostion. It was power that came to the holder naturally through years of practice and time as well as natural gifts and talent level.

Blood, sticky and warm, flowed with each beat of her heart against the spot on her side where she pressed her hand. She realized he didn't know she'd been shot, hadn't heard what she'd said to the jackwagon who'd shot her. "I'll be fine." She felt her side and found the exit wound. Straight through.

A nearby mage went on the offensive and she grabbed hold of his spell and yanked. He fell to his knees as she bent it and turned it back on him using the spell Edwina had shown Dominic and that he'd further enhanced to create the feedback loop. Already unstable because it wasn't his magic to use to start with, it broke easily, conforming to Meriel's intent.

Nell stalked in and dragged him away by the back of his collar. She didn't ask where. Didn't want to know.

Fighting broke out in earnest. Dominic had told her to stay back and safe and she did it. Her vision was a little spotty as she continued to work her magick from where she'd leaned against a far wall, sheltered by an old metal desk.

ALSO, Nell told her that if she got into the middle of things she'd kick Meriel's ass. She was the leader now, she had responsibilities to stay safe and let the others do their job.

That and she was bleeding. A lot. She remembered her first-aid training and focused inward. She found the wound, a bright, red spot of pain in her othersight. Best as she could, she knit what she could back together and built a sphere of protection around it. It wouldn't cure her, but it would hope-fully slow the bleeding.

What normally would have taken a great deal of her time and a lot of magick was done easily and quickly. The magick from the font had amped her power up considerably. She had no compunction about siphoning all the excess energy from those in the room who meant to cause harm. And weakening them was just another benefit.

Meriel kept the mages from draining anyone as Nell's team cleaned up.

Dominic walked back into view, the power arcing off him. Meriel widened her eyes. Her man was fierce and beau-tiful and he'd had enough of this nonsense.

He turned to where she'd crouched and narrowed his gaze. The magick still flowed strong between them. But she was hurt and sooner or later he'd figure out just *how* hurt.

One of the mages took a run at him and Dominic turned. As if in slow motion, he cocked his fist and rammed it into the other man's face so hard he stiffened like a board and keeled straight over. Another jumped on Dominic's back, knocking him down. Meriel couldn't risk the spell hitting Dominic and not his attacker so she made ready to run over there and cast the spell up close.

Only like some sort of scene from a movie, Dominic stood and actually threw the guy off his back and against a nearby wall.

Dominic straightened and turned again, this time to face Meriel. Something wasn't right. When he used his othersight on her, he saw the bloom of red on her side and nearly lost his mind.

"Meriel Owen!" he boomed, stalking over. Something or someone made to stop him and automatically, he shot out a spell, knocking whoever it was away.

"You said you were all right." He crouched, shielding her with his body.

Sweaty and pale, but fully conscious.

"Hey, I am all right. I'll heal. Now go! Your back is to the room."

Alarm raced through his system. "You've been *shot*. I'm getting you out of here."

"No, you aren't. They need us. The other turned witch is powerful. I'm not leaving and you're not either. I'm going to be fine. The bleeding stopped. The bullet passed through. Just hurry up and stomp this shit down so I can take a nap."

His hands shook as he touched her face. He fought with himself. She was right of course, things were hot just then and they were needed. But she was hurt.

"Look at me with your othersight. My magick is flowing, our bond is strong. I'm going to be fine and you can wait on me hand and foot when this is over. I promise. Go! We're here. Let's win. Go, team, go."

He groaned and kissed her hard, felt the sting of magic against his shields.

"I'm going to take care of this. You don't move."

He got up and scanned the room, not moving far from Meriel. He'd get this done and get her out of there.

Ah, there she was, her signature a slight echo of his. Enough to make his stomach turn to think on it.

"Gloria Ochoa, show yourself. You are in the presence of The Owen. You are in violation of our laws."

She stumbled forward and he saw how bad off she truly was. "Son! How I've worried about you." She turned big cow eyes and a trembling bottom lip in his direction as if they'd work. "They took you from me."

She moved closer and he put a hand out to stay her, not wanting her anywhere near Meriel.

At his left Gage hustled a mage out and Nell dragged a human that didn't look so good.

Dominic curled his lip.

"So worried you let a dark energy into my magick? I've had more than enough of your version of care, thanks, but no."

"Don't let her fool you! It was her." She pointed and . . . *damn it*, Meriel moved to his side and took his hand. He gave her a narrow-eyed glare that she chose to ignore, stubborn woman.

"I had to get you away from the clan witches. The possession spell was for your own good. Don't you see that?"

Dark, sticky magic pulsed from Gloria. Dominic blocked it.

"Give yourself over to my people and we can end it quietly." Nell stood nearby. "You'll be ours one way or another."

"So you'll just kill me? No way. I can tell you things. Things that will help you find other mages. There's a whole movement. They want to expose you."

"Where's the other one? The male?" Meriel asked Gage quietly.

"We've got a few in custody. One is dead."

"There was another turned witch, like her. Only stronger. He'd been turned a shorter time. Make sure."

"I'll double-check."

There was a loud crack and a creaking sound that brought the hair on his arms to stand. Something very bad filled the warehouse. Dominic watched in horror as Gloria began to call a gate. He brought his fist down onto his palm as he shouted, "Seal the doorway!" and shoved the full force of his magick at her. The gate slammed shut and Meriel stumbled a little, following up with her magick to seal the circle and contain the spirit Gloria had called. Trapping Gloria inside with whatever energies had already transferred through the gate.

The energy pulsing through him was so massive he was sure that if he'd felt this way even a month before he wouldn't have been able to handle it. Edwina had told him just a few hours before that the font, the clan, was a sword and a shield. As the magickal energies swirled through him, giving him more strength and stamina, making his intent more concrete, he believed it because he felt it. Connected to so much with this woman at his side.

He did, however, plan to kick her sweet little ass when she recovered.

She leaned into him and he shifted to put an arm around her and brace her.

"I'm all right," she whispered. But she didn't really look it. Pale and sweaty, he needed to get her medical help very soon.

Gloria choked back a shocked cry. She fell to her knees and the darkness she'd called swirled around her. She'd called something and it demanded life force for its payment. It couldn't get to anyone outside the circle so it began to consume her.

There was no telling the level of destruction it would cause if it got free of the bonds Gloria had given it when she pulled it from the lower realms. "If I pull the circle open, the spirit can get free. We can't take the risk. I'm sorry."

Dominic had to fight his instinct to turn Meriel away from the horror. Her features were set as she concentrated to hold the circle closed. Around them Nell's team engaged and then took out all the remaining mages and humans.

And yet, injured and dealing with a mess his mother had created, she worried for him.

"Don't be. You haven't done anything to be sorry for."

"What the hell? Meriel!" Nell approached, her gaze on Meriel. She met Dominic's eyes for a moment. "I can end this for her."

She meant his mother.

Meriel didn't say anything, letting him make the choice.

He nodded. There'd been enough suffering. It was time to end it.

Nell turned and spoke. There was a flash and then the stink of ozone and an empty circle.

"She's been shot."

Gage hurried over and Nell turned to address him. "Get your mother to my house right now. Meriel's been shot. Have someone bring a car up here."

"On it." He left again.

"Your house? Hell no! I'm taking her to the ER." Dominic picked Meriel up and she didn't argue, resting her head on his chest. A quiet Meriel who didn't argue was one that worried him.

She patted his arm. "Can't go to hospital with a gunshot wound. Gage's mom's a doctor. It's fine."

"Fine? This is far from fucking fine. Someone shot you. That's not fine. It's not."

Nell carefully interjected. "She's pulled bullets out of me before. She's good at her job and I wouldn't be suggesting it if I didn't think Meriel would be taken care of this way. But she's right, we can't take her to the ER or the police will be called and then what?"

"We can't expose the clan unless it's absolutely necessary. It's not."

With a growl of annoyance, he got her outside. If they were going on this fool's errand, he wanted it done as fast as possible.

"Loyalty to the clan doesn't mean being stupid," he muttered, putting her down gently as the car approached. Nell bent and rustled through a first aid kit.

"It's our clan now. You know it's not stupid." Meriel gasped when Nell wrapped her wound tight.

The sound tore at him. "Let's move this along then. You did your part. The longer we stand here, the longer you have a bullet hole in you."

Arel jogged up and jolted when he saw Meriel. "The other

turned witch is gone. We're searching. Can I assist?" He looked from Meriel to Dominic.

Meriel stood a little taller. "Take care of the search. Nell, give me your keys and call William to let him know we're coming so a bunch of bloody witches don't surprise him. And then clean this up. My blood, I'm sorry but there's a lot of blood where I was standing."

Nell exhaled hard, clearly torn between one duty and another.

She handed the keys over to Dominic. "I'll be there as soon as I can. The survivors have been taken into our custody. Everyone but the male is accounted for."

"I expect you know how to conduct some questioning. Don't worry about me. I'll be fine. I want you at these interrogations." Meriel winced and swallowed hard and then swayed.

Gage came roaring up in the car and threw his door open, scrambling out to get the other so Dominic could help her.

"I'm going to get blood on your seat."

"I'll bill you."

He ran around to the other side. "This better work, Nell. If it doesn't, I'm taking her to a hospital; I don't care about the rest. Get this place cleaned up before the early shift shows up for the other businesses and we get the cops called."

Chapter 30

HE sped out of the warehouse trying to keep it steady. He knew every pothole must have hurt.

"Keep with me, Meriel. Stay awake."

"You were totally badass," she said. "I'm not going to die you know. It hurts. I can't lie. But if the bullet had gone a little to the left, it'd have hit my stomach and we'd have a whole different conversation."

He groaned. "These are words I wish you would never, ever say in conversation again. Your job is to run the clan, not to get shot by fucking thugs. Piece of shit, I wish I could kill him twice. These people, Meriel, what could make them hate so much that they'd willingly go out to hurt others?"

He'd seen a lot of violence, but these humans doing the bidding of criminals like Gloria made no sense. Their hatred at what they didn't understand was staggering. Their willingness to hunt, kidnap and aid the mages in killing astounded him.

"People fear what they don't understand."

"Sounds like Simon when he's talking about how witches should come out to the humans."

"He's probably right. But when they find out about us they shoot us. It's an update on the burnings and drownings."

He sighed. Not like he could argue. But he knew she understood the world was shrinking every day. It still wasn't a conversation for that moment.

There was a balance to driving fast very late at night. Too fast and he'd get pulled over and then they'd really be fucked. But it was empty enough so there was no need to crawl along either. He pushed away his impatience to get her there.

She reached out and took his hand. He looked down for a brief moment, her fingers still bloody, tangled with his. He'd made the clan safer but she'd been shot. He hadn't made *her* safer.

"I can feel you trying to blame yourself in that head of yours. Stop it. You didn't shoot me. In fact, if I remember correctly, you took care of the guy who did. And then you went all superhero and punched a bunch of people *and* you used your magick. It's pretty impressive and sexy. So stop blaming yourself.

"I should have protected you."

"*You did.* Don't you see? Gloria and those mages were a threat to me. They aren't now. I'm here because of you in so many ways." She snorted and then whimpered.

"I don't know what I'd do—"

"Don't." She squeezed his hand. "Not gonna happen. You're stuck with me."

He tried not to turn too hard onto Nell's street. The house was at the end of a good-sized drive and at the top several cars already waited.

"Shit, that's my mother's car."

"Of course. You know she and Abe would be here. Sit still, I'll be around to get you."

William rushed out, followed by Abe. They stood back while Dominic pulled her from the car and carried her into the house.

"Guest room. Second doorway there." William pointed to where Gage's mother, Shelley, waited. The bed was covered and the room had been made sterile as well as it could be he guessed.

"Put her on the bed." Shelley moved with them and bent next to Meriel. "Hi there, honey. I think that shirt is ruined. I'm going to have to cut it off. Everyone but Dominic out."

Edwina sniffed and didn't move. "I'll be assisting. I have triage training. It's a long story."

"She did it for a Girl Scout camp I went to," Meriel said from her place on the bed. "Hello, Mother. Sorry I woke you."

"Yes, well, you've been doing it entirely too much of late. Your father and I would appreciate if you could stop getting yourself stalked or hurt." Edwina's gaze cut to Dominic. He saw and understood the emotion he saw there.

"Fine. Bathroom is through there. Get washed up and come back." Shelley grabbed the scissors and cut the shirt open and Meriel looked up into her friend's mother's face.

"Oh, sweetie pie, this is going to leave a mark."

Meriel coughed and it hurt. "Don't make me laugh."

"I'm going to give you something for the pain." She swabbed Meriel's arm and the cold shocked her back to attention. The prick of a needle and then the burn of the medicine as it shot into her system. Once that was done, Shelley began to weave a spell, her hands above the wound. Heat radiated outward as she did. The pain drifted away on drugs and magick.

"Gloves."

Dominic was there, she could smell him. She turned her head, feeling dizzy as she did, and managed a goofy smile. "See? I told you . . ."

MERIEL woke up with a dry throat. Once her eyes were able to focus, she noted the IV drip. Must have been some good stuff in there because she couldn't feel more than the tug of the stitches when she moved.

It was late afternoon if the slant of light on the walls was any indication.

She was really thirsty. Inside her the bond woke up and magick hummed through her. "Dominic?"

"Here. I'm here, baby." He came into the room quickly, holding a mug. "Your mother made tea. Hang on." He stepped outside the room again and she heard him call out for Shelley.

He was back wearing a smile. But he didn't fool her. She could see the lines from lack of sleep around his eyes. But when he kissed her on the forehead and sat next to her on the bed, his body touching hers, everything was so much better.

"You're awake." Shelley came in. "How are you feeling?" She looked at the wound, both sides, and changed the bandages. "This is healing well. You're going to be just fine. Are you in any pain? How's the medication?"

"How long was I out?" She sipped a little water and then Dominic helped her sit up.

"Day and a half. You needed to just let yourself heal and rest. Your body took care of it for you." Shelley carefully looked at her wounds and changed the dressing. "This is healing really well. I'm afraid you're going to have some scars, but you're going to be just fine."

"I'm okay. I don't need any more medication for now."

"Meriel, don't be so stubborn."

Dominic set his jaw like he did when he was going to get testy and it amused her. Filled her with a rush of love. "Hi there, you." She managed a goofy smile.

He softened immediately and brushed his lips over her cheeks. "Hello, to you too."

"You saved me."

Emotion flooded his features. "You've got that backward."

"Aw man, if you're gonna get mushy, let me go get a sandwich."

Meriel looked up to find Nell at her bedside. "Tell me what happened. Did they find the guy?"

"Not right now, Meriel. You can hear about it tomorrow." Shelley shook her head.

Edwina pulled up a chair and sat next to Meriel. "If you

scare me like that again I will break my promise to never strike a child. Do you understand me?"

Meriel nodded solemnly.

"You were correct, Gloria led us right to them. Keep on listening to your gut, Meriel, as long as it does not result in your being shot. Now. We have not found the other turned witch. But we have a name. Arel and Nell have had the surviving mage they captured in interrogation for the last day and a half. They've gotten a great deal of information. I took the liberty of standing in while you were unconscious, with Dominic's assistance of course. We're cooperating with our neighboring clans and several covens so far to get this man's information out. If he's seen, we'll be notified."

This was her clan now. It was her time to lead it. She looked to Nell. "So what's the story?"

Dominic grumbled under his breath but helped Shelley sit her up better so she'd be comfortable.

"Thank you." She sighed because he was so beautiful and he was hers and he was there, right there. His normally well-trimmed beard was scruffy. His hair was mussed up. He smelled good. Spicy and familiar and she couldn't stop staring at his pulse with the memory of the way he tasted *right there*.

Nell cleared her throat. "God, you two. Not the right time for that."

Meriel grinned at Dominic, feeling a lot better.

Nell got down to business. "There were six in all. We took in two prisoners. The turned guy's name is Cyrus Pasqual. Arel's crew is looking into his past to see what we can find out. Human says Cyrus has been with them for about six months. Gloria brought him around."

"And what does the mage say?"

"Not a whole lot."

"Make that change."

Nell cocked her head and then nodded.

"Okay then. I'm under the belief that once we indicate our willingness to go that extra step he'll tell us what we need to know."

Dominic nodded. She hated to even think it, but it had to be done.

"This group has been together about eight months. Gloria hooked up with one of the mages in Toronto and they came south. According to the human, they showed up at one of their *meetings* and told some story about how they'd lost people because of the witches. They told the humans that the witches to worry about weren't the Wiccans but us. He had a lot of information, most of it sort of true, but not entirely accurate."

"Best kind of propaganda, that. Bend the truth into a pretty lie." Nell didn't need to consult notes, but Meriel liked them. "Can I please have a pad or my laptop?"

"You should rest." Shelley gave her best severe-doctor face.

"I've got a clan to run and a psycho turned witch on the loose. I can rest in a little while."

Dominic heaved a sigh and reached down, bringing her laptop out. "I figured you'd wake up and want this."

Such a giant marshmallow. With a very flat belly. Mmmm.

Mind back on her work for the time being, she booted up as Shelley threatened everyone not to get Meriel excited and she left to go back to her day job. "Pain meds are right there. *Use* them if you need them. You won't benefit by being in pain. I'd like you to stay here at least one more night and then you can go home. I'll be back later to check in, but everyone has my cell. Call if you need me."

She thanked Shelley and turned back to Nell. "Go on."

It turned out the human had been relatively easy to get information from. A combination of being really scared after seeing not only what Gloria and the mages were capable of, but what had happened when they'd tried to harm Meriel's people. Their group was a cell of sorts with six members. The humans would do the scouting work to get around wards. They were usually dismissed for the part where they captured the witch. He'd taken care of body disposal though, so he may have been misled about what the others were doing exactly, but he knew the outcome and never spoke out.

"See what Arel wants to do with the human."

Dominic cleared his throat. "If I may I'd like to talk to the mage."

Nell shrugged. "Can't hurt."

"It can wait until later. I want to be with Meriel for a bit before she takes a nap." He shot her a look.

"You know where we are. I'll hold off on those extra measures until after you speak to him?"

Dominic nodded.

"All right. Call and we'll make him ready for visitors."

"Fine. Thank you."

Meriel spoke to her friend. "And Nell? I'd like you to put together three proposals for how you envision expanding your hunter team would work. I want specifics. There's no way around the fact that these mages are out to harm our people. I want to deal with a threat as soon as possible."

"I'll have them to you in a few days. I've jotted down some ideas already."

"You have until Monday. I spoke with Lark." She looked to Dominic. "She's the hunter for Gennessee. She and I had lunch last week when I was in San Francisco. She offered any assistance I needed if we wanted to go forward with an expanded hunter team."

"She'll need the training anyway. Gage talked with her a few days ago. One of their people is here now as it happens. He's in on the interrogations. I think Arel can help as well." Nell kept her attention on Meriel, which she appreciated.

Edwina stood. "If you'd like, you and Dominic are welcome to stay with us until you're feeling better."

"I wanted to thank you. For the seat. It made a difference. I don't know that I would have been able to stand and continue working magick if I hadn't had all the extra power. But it was Dominic who saved the day."

He snorted. "Says the woman who never stopped working, even when she had a bullet hole in her side and was gushing blood."

Edwina looked at both of them. "You've done me proud,

Meriel. Dominic too. I made the right choice. I knew it even before I transferred the seat to you. But seeing the way you handled this incident only underlines that. Expanding the hunter team will be essential, I agree. I wish this wasn't so dire. And maybe if we prepare ourselves we'll never need it. But we'll be prepared.

"For a long time I've thought my sister was paranoid. Now I can see she was right."

"Owen ground isn't the same as Gennessee. We don't have the same kind of trouble they do. Until recently we didn't need our hunters carrying firearms all the time like hers do. Our relationship with the Cascadia Wolf Pack is solid. The vampires here are fairly restrained. It's not the same in Los Angeles."

Edwina's features relaxed a little. "You anticipated it."

"I did. But it grew out of the need to have better diplomatic relationships with the other witches."

"Which is how you learned of this threat. It's all right to say I should have known."

Meriel wanted to shrug but the stitches still pulled a little. "I'm saying you can give yourself a break for not having foresight. You ran this clan for a long time in a peaceful period. Your leadership enforced the peace. That's important. And now we have new threats and we'll face those too. I hope I can do half the job you did."

Edwina reached out to squeeze Meriel's hand.

"As for the offer to stay with you, I appreciate that. I'll talk to Dominic, but I think I'd like to go home. It's closer to work and I have an office Dominic set up for me there if I need to work."

Dominic shrugged. "That's a given. You work there all the time." He turned back to Edwina. "I want to thank you too, for the seat and for the offer to stay with you. I'll ask for your assistance in keeping your daughter from overdoing until she's physically able to get back to full time."

Edwina laughed. "You've met Meriel, right?"

"The two of you are more alike than you think."

Edwina stayed with her for a while longer before leaving. "I appreciate your continuing to run the clan. It's easier for me to rest knowing you're doing it."

Her mother sniffed as if she'd do anything else. "Of course. I look forward to the day when you get that blank face of yours and tell me that perhaps I should take on a few more clients since you're running things and I'll have the time."

Meriel laughed and it didn't hurt a whole lot.

"You should sleep," she said to Dominic once they were finally alone.

"Too keyed up. You're awake now and I don't want to waste a minute. Anyway, I did sleep last night. You had a fever for a while but it broke yesterday early evening. I slept here with you last night."

"Are you all right?"

He snuggled closer, careful to stay gentle. "You got shot, Meriel. No, I'm not all right. But I will be."

"I mean about Gloria."

"How can you ever be all right when your mother is a mass murderer?"

"It's not about you. You're not responsible for what she does. How can you be? Look, you've been alive as long as she's been stuck and then turned. You didn't turn, did you? No. It's *her* weakness. Her inability to not be so selfish."

"She got you shot. I didn't protect you. She came to Owen land. I didn't protect our witches."

"Of course you did! Dominic, do you know how hard it is to close a gate the way you did? You had to make choices I don't envy in any way. But you chose me and our witches over your mother. I'm sorry." She wondered if he'd blame her on some level. Felt responsible for his pain.

"Sorry? For what?"

"You had to watch your mother die. For me. I'm sorry you had to choose."

"I chose you about ten minutes after I met you, Meriel. I didn't even know her. She was part of my life for six months when I was a baby and she sucked at it then apparently. And when she came back into it she tried to kill my woman and opened me up to possession. It's not like choosing between those two things is hard in any way. Certainly I wish she'd made other choices. I wonder if she could have been helped all those years ago. Would it have been easier though? To have known her and then watch all the horrible things she did? I can't help but wonder about all the might-have-beens with my mother, but the woman she was in that warehouse was beyond redemption. You had nothing to do with that."

"Aren't we a pair?" She let her gaze rove over his face. "Gosh, you're pretty. Even when you're sleep deprived and scruffy. Hell, because you're scruffy. I like that beard. Anyway, I'm not responsible for her and neither are you. You were strong and you saved lives. We did it together."

He took her hand and kissed her fingers. "Yeah. I love you Meriel. Therefore in the future, once this new hunter team gets all trained up and fierce, you will no longer be going out on missions of any kind."

"You got that right."

"Now, Shelley says you can't take a shower until after the stitches come out. But that you could have sponge baths. I'm the man to deliver. What do you say?"

Chapter 31

DOMINIC paused outside the door. He'd had a very lovely late afternoon with the woman he loved. They'd both needed the time together to reassure each other they'd be all right.

And they would. She was strong. He was strong and together they were unbeatable.

He didn't want any of that to touch what he was about to do, but they'd discussed it anyway. In the end, you were predator, or you were prey. Meriel understood that quite well and with these mages, they needed to be predator in the strongest of terms. He asserted, and she had agreed, that it was important for the leader to make this statement. Nell was fabulous at her job, but this was something Dominic was going to do because the point needed to be underlined in exactly the right way.

He was no stranger to physical violence and his magick, having been underutilized for so long, was now tight and toned and very, very powerful. He could do this and he would.

Nell opened the door and came out. They had been waiting to use any more severe methods of getting information from the mage until Dominic had spoken to them. "He's ready. Do you want backup?"

"No." He moved past her and into the room, pausing until he heard the locks engage again.

The mage they'd taken into custody two nights before sat on a bunk, head hung.

"You tried to kill my woman."

"You need to turn me over to the cops. You can't hold me here."

Dominic took four steps and drove his fist into the mage's face. The force of it sent him sprawling to the floor.

"I don't have to do anything, as it happens. Human cops have nothing to do with this. We take care of our own."

"I don't have to talk to you."

Dominic kicked him, hard. Twice, in case it needed to be underlined.

"I don't have to stop beating you down either. You see, we have a problem." Dominic moved away and sat on the chair near the door. "Let's go back to the beginning, all right? I'm Dominic Bright. My woman runs this clan. She's the one your dead friend shot. And you are?"

The mage glared through a swelling eye.

Dominic kept looking until the mage broke eye contact. "Tim Ifill. You can't hold me here! I demand to be turned over to the proper authorities."

"I don't give a shiny fucking penny what you want, Tim. I'm in charge here, not you. I hear tell you were in Gloria's little gang for at least seven months. Where you from originally?"

When he didn't get an answer, Dominic got up and cuffed Tim upside his head, leaving him on the floor again.

"Don't bother getting up. We'll be playing this game until you're ready to talk or until you have no ability to talk. I've had it. I'm happy to break other things if I have to. Two days we've been reasonably accommodating with you. Time's up."

"Accommodating! You broke my nose!"

"But I didn't shoot you in the head, which is what I'd really like to do."

"The other one tried the tough act, too." Tim sneered.

"I have to hand it to you, I figured you'd be smarter. I'm

amazed you got this far being so stupid. Until right now, we've been trying nonlethal methods to get you to talk. I'm bored with that. Meriel is bored with that. And she's recovering from being shot so she's extra grumpy." He heaved a sigh.

"As it happens, I don't think I need to punch you anymore. Though it'd please me just because. So, you can tell me what I want to know, or I can get it myself."

"Go ahead and try," the mage taunted, giving Dominic all the permission he needed.

He used the spell Arel had shown him earlier. The hunter from Rodas had told him it might take some practice, but Meriel was sure he wouldn't have any problem.

And he didn't. He walked right into the mage's head and looked around.

"You're from Cleveland. Long way from home." He shuffled through Tim's mind and found what he needed and then disconnected.

They weren't as organized as Gloria had claimed. But there were other cells and they'd begun to network and divide up territory. That was the most frightening thing. Like a pack of hyenas. "You're a lazy, lazy person."

"You're not supposed to do that! You're supposed to stay out of my head."

"Is that what she told you? Or what Cyrus told you? It's true, you know, that we're supposed to not take over people's will the way I just did." He shrugged. "It's also not all right to kidnap people and torture them by stealing their magick and then killing them. How many witches have you harmed? I'll get over my breaking of our rules. You gave me permission anyway."

"I didn't kill any of those witches! I can draw from them without killing. I never killed anyone."

"I was just in your head, Tim. It's a silly thing to lie to someone who's seen your memories."

"It was an accident the first time. The second one got away."

"She did. Her name is Kendra de La Vega. She's been

very helpful with the information about you. I'd love to chat with her ex-husband, but I get the feeling her present husband will find him first. And then he can't talk to anyone."

He stood again and Tim winced. *Good.*

"Here's how it works. We're done with being taken advantage of. We've declared a war on you and your kind. Only we don't have to steal magick. We're born with it. We are not victims and you made a mistake thinking we'd stand for this. They burned us. They drowned us. They stoned us and put us in mental institutions. We will never allow it again."

"What are you going to do with me? What have you done with the others?"

"They're dead. And if you don't want to join them, you'll help in our attempts to find your friend Cyrus. Maybe we'll let you leave."

"You can't do this!" He got up and rushed at Dominic, meaning to knock him down.

Dominic stood aside, grabbing the back of the mage's shirt and tossing him back to his bed.

"I can do lots of things, Tim. If you want to find out just what that means, you keep pushing. I'd advise you not to test me anymore. I don't like you. I don't think you *deserve* to be alive. It's up to you. I'm happy either way."

He rapped on the door and Nell let him out.

"Do you want ice for your hand?" She motioned to his bloodied knuckles.

"No, I'm going to wash up and go back to Meriel. Abe is in charge, but you know how Meriel is, she's probably faxing and ordering people around already."

Nell grinned. "You can't keep her down."

"No." He sobered. "I know you heard what went on in there. We've got a problem. This Cyrus is powerful. He only turned a few years ago so he's not as far gone. It was his idea to hook up with the human separatists. He's the one who recruited the mages and created their little group."

She took notes while he explained what Tim had in his head. There were good dates and times. And sadly, a list of those witches they'd harmed.

He wrote down several names. "These are the witches they've killed. We'll need to find their people to tell them what's happened. Meriel wants to call a meeting with the other clans and covens and whoever else wants to attend to fill them in on this issue. I made her promise to wait until tomorrow. If I'm around, I can help."

Nell nodded, taking the paper. "We hit the safe house the human told us about. I don't think Cyrus went back there though. Gage is going through everything we took. I'll report to Meriel when I get home."

"Don't overdo." He touched her belly briefly. "Meriel wanted me to remind you."

"She's one to talk. I'm pregnant, not recovering from a gunshot."

"Tim is going to start jonesing for a fix very soon. Don't take your attention from him."

"He can't draw in here. Magic won't work. Arel is giving me a primer on how to make these facilities more mage-proof."

"Thank you for letting us stay in your home. I keep meaning to say that and then something else happens and I forget."

She rolled her eyes. "Of course. Meriel is my sister in every way but biological. I'd do anything for her. And thank *you* for helping William."

Just a week before, he and Simon had come to an agreement with William Emery. William would run the human part of the club.

"Helping him? He's helped me. Just having him around has lessened my workload considerably. And he's a smart man. He's got great ideas and a lot of experience running nightclubs. I think this will work out well. Despite all the mage stuff, the rest is good." He bent to kiss her cheek. "I'll see you later."

"Definitely."

He went outside, taking a deep breath of the evening air and pushing away all the ugliness. He had a woman to get home to.

Turn the page for a special preview of
the next Bound by Magick novel by Lauren Dane
Coming soon from Berkley Sensation!

Chapter 1

LARK shouldered her duffel and headed down the Jetway, hoping to avoid the cute and nice-smelling hipster college student who'd been trying to pick her up since they took off.

He was a pretty tall guy though, so by the time she caught sight of the escalators down to baggage claim, he'd caught up with her.

"Hey, do you need a ride or anything?"

"No, thanks. Someone's meeting me here."

"Do you want to get together? You know, while you're in town?"

If she were just a regular old human woman, she'd be all over this cutie pie like icing on cake. But she wasn't regular anything, and she'd only break him. It was inevitable with humans, which is why she never allowed herself to partake in anything they had to offer.

Her life was filled with weapons and other not-human beings with weapons, or those she had to use her weapons on. Human men never understood it, the life she led. She had to hide her true nature from them, and that was never a good way to have a relationship.

"I appreciate the offer. But I'm here for work, and my time is pretty much booked until I go back home."

He frowned, apparently unused to his charms failing.

"Oh. Well." He continued to walk alongside her as they approached their carousel. And that's when she saw the giant, beautiful man holding the sign with her name on it.

Mentally, she wiped her brow and fanned her face. So masculine the heat and power of him radiated outward in waves. His hair was thick and dark, cut perfectly. A tousle of hair that made her instantly think about what he'd look like right after a long, slow kiss. Denim covered unmistakably powerful thighs and long legs.

Lark had always tended toward men who were of the cute, college hipster type. Scruffy beards, lanky, sexy glasses. The kind of men who not only wore scarves, but looked totally adorable in them.

Sign Guy was not one of those men. At all. He was one of those capital *M* Men. The kind she enjoyed working with because they were smart, strong, independent and yet controlled. She imagined though, a man like him would be a hell of a lot of work to have a relationship with.

His eyes were of the slow, sexy type. Though, she noted, he looked around the room just like she did. An *Other*. Her heart kicked and her attention honed in on him.

"Well, have a great quarter. Nice chatting with you." She said it offhand as she wandered toward Sign Guy.

A shifter. She paused, cocking her head. Not quite. The same, but slightly different. Not Fae, though his magickal signature was similar.

His attention had been snagged as she approached. The man was a predator after all; he was sure to notice anyone who got near. His nostrils flared as she knew he took her scent in.

"I'm Lark." She held her hand out for him to shake.

He smiled, a slow, sexy smile designed to part women from their underpants. The hand that took hers easily engulfed her fingers.

"Simon Leviathan. Meriel sent me."

Lark nodded. "She said she was sending a friend of the clan. Thanks. I appreciate the ride." Her suitcase hit the conveyor belt. "Can I leave this with you while I grab my bag?"

"Which one is it?" He took the bag she'd been holding.

"The red one."

But before she could move, he'd already taken three steps to the carousel and had grabbed her bag.

"That all?"

"Yes, thanks. I can get those." She reached for the duffel, but he just sent her a raised eyebrow and turned slightly to continue holding the bag.

"I'm sure you can." He squeezed her upper arm with his free hand and then paused. "I'm really sure now. But I can hold them just as easily. We need to go upstairs to head to the parking garage."

And then he sort of ushered her just exactly where he wanted to go.

She was still mildly annoyed at how he just sort of took over. Interesting that she let him get away with it, she thought to herself as she got her seat belt snapped. While she remembered, she sent a quick text to Meriel letting her know Simon had met her and was taking her to her hotel.

He slid in on the driver's side, and though the car was pretty large—she hadn't been surprised by the big black Cadillac—he seemed to fill every inch. Tinted windows. Swank interior. Smelled good too.

He paused before he turned the engine over. "You look tired. Would you like to go to Meriel's? Or straight to sleep? I know you've got the meeting with Clan Owen's governance council tomorrow."

Surprising how easily she found herself responding to him, a near stranger. She'd heard Meriel refer to Simon, knew he co-owned a nightclub with Meriel's man, Dominic. That Meriel had trusted him to pick Lark up told her that he was to be trusted, even if her gut hadn't already told her the same thing.

"It's already nine. I've gone over my presentation several

times." Including once with her sister and father, and, really, she couldn't think of anything she wanted to talk about less right then than mages and death magic. "I've eaten and slept this stuff for the last few months. I'm as prepared as I'm going to be. I think."

"Are you hungry?"

"Um. I figured I'd get room service when I got to the hotel." She'd been in such a hurry after her last meeting with her sister, Helena, that she'd missed dinner, though she did eat a giant bag of M&M'S on the plane.

"Do you like steak or are you a vegetarian?"

He said *vegetarian* as if it were a suspect class.

"I like steak. Vegetables too."

He hmmed, but it was laced with suspicion. "You'll be staying in Meriel and Dominic's old apartment."

"I don't want to intrude on them." She liked Meriel, but that didn't mean she wanted to stay with her. A hotel meant she could walk around in her underwear and eat ice cream from the carton. She had to be nice and polite and make small talk if she stayed with people.

"They don't live there. They recently bought a house and had two months left on the lease."

Well that was nice, actually. An apartment meant she'd have a kitchen and some room. Of course that meant she'd have to go grocery shopping. Though if she knew Meriel as well as she thought, that fridge was most likely well stocked already.

"Cool. Thanks for the ride. You're not a shifter."

He continued to look at the road but one of his brows rose.

"I'm sorry. I have a hard time telling the difference between blunt and rude."

His mouth twitched.

"I'm Lycian."

She leaned closer and breathed him in. "Oh! I've never met anyone from the other side of the Veil but a Fae warrior."

Simon had no idea what to make of this woman. His wolf liked the way she smelled. Sharp like he did. Like a warrior did. But she had blue streaks in her hair. Hair she most likely cut herself. Maybe not even in front of a mirror.

She most likely listened to bands no one ever heard of and went to shows in clubs with sticky floors. Clearly she liked shopping in thrift stores and probably had gloves that were once someone's sweater.

The smudge of her energy was bright and clear blue. Blue like her eyes. Earnest eyes, but the shadow of a warrior lived there. Even as she rattled on at random, her gaze roamed, keeping track of where they were and who was near.

"How long have you been here? And by the way, if I, you know, fall over the line into rude, please just poke me and say so. That's what my family does."

"I have been here for ten of your years."

"I bet your house has very clean lines. Nothing fussy. You don't have knickknacks and I bet you fold your shorts."

"I don't follow."

She sighed. "You're a very spare guy. I mean you don't have any fuss about you. You don't use four words when three will do. It's an admirable trait. One I do not possess. I bet you don't leave your clothes on your bedroom floor or have stacks of magazines anywhere."

"Tell you what. I'll make you a steak at my house. You can see for yourself."

He caught her grin.

There was an odd sound and they both looked around. And then she cursed and dug into her coat pocket. *Hubba Hubba, Hubba Hubba*. That's what it kept saying.

"Clever," she said as she answered the call. "Oh yes, I'll totally take you back now. What do you want?"

Much like a shifter, he had excellent hearing, so the other end of the call was audible.

"Why you gotta give me such a hard time?"

"I'm working. And hanging up now."

"I forgot to tell you. I put a new grip on your Sig. I think the balance should be better. And you should take me back."

"Thanks for the tip on the Sig." She disconnected.

"What did he do?" Simon asked.

She laughed. "You assume he's the one who messed up."

"If it had been you, he wouldn't be the one begging to be taken back." He had enough experience with such events. Enough that he'd ceased having anything more than flings.

"I'll tell you, but only if you have some vodka at your house to go with the steak."

"I have whiskey and some tequila. Will that do? I own a bar; it's not as if I can't stop to get vodka."

"You're very accommodating for a guy who just met me less than an hour ago."

He liked taking care of people. And he was intrigued by Lark Jaansen and her colorful contradictions. She pleased his senses. In an entirely platonic way, of course. He sure as hell wasn't going to be nailing her, but that didn't mean she wasn't interesting to man and wolf.

"You're one of Meriel's. She's the woman of a man who is like my own brother."

He got off the freeway.

"To answer your question, whiskey is fine. Or tequila. Thank you."

His phone rang this time and when he answered, Meriel's voice sounded over the speaker.

"Is Lark with you?"

"Yes, of course." He turned his attention to Lark as he took the steep turn on the drive up to his house. "I thought you said you called Meriel?"

"I texted her to say I had arrived and was with you."

"Texting is not calling. She's here with me, Meriel. I'm going to feed her. She's a little thin. And give her a drink. I'll be sure she gets back safely. Tomorrow all you witchy types will have your war talks and all that jazz. Let the girl have a good steak and a decent night's sleep."

"Gage is going to pick you up first thing, Lark," Meriel said. "We'll get you a car as well. Our old place is warded up tight. No worries at all on that front. No one will breach your security there."

"Good to know about the warding. I expected nothing less. As for Gage, yes, I spoke with him before I left L.A.

I'm good. I promise I can take care of myself, Meriel. I'll see you tomorrow afternoon. Appreciate the use of your place, by the way."

"We're climbing the hill to my place," Simon interrupted. "Cell service is going to get sketchy. Talk to you later." He hung up and Lark laughed again.

"World-class skills, Meriel Owen. I've yet to meet a cannier witch when it comes to politics. She constantly pisses people off and yet they always listen to her. Take her seriously. Clearly you're like she is. Just because I've never met a Lycian before doesn't mean I can't see you're clearly a superior specimen. I mean, top of the food chain in Lycian speak or whatever. Why aren't you back home ruling the pack?"

"I'm the third son. My oldest brother already leads the pack in my father's name. My next youngest brother is his right-hand man."

"Ah, so like you have the heir, and then the spare, and what about you?"

"There are corollaries. I've got eleven brothers and four sisters. We each found our place and path. Mine led me here."

She leaned forward, gripping the dashboard, getting her fingerprints everywhere, he was sure. "Holy crap. Simon, is that your house?"

Pride warmed him as she gawked at the grounds and the edifice of the house through the windshield.

"They've been building it for three years. Just finished everything a month ago."

"You could totally play basketball in here." She got out once he'd closed the garage door.

"I have a basketball court. Do you play?" He motioned toward the doors that led to the breezeway between the house and garage.

"Of course you do. Oh, my weapons are in my suitcase. I shouldn't leave them out here. They're kitted for taking down things far worse than a deer."

The wolf inside him responded to Lark immediately because she was like him. A warrior to her essence.

"We can talk weapons while I get the steaks started." He grabbed her bags from the trunk. "Come on." He indicated the door to the breezeway. "Rest assured that this ground is safe." He bowed his head and she realized he meant it. He took it as a matter of pride and responsibility that anyone on his land would receive safe passage. It was old-school honor.

"Thank you. This place is amazing. I'd like to be outside for a little while. Would you mind?"

"Let's drop this in the house and I'll take you to the gardens."

As she let him lead her to the main house, she couldn't help but admire everything she saw. The house sat on a large lot with a view from every window.

And she understood why he wanted to let her be in the gardens. He took her to the heart of his house and she felt the deep well of his connection to the land beneath them.

He put her bags down in an entryway.

"She likes you here. The earth," she added, following her senses through his house, looking up at the soaring ceilings and walls of glass. It was just as clean and elegant as she'd imagined it would be. But with a surprising warmth and masculinity.

"Meriel says this too. It's reassuring to hear it from another person I suppose. Welcome to my home, Lark Jaansen." He bowed courtly.

"Thank you for having me here. This is beautiful." She turned in a circle when he took her to his living space. "I was right." She smiled at him.

"Should I be flattered?" He flipped a switch and the walls of windows opened up to a deck with a view that had her moving outside before she'd known to do it.

"Yes. It's not serial-killer scary-neat. It's clean and simple. You've created a place where nature is totally inherent to the overall design of the house."

Three levels of decking and entertainment areas sprawled down the slope of the land.

"I wanted to occupy the land and still respect the shape and sense of wildness."

Her breath caught as she stepped from her shoes and pulled her socks off. The intensity of connection to the well of magick at her feet shocked through her system. The font clicked into place as it accepted her, as the land at her feet recognized her as Owen through her connection to Gennessee. Their foremothers were the same and their magick still flowed strong here.

She breathed in deep, simply letting the energy hum through her system. "This is stunning, Simon. Truly." She continued to meander and he steered her around one path and directed her back up toward the house.

"You're not wearing shoes; that path is for shoes. Would you like a drink?"

"Yes, thank you." She looked out over the mountainside and to the world below. "It's crazy to me when I visit. Such a riot of nature here in this place. And yet just ten minutes down this mountain and you're back into the buttoned-up control of a city. At home it's different. My magick isn't stronger or weaker, really, it's just that the ways I access my magick are different. So much light, the salt of the ocean, the energy of all that humanity hums through the concrete."

She followed him back inside and toward the large, open kitchen that shared the heart of the house.

"And here it's as if I breathe the magick in through my pores."

"Would you permit me to choose the drink?"

She shrugged. "Sure, why not?"

He went to a bar and studied it for long moments before he pulled a bottle out. She leaned against the counter and watched as he pulled two black stones from the freezer and put them in glasses. He poured the amber liquid—scotch; she could scent the oak of it—over the stones and then once again with the second glass.

"One of my brothers has a boutique whiskey distillery. Try."

She breathed in the scent of the whiskey before she took a sip. The smoke of it danced across her tongue.

He didn't pester her to ask what she thought. Instead he moved to the sink to roll up his sleeves and wash his hands.

"I like it. I'm not normally a whiskey drinker. But for this I'd make an exception. Can I help?"

He paused to look her over. "There are tomatoes over there on the counter. Fresh mozzarella in the fridge."

She moved to wash her hands. "Do you have balsamic and olive oil?"

He snorted at her audacity. "Do I look like a man who wouldn't have olive oil and balsamic?"

"I notice you're less terse. Is it the whiskey?"

He laughed, putting the steaks on the grill on his center island as she cored and seeded tomatoes.

"I'll let you know after the next glass."

Chapter 2

"SO we've seen a distinct reduction in overall crime in our community since we've instituted this system of tactical units."

Edwina Owen looked Lark over, one brow up. "Your hunters use human firearms and weaponry. That's a complicated matter and raises the chances of discovery by human authorities when we obtain the necessary licenses."

"It does indeed bring us into more contact with the human authorities. But Clan Gennessee can't afford to lag behind what criminals of all sorts use to commit crimes. We have a higher concentration of incursion into our community by outside groups. Drugs and organized crime are on the rise. I can use magick, of course, and I do. But everyone gets depleted and a bullet does the trick in a pinch."

Lark addressed the full governance council of Clan Owen. Nell and Gage were there as well, representing the hunter corps.

"And now the mages are working with turned witches and human separatists. They use guns. The human organized criminals we found last year had been working with witches to run a brisk business in prostitution and drugs. They use guns too. They use guns and explosives and they'll hit a crowded street party filled with children just as easily as choose a military target."

Meriel looked to Nell. "What do you think?"

"She's right, and you'll bear the scar that underlines her point."

Meriel touched the place on her side where she'd been shot only two months before by mages.

Point made, Nell continued. "We found explosives in that warehouse. Homemade timers. Several small frag bombs. These people want to hurt us, kill us, take everything they can from us and they're not only going to use magick. In fact, they won't because we're superior at it."

Lark nodded. In total agreement.

"This isn't Los Angeles." Edwina wasn't going to make this easy.

Lark shrugged. "No. It isn't. You have a fairly decent relationship with your local wolf pack. Ours can be contentious at times. The largest vampire population in the United States is concentrated in the Los Angeles metropolitan area. Overall your crime rate is lower. And yet your leader was shot in an attack by mages. Here on Owen land."

"And this wouldn't have happened on your watch?" Edwina Owen, who until only recently had held the seat of Clan Owen, was clearly insulted.

"It is not Gennessee's intention to insult you. Your land is different. The challenges you face are different." She looked to Nell, who, thank goodness, understood exactly why Lark was there.

"What I *am* saying is that I have a tactical team trained specifically to deal with hostage situations. Our job gets bigger each year. There was a time when all hunters did was round up witches who broke the rules of the clan. Seven months ago one of our witches had thrown in with a group running a meth lab. Oh true love. I had to send in a team to clean that up. Because I'd made connections with the local authorities, I was also able to get them involved to clean up the biohazard the lab had created."

"My sister has less problems with being discovered by humans than I do."

Meriel had warned her to be prepared for such an attack, and so she was. She stood her ground. Gennessee had nothing to apologize for.

"With all due respect, Ms. Owen, that doesn't make it any less likely to happen. Being discovered will happen eventually. It's not dependent on whether or not you believe in doing it. You tie the hands of your hunters when they're not trained as they should be. They're your best defense against external threats. Now we're being hunted for our magick. We can be predators, or we can be prey. I know which I plan to be."

Meriel gave her a discreet thumbs-up.

"If I may speak?" Nell stood and, even with the swell of her growing belly, continued to look entirely capable.

"Yes, please do." Meriel motioned to Nell to continue.

"I've been quite open about my support for the idea of expanding our hunter teams to specialty units. I *do* believe that we'd have been far better able to meet the threat those mages posed us two months ago during that showdown if we'd had teams like Gennessee. We aren't just sage-burning kitten-huggers. We face threats darker and larger than ever before."

Meriel leaned back and looked them both over. Edwina stayed silent. Meriel had taken the reins of leadership of Clan Owen just a few months prior, but the changes had already begun.

That had to be hard on mother and daughter both.

"What is your sense of next steps then, Nell?" Meriel asked.

"With the permission of the governance council, I would like to set up some special teams. Get them up and running, get people trained. Lark has offered to help with this project. And in addition, Lark and I, in conjunction with Arel from

Rodas Clan and several other hunter team leaders across the United States and Canada, would like to set up one large unified team to deal with the threat the mages pose. We've got a turned witch on the loose who's working with the mages. And that's just the one we know about. There are others. There will continue to be others."

Dominic Bright, Meriel's bond-mate and soon-to-be-husband, sighed. "Nell and Lark are right."

"Make it happen. Keep me apprised. Lark, I'd like it if you could help not only the hunters here, but our rank and file membership."

"I'm under orders to share and help as I can." Which was sort of true.